The Caspian Monster

Larry Jeram-Croft

The Caspian Monster

Copyright © 2011 Larry Jeram-Croft
All rights reserved.

Also by Larry Jeram-Croft:

Fiction:

The 'Jon Hunt' series about the modern Royal Navy:

Sea Skimmer
The Caspian Monster
Cocaine
Arapaho
Bog Hammer
Glasnost
Retribution
Formidable
Conspiracy
Swan Song

The 'John Hunt' books about the Royal Navy's Fleet Air Arm in the Second World War:

Better Lucky and Good
and the Pilot can't swim

The Winchester Chronicles:

Book one: The St Cross Mirror

The Caribbean: historical fiction and the 'Jacaranda' Trilogy.

Diamant

Jacaranda
The Guadeloupe Guillotine
Nautilus

The Caspian Monster

Science Fiction:

Siren

Non Fiction:

The Royal Navy Lynx an Operational History
The Royal Navy Wasp an Operational and Retirement History
The Accidental Aviator

Prologue

1967, the Pentagon, Washington DC

The room was quiet as usual, just the hum of the air conditioning and the odd cough to break the silence. Sitting at the rows of desks, the analysts concentrated on their work. One man, in particular, was frowning as he stared intently at the black and white photograph before him. He was looking through a stereoscope at the black and white image. Muttering to himself he took the next one in the pile. Within half an hour he had selected four in particular and then called over his superior. The new man looked at them as well and then they conferred for some time. The supervisor went to his desk and made a call. Two minutes later, the phone rang and after a brief conversation the two men collected the photographs and headed for the small conference room to one side of the main office.

They were met by their boss.

'Right boys, what've you got for me now?'

The supervisor nodded to the analyst who put the first photograph onto a projector so they could all study it.

'This came in this morning Sir. One of a roll from the latest Blackbird flight, I've got to say that machine has really opened up our eyes. I bet the commies are really grinding their teeth now.'

The other two men nodded. This fantastic new spy plane of theirs was really starting to deliver the goods.

'Anyway, these photographs were taken on the northern end of the Caspian Sea. What we seem to have here is a new aircraft. I've done some rough calculations and it seems to be very large. It's about three hundred and fifty feet long and it's only partially complete. You can see the massive tailplane quite clearly but it looks like the wings are yet to be fitted.'

The Caspian Monster

The Boss, who used to be a pilot, was looking sceptical. 'Sorry but something's wrong here. Those wings look finished to me but what the hell is that sticking out either side of the cockpit area?'

'From what I can gather Sir, they're jet engines. I counted eight of them.'

'What the hell? Eight goddam engines and they're in the wrong place. And more importantly, what on earth is it that thing they're building the machine in. Why isn't it in a hangar and covered up? They must know we'll see it.'

'Sir, it looks like a graving dock to me.' And seeing the puzzled look on the Boss's face he continued, 'a dry dock, the sort of place they normally build ships.'

'So, it's a sea plane then but it still looks all wrong to me. OK guys, get the aerospace experts on to this as soon as you can. Shit, I've no idea what this monster really is but we better find out and quick.'

Chapter 1

The Soviet Republic secret test base east of the Urals

The night was pitch black and clear. The stars were out in all their northern glory, made even more striking by the lack of a moon to dim their sparkle. The air was completely still. It was as if the whole airfield was holding its breath.

Major Yuri Alexeyev exited the bus with his support crew and a lump caught in his throat as he saw his aircraft waiting for him on the hardstanding. His heart swelled with pride, while at the same time he felt the familiar palpitations of controlled fear that always preceded a flight where new limits were going to be set. But his overarching emotion was pride. Pride that he had been chosen to conduct the flight in the first place and pride in the achievement it would bring.

For too long the damned Americans had been able to overfly his country with impunity, first with satellites and now with an amazing aircraft. All that was known was that it flew incredibly fast and high and nothing in the Soviet arsenal could intercept it. Many years ago, the Americans had done the same thing with their U2 spy plane, right until it had been shot out of the sky. But now they had this new machine and his government were determined to dish out the same medicine to them. With this new aircraft, they would do just that.

Yuri remembered the first time he had set eyes on it soon after joining the programme. He had been taken into a large camouflaged hangar and there it was squatting like a giant, angry, black insect. It looked like nothing he had ever seen before. Clearly, it was meant to fly but the configuration and size was simply disorientating. Firstly, it was the biggest aircraft he had ever seen. Bigger even than the new American 747 jet. Then there was the shape. It was like a large letter 'W' with a slim fuselage piercing through the middle. At the apex of the pointed wings were clearly engines of some sort but their asymmetric shape seemed totally illogical. However, he soon learnt the reason. The problem with very fast aircraft was that they were absolute bitches to control at slow speed and so a way had to be found to make them controllable for landing and takeoff. The beast would fly at slow speeds like this with the wings opened up but as she got faster, the wings and engines retracted into the fuselage until they formed one slim delta shape with the engine exhausts trailing the rest of the body. This was necessary because of the unbelievable power and therefore heat the engines generated. And today he was going to find out just how much that would produce in terms of performance.

This was not his first flight. Indeed he and the rest of the test flight crew had racked up an impressive number of flying hours on her already. But tonight he was going to take her to the limit. They were finally going to use the extraordinary engines at full power. In the past, the USSR had been keen to trumpet their successes. The first satellite, the first man in space, the first space walk, the list went on and on. Unfortunately this time, the world would not know of yet another Soviet aerospace achievement, secrecy was too important. But eventually, he knew his name would enter the record books.

Putting aside his thoughts, he walked over to the boarding lift and climbed onto the platform. It whirred into hydraulic action and carried him up the considerable height to the absurdly small cockpit. As soon as the lift stopped, he climbed in with the help of two of his crew and connected his umbilicals and did up the straps. All the time he was conscious of the overpowering smell of kerosene from the leaking fuel tanks. It had proved impossible to make tanks that sealed both at ground temperature and at the incredible temperatures generated by high speed flight. The answer was to let them leak and simply top them off just before takeoff; something that was occurring now as he got ready. He glimpsed the fuel bowsers stationed on each wing. Finally, he closed the helmet of his pressure suit and all external input disappeared.

Once secure, the crewmen gave him a thumbs up and cheerful grins before disappearing from sight on the lift. He was on his own. Reaching into a pocket, he pulled out a worn photograph of Anna his wife and Gregor his son which he stuck under the edge of the cockpit coaming. It was a little ritual he always conducted on test flights but only when he was finally on his own. The last thing he wanted was the good natured ribbing it would generate from his colleagues if they found out. But somehow, having them with him on these flights always seemed to settle his nerves.

It was time to start up. For such a complicated machine, it was absurdly easy. He quickly ran through his cockpit checks and once all the switches were made, he simply pressed a button. One and then the other engine started without any further input from him. The system was completely automated, unlike earlier Soviet machines. He looked at each wing and saw that the fuel wagons were driving clear and called on the radio.

'Tiger one, ready.'

Immediately, the control tower responded. 'Tiger one clear to take off, the chase aircraft are already on station, your telemetry looks good. You are clear for full envelope test as briefed.'

With a short acknowledgement, Yuri concentrated on getting off the ground. The aircraft was already at the end of the runway, so all he had to do was release the brakes and open the throttles. But from previous experience, he knew he would have to concentrate like mad. The plane was not easy to control at slow speed, despite her unique design.

He pushed the throttles firmly to their maximum forward position and engaged full afterburner. The acceleration was good, nothing like a modern jet fighter just a firm never ending push in the back. The runway lights started to blur as his speed slowly increased. With just enough runway left, he finally reached take off velocity and lifted the nose into the sky. Immediately, he retracted the undercarriage and carefully brought up the flaps and she slowly got faster and faster. Entering a gentle climb, he was soon able to bring the wings into their interim position and accelerate even more. A check around the cockpit reassured him that all was well. He was now getting high and already approaching supersonic speed. It was time for the first of her little tricks. The engines he had used for takeoff were conventional bypass turbo jets. However, they were encapsulated inside much larger ducts. This allowed air to be channelled around the conventional engines in a special way. He ignited the burners in the ducts and the ram jets added their thrust. The kick in the back was impressive and he pulled the nose up almost vertically to keep the speed within sensible limits and rocketed up into the night sky. At 32,000 metres, almost the edge of space he levelled off. He had briefly glimpsed a pair of the Mig 25 chase planes on the way up but from now on, all they would be able to do was watch him in the distance in relays.

So far, so good and just as on all previous flights. Now it was time for the really clever bit. He fully retracted the wings and there was a gentle clunk as the engines mated with the sides of the fuselage. The machine immediately accelerated to just under Mach 3. His engines were now going to operate in yet another way. It had already been tried on previous flights but only to prove the function. Now he was going to prove the performance. The intakes of the engines had large bell shaped structures in them. He selected the setting that completely blanked out the small turbo jet intakes and did very clever things with the supersonic shockwaves in the engine ducts. When he was fully ready, he called ground control. He knew that the telemetry was telling them all they needed to know but this was his final chance to ensure that everything was ready for the test.

They responded immediately. 'Tiger one, you are go for full burn, good luck.'

Grunting to himself in acknowledgement, he made the final switch that changed the fuel in the engine ducts from kerosene to liquid hydrogen, the other fuel he was carrying and then he pushed the throttles to maximum.

'*Dear God,*' he thought, as he was punched in the back. Anyone close enough would have seen the now slim black dart disappear on two jets of flame. The flaming exhausts trailed behind the aircraft with a peculiar pulsing pattern that left odd regular diamond shapes in the sky for miles behind.

Watching the speed, he saw the Mach number steadily increase from 3 to 3.5 to 4 then 4.5. He was now entering completely uncharted territory. Until now, the only people to travel this fast in atmosphere were the cosmonauts as they re-entered from orbit in an uncontrolled, unpowered descent. But he was doing it in controlled flight and under power. The power that was being generated by two hydrogen powered semi rockets that were gathering oxygen from the incredibly thin atmosphere around him. A feat that was only practical when travelling at such incredible speed.

The speed was still increasing but the acceleration was slowly reducing. Mach 5 was eventually reached and finally, it steadied at just over 5.5. He grinned to himself, all onboard systems looked good. The skin temperature was high but steady, fuel flow gave him another thirty minutes at this speed should he want it but by then he would probably be in the middle of the Atlantic, not a good idea. He knew that if he pulled the nose up now into a ballistic arc he could even get close to entering a low earth orbit. All the calculations said it should be possible. The only problem would be getting back. His engines needed some atmosphere to breathe and he had no heat shield. No, he wouldn't try that. He looked out at the outside world for a second and it suddenly came to him how high up he was. The sky above was pitch black and the atmosphere or at least most of it, was lit up below him by the rising sun. But the horizon was clearly curved. He felt like a God looking down on a toy world. For a moment he was overcome.

The radio brought him back with a bump. 'Tiger one, you need to start your turn in no later than one minute.'

Forcing himself back to reality, he prepared to start his turn. This was imperative to stay in Soviet airspace and ensure that his country's enemies weren't able to track his flight.

'Roger control, starting to decelerate and turn.'

He reduced throttle and the aircraft slowed to Mach 4.5, the fastest it was deemed practical to attempt to manoeuvre. Even so, his radius of turn would cover hundreds of miles. He then slowly rolled the aircraft to the left. At first, all went well and the aircraft's heading slowly started to change. Then he felt a low tone, almost like an organ pipe. The volume slowly built up until it was a noise that could be heard reverberating throughout the aircraft. He scanned his instruments and saw that the starboard engine was running considerably hotter than its sister. Holding things steady he called ground control and told them of the symptoms.

'It's alright Tiger one, hold the turn you must reverse your track. We see the same as you but it appears steady.'

Without warning, the starboard engine flamed out. The immediate asymmetric thrust flicked the aircraft hard back to the right and suddenly Yuri was fighting for his life. This wasn't the first time he had been in an aircraft that was out of control but he'd never experienced such a violent departure from controlled flight like this. In these situations in the past, pilots had lost their lives purely by being shaken so hard that they had blacked out. In this machine, the seat immediately reacted and clamps shot out and gripped his helmet to stop his head flying around uncontrollably. Even so, the violence of the out of control aircraft was making his vision grey out. With no guidelines as to what to do, he realised he had very little time before he lost consciousness. His hand was still on the throttles and he managed to slam them both shut. With a total loss of thrust at this high speed it was like hitting a brick wall. He was flung violently forward against his straps but now he could see the Mach number dropping fast. As it dropped past Mach 3 he deployed the wings to the semi opened position and wrestled for control. No matter how he deployed the controls, he couldn't stop the tumbling. He saw through his peripheral vision that both engines were now flamed out and he knew that unless he could restart one of them, his hydraulic power would soon be gone and then he would just be a passenger in a tumbling, crippled pile of junk. Try as he might he couldn't get his hand to the restart switch. The violence of the motion was just too great. Managing to press the transmit button on the control column he yelled, 'Tiger one out of control, no hydraulics, engines flamed out, ejecting.'

He knew if he tried to eject with the aircraft going too fast he wouldn't survive. In fact, he wouldn't be ejecting in the conventional sense, rather the whole cockpit section would leave the aircraft and descend on its own parachute but even so, if it was too fast, the stresses would be enough to smash the escape capsule to pieces. His vision was now almost gone and he realised he only had seconds before he lost consciousness. He made one last prayer that he had slowed down enough. The last thing he saw through a red mist of pain before pulling the ejection handle, was his wife and son smiling at him, then the world went mercifully black.

Chapter 2

Bardufoss, Northern Norway

The Royal Marine Major was standing at the podium of the overheated room in front of a large map of Norway and the Kola Peninsula. He was pointing out features on the map with a long stick.

'Right, just to recap, if we end up at war with the Soviets they will almost certainly send several divisions down through here as part of a flanking attack and it will be our job to stop them. This is why we need to be trained to fight in the Arctic and why you navy types need to be able to fly in these extreme conditions. For fuck's sake, is anyone here listening or even awake?' This last was said in exasperation as he looked around the room. The dozen naval aircrew present were all exhibiting signs of strain. Mainly the strain of trying to keep their eyes open in the cloying atmosphere. It might be below minus twenty outside but the warmth of the room, coupled with the results of the previous night, were clearly taking their toll.

'Right, you bunch of pissheads, let's take a break. That's enough for this morning. But don't think I'm being easy on you. After lunch, we're all going on a little five mile stroll through the snow. The start of your arctic familiarisation and believe me you won't be falling asleep during that,' he finished with a feral grin.

Lieutenant Jon Hunt and the rest of his guilty partners in crime got up from their seats and gratefully made their way back to the mess for some respite from the mornings seemingly never ending, droning briefings.

Two days ago, they had flown four Sea King Mark 4 Commando helicopters up to Bardufoss in Norway, one hundred miles north of the Arctic Circle. The rest of the squadron had followed, courtesy of the RAF, in Hercules transports. The airfield at Bardufoss belonged to the Norwegian military but in an arrangement with NATO part of the airfield was leased to the Royal Navy. It was used it as a training base to give their helicopter crews and maintainers the skills necessary to operate in the extreme conditions of an arctic winter.

Jon had flown one of the aircraft and although he had been through the training some years before, they were all still required to refresh in survival techniques, so he had been required to sit in on the initial briefings. Once survival was over, as the senior Flight Commander, he would then manage the squadron detachment while most of them carried on with full operational training.

Heading first to the heads, he splashed cold water over his face and looked himself in the mirror. *'Bloody hell,'* he thought, seeing the reflection of a dark haired, good looking, thirty year old, who had clearly been out on the razz the night before. That is if the bloodshot and baggy eyes he could see staring back at him were anything to go by.

He next went to the bar and mixed himself an extremely powerful Bloody Mary which he knocked back, hoping for some relief.

'Ah, a hair of the dog old chap,' said a voice from behind him.

Jon turned and saw the tall lanky frame of Mike Turner, his old friend from flying training days and now quaintly titled the Senior Naval Officer Bardufoss or 'SNOB' to his friends.

'Wotcha SNOB,' responded Jon. 'Gonna join me? Methinks you might need it even more than me.'

'You're not fucking wrong, that was some piss up last night. The Noggies sure know how party. Bloody hypocrites the lot of them. Buying booze over here is almost impossible but as soon as we open our duty free bar they're over here like a swarm of locusts. Still, it's always good manners to have a welcoming party each year when we open up.'

'Yeah but on the bright side, they brought their women with them. Frankly, I think that they're worse than the men. What's that saying? 'In the summer they fish and make love but in the winter they can't fish'.

SNOB choked slightly on his drink. 'That about sums it up. Anyway, how did you get on with that little blonde I saw you canoodling with late last night?'

'Mind your own bloody business. Inga and I are just good friends.'

'Yeah right, so how come you didn't get back until 0400? Hah, answer that.'

'For the same reason you were seen sneaking back just after me. At least my young friend is single.'

'Are you casting nasturtions on my morals young man? Anyway, her husband was so pissed he'll never know.'

'Don't you believe it matey. Mind you, none of them ever seem to mind. A bottle of scotch goes a long way up here. Anyway, we really ought to talk business at some time. My lot are off for a little fresh air this afternoon with their Royal Marine chums, so how about you and I do some planning?'

Five days later and it was the last day of the survival course. Jon was completely exhausted, as were the rest of his team. Things had started off relatively easily, with a night in tents with all their usual equipment. Getting into tent routines and just living in temperatures of minus double figures took some basic skills. Slowly, as the days progressed, they lost more of their equipment and got less and less sleep. The marines seemed to take fiendish delight in inventing new ways of making their lives bloody difficult. But as was repeatedly said, it couldn't be worse than if the Russians were attacking, so use the experience to learn. At least they knew it would end in a hot bath some time soon.

Last night they had been bounced by the 'enemy' and now they were down to the most basic kit on yet another march to another location. They were high up on a snowy plateau somewhere. The going was quite good on their cross county skis, commonly known as 'pussers planks' but even so Jon was finding it hard work, especially as the temperature had dropped to a mind numbing minus twenty eight degrees.

'Shame it's not down to thirty,' he said to Dave one of his pilots and walking companion. 'Because then the Royals call a halt to training and wait for it to warm up.'

'No fucking chance now, not with only one night to go. My God, will you look at that.'

It had been dark but as they were speaking, the sun started to make an appearance. A tiny sliver of gold suddenly appeared on the horizon before them. Jon was standing next to a tree completely smothered in snow. Suddenly, it turned pink and then little flecks of gold appeared in the snowflakes on its surface. The pink slowly turned to gold everywhere as the top of the sun grew on the horizon ahead and the band of colour could be seen travelling across the snowfield as the sun chased it away.

Jon looked around and saw that everyone else was standing mesmerized by the beauty of the moment, even the hairy arsed Marine Sergeant who had been their nemesis for the last five days. He knew it wouldn't last.

'Right, you lot of poncy sailors, that's enough gawking. No one said to stop, we've got surviving to do and snow holes to dig.'

'Didn't see you ignoring the view Sarge,' observed Jon wryly.

The Sergeant had the grace to smile back and replied in a low voice, 'now you know why us Royals love working out here Sir but I'll deny I said that if you quote me.'

Jon chuckled and then got back on with the grim task of sliding one ski in front of the other.

Later that evening, he was surprisingly snug and warm. They had marched for another couple of hours that morning and then stopped just below the edge of the plateau, within the main tree line. The rest of the day was spent learning about and then making various sorts of survival shelter. Some were made under the base of the fir trees where the snow hadn't penetrated. The chamber that was exposed, when dug out from the side, could be remarkably comfortable. Some were constructed above ground, made out of branches and fir fronds. Jon and three others had been given the task of digging a snow hole in the side of a large drift. They had taken it in turns to excavate the cave in the deep snow and despite the cold, had soon found that it was necessary to strip right down to their shirts to stop sweating. Frozen sweat in the Arctic was a very bad thing. So now here they were, huddled together inside the hole. Their body warmth was being supplemented by the heat of the flame of a single candle that was also providing their only light. It was surprisingly snug. Although pitch dark outside, it was actually still very early in the evening, the Arctic winter having now set in. No one felt like sleep just yet, despite their exhaustion.

'I almost killed a Royal Marine today,' someone chipped in.

'Deliberately or by accident?'

'Oh, definitely with malice of forethought.'

'Oh and you failed I take it?'

'Yeah, I had just fallen over for the millionth time and snow was balled up on the base of my skis. Some bloody Lance Corporal comes over and says, 'we didn't wax out skis today did we Sir,' in that superior tone they always use. Bearing in mind they never give us any fucking wax, I decided I was going to kill him. Unfortunately, spearing a Royal with your ski stick is just not possible from the prone, stuck in a snow drift, position.'

They laughed, all having experienced something similar in the past.

'You can get your own back on them, you know,' said Jon. 'Anyone here remember Cook Smith and the torch?'

They pressed him for the story.

'Right, well, we'd all been on the rifle ranges in Germany during our last training trip there. Most of the squadron actually, we were going to do a night shoot but had an hour or so to wait until it got dark. The lads and officers were all mixed up but sitting on the ground in three lines. Smithy had acquired a very foul, smutty book and was reading to everyone to pass the time. To everyone's approval I might add. He had just got to a completely disgusting bit about anal sex and we were all listening intently when the Colour Sergeant decided enough was enough and he would take charge of our entertainment.

'Bloody Royals, always having to interfere.'

'Ah, but it backfired big time. He called Smith out and told him to stand clear to stop him being a bad influence. He then got us all to our feet and started making us do silly things like dance a Can Can. Meanwhile, Smith had spotted one of those big green torches we use for setting up tactical landing sites. Nobody could work out what he was doing at first but then we all twigged. You see, the Colour Sergeant was wearing a Clansman radio as a backpack and the aerial was sticking up behind his head. Smithy was pointing the torch at his back and appeared to be wiggling his hand. We all got it at once. He was radio controlling the Royal Marine! After that, it slowly became chaos. We all started laughing and Colours couldn't work out why. That just made him angrier. But of course, he was only really getting angry because Smithy was controlling him that way, which made it even funnier. On several occasions, he spun around to see if there was something happening behind him but all he saw was Smith with the most innocent look imaginable on his face. As Colours slowly lost control of the situation, Smith waggled his controller faster and faster. The Royal got more and more angry and we were literally falling around laughing.'

'How did it end?'

'Well the Boss had to stop it eventually but I'm pretty sure that even now the Colour Sergeant hasn't worked it out.'

The conversation then slowly got serious.

'Do you think we're we really ever going to have to do all this survival shit for real?' someone asked.

Jon answered. 'Quite possibly, you guys haven't flown out here yet but I have. For a start, the whole bloody country is held together by wires and nearly every year despite all the surveys we do, some clown manages to hit some. They're mainly for logging but there are loads of high tension power lines as well. If you spear in on route you don't want to stay in the aircraft believe me, it's just a bloody great fridge. So yeah, you might well need some survival skills.'

That got a grunt of acknowledgement from somewhere. 'And what about if the bloody Russians really attack? What are we actually going to do?'

A chorus of 'Run Away' greeted the question followed by the usual ribald comments.

But despite the levity, it brought about a general discussion. The Cold War was something they had all been brought up with. Ever since they could remember, the Superpowers had confronted each other over the plains of Germany and up here in the frozen north. Tension had ebbed and flowed but no one doubted that the threat was still very real.

Jon summed it up. 'You know guys, it's only a few hundred miles to the east of here and you get to Murmansk, the base for their northern fleet and my God it's big. Not much further and you're in the Baltic and another fleet. You all know how much kit they've got. We see the photographs all the time. Only a fool would underestimate them.'

'Yeah but is it really any good? Look at those crappy old turbo prop Bear bombers we see all the time. You could shoot them down with a rifle and everything they build looks so agricultural.'

'Yes, I would agree but the only problem is that they've got fucking shed loads of the stuff. You think about it, send forty old propeller driven bombers to attack a fleet. Very few need to get through to really ruin your day. They carry some very serious missiles you know. Same goes for their ships, tanks and everything. Their quality may not be as good as ours but by God, they've got the quantities.'

The conversation drifted to a halt as sleep took hold but it was quite clear that everyone of them felt they were here for a very good reason, no one doubted their purpose.

Chapter 3

Moscow

Yuri Alexeyev looked at his wife and son. They weren't smiling. Anna was scowling at him over the breakfast table and his son didn't look too friendly either. Yuri suspected they had been colluding and now he was about to get the results.

'How much vodka did you have last night Yuri? You didn't get back until three in the morning. When are you going to start your life again? This can't go on,' his wife asked grimly.

Yuri looked at Anna. To him, she looked exactly the same as the day they'd married slim, dark haired and brown eyed. He still loved her as much as the day he set eyes on her. But that didn't mean he had to put up with this continual criticism. He was head of the household and he decided to when to come home, not her. The nagging headache didn't help maybe she was right but he was damned if he was going to admit it.

'If I want to go out and drink with my friends, I will and none of your incessant nagging is going to stop me.' He retorted angrily and made to get up from the table.

'Dad,' said Gregor entering the family debate. 'We're only worried for you. Ever since the accident you've changed. Can't you go back to your work?'

Yuri knew that this was the real core of his problem and it was one he couldn't see a way around.

'Look, you know I can't tell you what I was doing, apart from the fact that it involved flying. Look at me, do you think I will ever fly a plane again?' And he brandished his metal leg at them from the side of the table. 'Who do you think is going to let a cripple fly?'

The Caspian Monster

It was almost two years now since he had been rescued from the wreckage of his escape pod somewhere in the Siberian tundra. He remembered nothing about it. His first recollection after the accident was of a white suited doctor leaning over him and telling him he was alright. That was a bare faced lie but he didn't know it then. Eventually, he found out that his legs had been badly crushed when the pod hit the ground too hard because one of its three parachutes had failed to open. Had he been conscious, he might have been able to parachute out of the pod and make a safe landing on his own. The system was built for that but the violence of ejecting at a speed far in excess of the stress tolerances of the design had knocked him out cold. They told him afterwards that he now had the dubious honour of being the world record holder for the fastest ever successful ejection. Somehow that didn't offer much consolation. Especially when the doctor finally came clean and said that one of his legs would have to come off. Luckily for him, it was below the knee but Yuri saw his career disappear along with the limb. They had all been very considerate, even allowing him to convalesce at home on full pay until he was medically discharged. He had even been given a medal and a modest pension but with what seemed like almost indecent haste they removed him from the test site and off the programme. No one, it seemed, wanted a failed and crippled test pilot.

So here he was now, in his Moscow flat with his family, slowly descending into a despairing apathy. But knowing it and doing something about it were two different things.

Anna looked him hard in the eye. 'Yuri Alexeyev, you're better than this. Many people have got over worse and carried on with their lives successfully. Anyway, if you won't do anything about it then I will. In fact, I already have.' She stared defiantly at him.

'What have you done woman? You have no right.' Oh my God, had she gone out and got him some boring job behind a desk? That really would be the end of him.

'No right? How dare you,' she shouted at him. 'You want to work again, maybe even fly but you do nothing but drink vodka and live in self pity. Well, clean yourself up, because I've arranged an appointment for you at the Kremlin with my uncle.'

Yuri looked startled. 'What? How on earth did you do that?'

'Family counts, you should know that. I pulled a few strings. You're expected at his office at two o'clock, so you'd better have a shower and shave and get ready.'

For once Yuri didn't know what to say.

At one thirty, dressed in his best suit, he presented himself to the Kremlin. Anna had refused to tell him what the meeting was for and he suspected she probably didn't really know all the detail anyway. But being related, even by marriage to the Soviet Defence Minister, was clearly not a bad thing. At the main reception, he found that indeed his name was on a list and a guard took him up in a lift to the third floor. He was deposited in a bland office that held a few chairs, a table with some very old magazines and the most formidable looking woman he had ever seen sitting behind a desk. He announced his presence which she barely acknowledged, gesturing to a chair and merely saying that he would be seen soon.

Time passed slowly and he was starting to worry when the phone rang and the dragon lady picked it up and then looked over at him. 'Minister Ustinov will see you now.' And she pointed to the door.

He got up and was about to reach for the door handle when it opened and the bespectacled smiling face of his uncle-in-law held out his hand in greeting.

'Yuri, good to see you come on in,' and he waved him past into the inner office.

Yuri was surprised to see another man there who stood up as he limped in. He saw him look at his leg and prayed that whatever was coming, it was not going to be an issue.

The Minister introduced the stranger. 'Yuri, this is your namesake, Rostislav Alexeyev. He is the head of the Soviet Central Hydrofoil Design Bureau and something of a protege of mine.' The two men shook hands, sizing each other up. Yuri saw a tall thin man with a careworn face and an alert intelligence behind his pale blue eyes. But his mind was buzzing. *'Hydrofoils, what the hell was this all about?'*

As if reading his mind, the Minister continued. 'Yuri, I'm sure you're wondering why I have asked you here, please be seated.' And he indicated some leather armchairs arranged around a small circular table.

'First of all, the call from your wife came at a very appropriate moment. Rostislav here has a particular problem that you can help me with. Now, I understand that the medical profession have said you can no longer fly military aircraft, is that so?'

Yuri responded with a trace of bitterness in his voice. 'Yes Minister and nothing on my part would convince them otherwise. Did you know the British had a fighter pilot in the Great War with no legs at all? And all I've got is the lower part of one missing.'

'Yuri calm down. I know you were one of the top test pilots in the Union. No, in fact, you were the top pilot and your skill was not all in your left foot,' he added with a grin. 'Rostislav here is also running a classified programme and has also suffered a setback. He is looking for a highly qualified and experienced test pilot but also one with an engineering background like yours. In fact, you're exactly what he needs. That's what we were discussing before you came in. I hope you won't mind moving your family to the Caspian Sea by the way?'

Getting more and more confused Yuri looked at the Minister. 'No, we'll move where we have to. But hang on, you keep talking about test flying. If I'm not allowed to fly military aircraft, then what use am I?'

'Ah, but how would you like to fly a military ship?'

Chapter 4

Bardufoss

Christmas had come and gone. With no direct family at home, Jon had volunteered to be the duty officer at Bardufoss over the break, much to the gratitude of the other officers in line for the job. The period would have been quite a trial except for the fact that he had spent the majority of it with the beautiful Inga. And that might just have had something to do with his decision.

But now, post New Year reality was setting in. The place was starting to buzz again. Last night, several Hercules had landed and the support staff and engineers were hauling the Sea Kings out of the hangar and getting them ready for the next training course that started on the upcoming Monday.

He was also expecting two more Sea Kings from Yeovilton so that when training was complete the six aircraft could be deployed to the end of season Arctic exercise that was planned for the end of February.

He was looking forward to their arrival. Not only would SNOB be on board and he could hand back his administrative duties but his friend Dave Brown, the Squadron Senior Pilot, would also be there and that meant Jon could get back to solely concentrating on doing what he really loved and that was flying. His duties prior to Christmas had kept him on the ground far more than he would have liked. However, the aircraft should have arrived at 1130 this morning, just as it was getting light. It was now gone 1400 and if they weren't here soon it would mean them arriving in pitch dark. Not a problem for the aircrew but it would make securing and servicing the aircraft much harder for the engineers. More importantly, why hadn't they radioed ahead and updated their ETA?

Suddenly, he heard the familiar sound of two Sea Kings flying directly overhead just as the telephone rang. The control tower confirmed that the aircraft would be landing shortly. Still wondering why they were late, he made his way down to the flight line building to welcome them back.

From the line shack, he watched the two aircraft ground taxi to their spots and shut down their rotors. The Sea King could also power fold its rotor blades for ship operations but they didn't do that here. It was just another thing to go wrong. Soon, people were climbing out and emptying kit onto the trolleys provided. The aircrew exited the forward doors and made their way towards him. Jon could recognise SNOB but nowhere could he see the sight of the Senior Pilot.

As the aircrew entered the shack, a tall sandy haired Lieutenant Commander, who Jon had never seen before, demanded in an imperious tone, 'right, where's the duty officer? I'm not at all happy with this.'

Slightly nonplussed, Jon stepped forward and held out his hand. 'Hello, my name is Jonathon Hunt. I've been guarding the place over Christmas. I guess you could call me the duty officer.'

The tall man looked at Jon as though he had crawled out from under a stone. 'In my navy young man, Lieutenants call Lieutenant Commanders, Sir. Now, sort out the aircraft and come and see me in the main office once you've done that.' And he turned his back on Jon and started to sign in the aircraft.

Jon looking slightly bemused, saw SNOB come in and raised an eyebrow in query. His friend gave him a conspiratorial grin but shook his head.

So, Jon did as he was told, even though the ground crew knew exactly what to do. If nothing else, it kept him away from the newcomer for a while as he gathered his thoughts. The first thing he did was track down SNOB and ask him exactly what was going on and where the hell was the Senior Pilot?

The Caspian Monster

SNOB gave a short bark of a laugh at the question. 'Sorry mate but that is the new 'Splot' his name is Ewan Bailey. Your mate Dave Brown fell off that stupid Harley Davidson of his coming back from the pub and is going to be out of it for several months. He was due for relief anyway at the end of this deployment, so they got his replacement in early. And boy you are really going to love him.'

'Yeah, I think I've already worked that out. So anyway, how come I don't know him? It's not that big a club.'

'Ah well, while you were poncing about in the Lynx world, he transferred in from an Anti-Submarine Squadron. He did a tour with the training squadron as he's also an instructor and now he's got the Splot job. Oh and before you ask, he is universally known as the biggest wanker this side of the black stump. What's even worse, is that he is almost passed over for promotion and is looking at this job as his final chance to make a name. So you'd better watch out.'

'Oh great, just what we need. Hang on, is he Arctic trained?'

'Nope, he's here as a student just like the rest of the newcomers but don't expect that to help. On the way up here, he's been telling us all how we should really do it and what changes he's going to make. Bearing in mind that I'm the one actually in command here and the same rank as him, you would think he would be more circumspect. But I haven't said anything yet. I'll keep my powder dry for the moment. But look matey, be careful this guy is poison.'

'Thanks for the heads up, I guess I'd better see what he wants now.'

A few minutes later and with some trepidation, Jon knocked on the door of his own office where the new man had apparently decided to take up residence.

A curt 'come in,' had answered his knock. He stepped in and stood in front of the desk. The newcomer studiously ignored him.

He eventually looked up at Jon and studied him in silence. 'Ah, now I know you. You're Lieutenant Jonathon Hunt the Lynx pilot,' and before Jon could respond. 'You're the clever dick that shot down a Pucara in the Falklands, am I right? They gave you a DSO. Well, let's get one thing straight, I don't care about your past, only about your current performance. From what I've seen already, this place needs some serious waking up and I'm the one that's going to do it. Understand?'

Jon was completely taken aback and didn't have a clue how to respond so simply nodded.

'Right, well we'll start by tidying my office, you can help.'

'Er, Sir, this isn't your office, its mine.'

'What? If I say it's mine then that's an end to it.'

'No Sir, sorry but you have a much bigger one two doors down the corridor. Surely you don't want to share with the other trainers. That's why there are two other desks in here.'

Jon could see the thought processes going through the man's mind and would have smiled except it would have only poured petrol onto the fire.

Eventually, the realisation that there was a much better office for him won through. 'Right, well, thank you for that,' he blustered. 'You'd better show me the way then but remember what I said. Things are going to change around here.'

Later that evening, there was a gaggle of aircrew around the bar. The new Senior Pilot had yet to make an appearance and mutinous rumblings were already under way. It appeared that within the space of a week, the new Splot had managed to alienate just about all his aircrew and if rumour was to be believed, most of the engineers as well. However, as the next most senior squadron officer, Jon found himself in the unusual position of having to defend his superior if for no other reason than to maintain the chain of command.

'Now, pack it in you lot, give the man a chance. Let him get settled. He may not be as bad as he seems,' said Jon forcefully, not really believing a word of it.

'That's alright for you to say Jon,' came a voice from the crowd. 'But I've got a mate on an ASW squadron and what he says about the guy only confirms what we've already found out.'

'That's enough, change the subject,' and then he added with just a note of smugness. 'And remember one thing guys, he's going out on arctic training just like the rest of you lot and things can be quite testing out there. Especially if I have a word with my marine chums. Now, whose round is it? Because it bloody well isn't mine.'

The next morning, Jon was leafing through the morning signals when the phone rang. It was the Squadron Commanding officer back at Yeovilton.

'Morning Jon,' came the friendly voice of the Boss over the phone. 'All going well I trust?'

'Fine Sir, the new Senior Pilot and the rest arrived safely yesterday. When are you coming out?' asked Jon, praying that it would be soon.

'Not until the end of Feb, for the exercise I'm afraid. You'll have to soldier on without me. We've got a couple of issues back here I have to deal with. Now look, the reason for ringing is that you are going to have two visitors tomorrow. They are flying out and should get to you at midday. Apparently, you'll know them on sight. The problem is that they'll have a little job for you and it's highly classified. So much so, that even I'm not cleared for it and look, just as importantly nor is the Senior Pilot. It's got something to do with the security clearance you achieved last year during the Falklands. Operation Dragonfly I'm told, whatever that was. Anyway, the point I am making is that you will have to tell Splot to let you get on with this on your own. You have one aircraft and a ground crew at your disposal and you have free rein to pick who you want, is that all clear?'

'Sort of Sir, can't you tell me anything more?'

'Sorry, not really, I don't actually know any more. Your man tomorrow will give you the full story. Oh and good luck with the Senior Pilot. Jon, I know he can be difficult but give him a chance please? I won't say anymore, I'm sure you know what I mean.'

Jon put the phone down and stared at the wall. Well, it sounded like something interesting was coming up and hopefully, it would get him off base for a while. But what on earth was it?

Chapter 5

Near Astrakhan on the Caspian Sea

Yuri stopped the car and looked out over the sparkling blue waters ahead of him. He drew in a breath of crisp sea air. Suddenly, he felt alive again and optimistic about the future. The move to the Caspian Sea base was proving remarkably easy. Anna and Gregor would follow on but he was pleased with the little house provided in the local town. Now he was driving his relatively new Lada to the base, his new working home. As he got closer, so did his pent up curiosity. The actual base was several miles out of town around a rocky peninsula. He guessed that it was because of the need for some level of secrecy but quite why was still a mystery although he had a few theories of his own. As the buildings came into sight, all he could see was two enormous hangars and a relatively small office block. He then realised that actually, the building was quite a reasonable size it was just that the hangars dwarfed it so much. Leading from the closed doors of both hangars, were two massive concrete slipways that led into the sea but what they were used for was far from clear. The place seemed deserted. There was also what looked like a dry dock for ships.

The uniformed guard checked his pass at the large main gate and directed him to the car park by the office block. He entered the building and was surprised to be greeted by his new boss who was waiting for him in the lobby.

'Yuri, so good to see you at last, welcome.'

'And you Rostislav.'

They shook hands and he was ushered into a small conference room. Judging by the number of people they passed, it was clear that despite the inactivity outside, the place was actually very busy. Yuri was desperate to know what on earth they were doing. He still hadn't been told that much about his new job merely that it involved some sort of flying and that he would be able to do it despite his injury.

'Yuri, I really must apologise about the secrecy but I always find it useful to introduce people to my babies while they don't have any preconceptions. I hope that's alright?'

Almost bursting with curiosity, he just nodded.

'Right, now as you know, this is the design bureau for hydrofoils but we haven't designed one of those for years. We've been concentrating on a different form of machine, something that the West doesn't have and something that could revolutionise our armed forces. Please, no questions just come with me. We will go and visit the hangars.'

So saying, Yuri was led out of the room by a back door and across to the smaller of the two buildings. At the side was a normal size door which looked tiny in the massive wall. Rostislav pushed it open and ushered Yuri inside.

He had a feeling of Déjà Vu. It was just like the day he been introduced to the Tiger all those years ago. This was yet another incomprehensible machine of enormous size. But as soon as he could take in the dimensions and configuration, the pilot in him was screaming that it was all wrong. It had eight jet engines, four either side but they were mounted high up and either side of the cockpit in exactly the wrong place. He then noticed two more half way up the enormous tail which was topped by a massive 'v' shaped tail plane. The hull was obviously boat shaped and he could understand that bearing in mind that they were on the shore of the Caspian Sea and there were those massive slipways. This was clearly a sea plane of some sort. But what was totally wrong were the wings. They were in roughly the right place, quite broad and finished in massive end plates. *'But they were far too small'* he realised. This was madness. What the hell was this thing? He turned to his boss who was smiling.

'The look on your face Yuri is the same I see every time I show them my Ekranoplan for the first time. Let me give you some facts. It travels at over 400 kilometres an hour, weighs over 500 tonnes, yet can lift almost 1000 tonnes at that speed. And yes, it does fly but only at about 20 metres above the sea. Because of this, it is actually classified as a ship, not an aircraft which is why we are able to clear you to operate it.'

'Ekranoplan? What does that mean? How does it fly even so close to the sea?'

'Simple, it uses ground effect. Come on, you're a pilot, you know that the closer to the ground you get, the more lift you get. With some aircraft, it actually makes them quite hard to get back onto the runway.'

Yuri nodded. He had experienced that, particularly with gliders.

'So, we use that effect. All the engines are used to accelerate it through the water until we get enough speed, then we lift off into the air cushion produced under the machine. We can then shut down most of the engines as it's incredibly efficient once flying. So, the range we can achieve is enormous. With that lift capacity and speed, it makes a very effective marine assault vehicle. It is extremely hard to detect by radar as it travels so low. We are also working on other variants. The potential is endless.'

Yuri couldn't help but notice the almost evangelical tone in his Boss's voice. But clearly the monster did fly and his heart leaped when he realised that he would soon be flying it.

'Come, you can look over her,' and he led Yuri inside the capacious hold.

Three hours later they went back to Rostislav's office.

Sitting back in an office chair and drinking tea provided by his new boss's secretary, Yuri's mind was whirling. On the one hand, the machine he had been shown was amazing and the fact that he could be flying it had regenerated all his enthusiasm like nothing else could. Unfortunately, he still had serious doubts about the whole situation and despite the tour, they were not going away.

'Rostislav, thank you for showing me the incredible machine and believe me I can't wait to get involved in the programme but forgive me for asking, why me? This is obviously a mature project and you must have many pilots with far more experience. Why bring in a complete stranger at this stage. I'm sorry, I really want the job but it just doesn't make sense.'

Rostislav looked at his new recruit shrewdly wondering how much he should reveal. He had taken a liking to this man as soon as they had met and his test flying and engineering experience were just what he needed. But there was far more to the move than that.

'Yuri, I'm going to be totally honest. There are two major reasons for recruiting you and they don't include your obvious expertise to do the job which on its own would be enough.'

Yuri just nodded. It looked like his suspicions were correct.

'Firstly, what I haven't told you is that the machine you have just looked at is our second prototype. We only use it for ground and system tests and it will probably never fly. But the first one did. However, two months ago it crashed and we haven't been able to recover it. It's just far too heavy for any lifting equipment we can get hold of.' He held up a hand as he saw the question forming on Yuri's face. 'We think the pilot failed to use full power on the main engines and although significant speed was achieved, it wasn't enough and it didn't take off. However, when he throttled back, the nose dug in and it literally dived in nose first. I say 'we think' because we don't know where the pilot is. Divers went down and recovered the bodies of the engineering crew but the pilot was missing. We don't know whether he escaped or not.'

'Hang on Rostislav, why would he want to disappear? If that's what you're insinuating.'

'Well, why not use full power? It's a known handling problem with these machines. Look, this brings me onto the second issue I mentioned and its politics pure and simple. If it wasn't for Minister Ustinov, there are enough people against this project to shut it down. There is a strong lobby in government for reductions in defence spending and any programme that doesn't have immediate potential is under threat. As it is, I have just received orders for over a hundred smaller machines with several different variants and it's this programme I need a new chief test pilot for. And I need that test pilot to be untainted with internal politics and someone I can trust. Because, believe me, there are enough people out there who would like to see this programme fail.'

Yuri thought carefully and then nodded. Clearly being related to the Minister was the key issue here. Nepotism was a way of life in Soviet politics but he couldn't see why he should object.

'I can understand that,' he left the issue of his uncle unspoken. It was clearly understood by both men. 'But if I take this on, I want the final say on the flight test crew and the management of the test programme itself.'

'I wouldn't have it any other way Yuri,' and he reached over and shook his hand. As he did so he wondered what Yuri would have said had he revealed his other reason, the overriding one for recruiting him. He thought, *'No, it may not come to anything anyway and then he will be better off for not knowing.'*

Chapter 6

200 metres below the Arctic ice

Captain Andrei Orlov was dog tired. His Shchuka class submarine was the fastest and quietest in the Soviet Northern Fleet. His job was to get out into the Atlantic Ocean and hunt the enemy. Unlike surface ships, the winter ice didn't affect his movements. He had spent several intense days planning this patrol. The most important part was getting out into the Atlantic undetected. They had sailed in darkness when no American satellites were anywhere near. Slipping below the surface as soon as they could, they headed out under the ice of the polar cap. It was proving to be a very cold winter this year and the ice was providing even more cover than usual. Consequently, he was quite sure no one had seen him depart, either from the shore or the sky. He had been given a free hand to decide his route and he had decided on a circuitous track. His initial heading had been towards the pole and he only doubled back towards his exit point when well clear of Soviet territory. However, in the end, he had been constrained to his exit point, as his orders required him to patrol the Atlantic, not the other side of the world. But this still gave him hundreds of miles of choice when it came to picking his exit from the ice.

At first, he felt confident that he had made it. Sneaking slowly clear of the pack ice at the edge of the Arctic Circle, not far from the Faeroes, all had seemed quiet. At last, he finally decided he could rest and had slid gratefully into his bunk when a yell from the control room jerked him back to full consciousness. The sonar operator using their passive hydrophones had picked up the whir of a propulsor. It had quickly been translated into the tell tale signature of a British hunter killer submarine. For the next day, no matter how he tried, Orlov couldn't shake it off. What was worse, it was clear the

British could retreat at will and then find him just as simply whenever they wanted. It made him wonder how many times he had been tracked in the past and had never known it. However, this British captain may have made a big mistake in being so aggressive. By showing how clever he was, he was also showing how capable he was and telling the enemy that was a rash thing to do. When he returned from this patrol, he would be asking some very serious questions.

Several hundred miles away and several hundred feet above, the sonar operator finally sat back in his chair. His supervisor looked over at the blank screen and patted him on the shoulder. They had been tracking the Soviet Victor Three submarine for almost two days but now he had been handed off to the Royal Navy and they could relax.

'Well done everyone, that was a long one. He didn't want to get caught that's for sure. But good work,' he announced to the whole room. 'Now keep your vigilance up. I expect another will be along soon. That's why we're here after all and we don't want any slipping through the net.'

Privately, the supervisor wondered how long this could go on. Surely the dumb Soviets would eventually realise just how bloody noisy their submarines really were.

Of course, none of this solved the other problem they were facing up here. With the ice so thick this winter, how on earth were they going to get resupplied?

Bardufoss

The small executive jet touched down at Bardufoss just after midday as expected. Jon went over to the Norwegian side of the airfield in a Land Rover to pick up his mysterious passengers. Despite the Squadron CO briefing Jon personally on the phone, the Senior Pilot had got wind of the arrival and ordered Jon to bring the newcomers to him after they had been collected. Jon had shied away from a confrontation as he wasn't really sure of his ground. Hopefully, all would come clear once he knew who he was meeting. In his heart, he knew he was hoping to be able to palm the problem off onto the newcomers. He felt a bit guilty about that but then it was their problem really. The mention of the codeword 'Dragonfly' had made his heart skip a beat when the Boss used it. But quite what a clandestine operation during the Falklands War had to do with the current situation he was dying to find out.

He saw two figures climb down out of the jet. One was quite tall and heavily built, the other smaller and limping slightly. Jon recognised them at once. The tall one was Brian Pearce, until recently the Observer from his Lynx Flight during his previous appointment. The other was called Rupert Thomas and when Jon last knew him he had worked for MI6. He assumed he still did. His limp was a legacy of a little adventure they had all shared before the shooting war had started down south. But what on earth were they doing here?

The door to the terminal let in a cold blast of air and then he was shaking hands with his old colleagues.

'Bloody hell, you two were the last people I expected to see. What on earth is going on?'

'Not now, not here,' said Rupert looking around. 'We'll brief once we're somewhere secure. Anyway, how are you? Long time no see.'

'Pretty good and you Brian, you're looking well.'

'Yes, well, a shore training job is a lot less stressful than being flung around the sky by some maniac bloody pilot.' Brian's warm handshake and massive grin belied his words.

'Ok, I've got a Land Rover outside. Let's get your kit and get you over to our side.'

So saying, he bustled them outside and into the waiting vehicle, chucking their bags into the back.

As they drove around the airfield he explained the layout. 'The officer's mess where we're going is called Milliways just in case you hear people using that term.'

'Ah the 'Restaurant at the End of the Universe',' acknowledged Brian. 'That seems quite appropriate. It is a bit like the asshole of the world up here. Is there anything else to see other than snow and pine trees?'

Jon laughed. 'No, not really, although you should see how the Noggies decorate the insides of their houses to compensate. I hope you like primary colours.' But he acknowledged the truth of his friend's remark. The area was white, flat and barren. Just the runway was cleared of snow.

They chatted happily, catching up on their news until Rupert noticed a piano sitting forlornly in the snow by the wall of the officer's mess they were fast approaching. 'Don't tell me you have sing songs out in the snow Jon? I know Arctic training is meant to be tough but that's just silly.'

'Ah,' said Jon. 'Yes, that's our piano but it was stolen recently by the Norwegian Huey helicopter squadron. We've only just retrieved it from about four thousand feet up the side of a mountain. It's going to have to be repaired a bit first. Mind you, no one here can play the bloody thing, so it's not a priority. Of course, we're going to have to get our revenge on the Noggies. We're just biding our time. Right, here we are. I've got you cabins next to mine where you can stow your kit and then we'd better find somewhere to talk. Oh, by the way, our new Senior Pilot arrived the other day and he could be a problem.' He started to explain why but Rupert cut him off.

'Jon, don't worry, he may outrank you but for this operation but I have been given the authority of a Brigadier, so I can sort him out.'

'Just as long as you don't try to dress and act as one please,' said Jon looking slightly worried. 'I remember last time you tried to be a Royal Marine. You ended up with a broken leg and dropped me deeply in the shit.'

The Caspian Monster

'Hmmph, well that's not quite how I remember it but you're right. No, this is just to ensure I can overrule anyone who wants to interfere and it sounds as though it was a good precaution to take.'

Half an hour later, they were ensconced in one of the small briefing rooms and Rupert was opening his briefcase when the door flew open.

The Senior Pilot was clearly out of sorts yet again. 'Hunt, I told you to bring these visitors to me as soon as they arrived.'

'Sorry Sir,' said Jon, who wasn't sorry at all. 'I thought it best to get them settled in first.'

'Don't think young man, just do as you're told,' and then turning to the two newcomers he turned off his scowl and held out his hand smiling. 'Gentlemen, Ewan Bailey, I'm in charge up here.'

Rupert shook his hand. 'Ah, you must be SNOB. I rather like that title. I'm Rupert Thomas and I'm in charge of this little operation.'

Ewan looked slightly discomforted. 'No, I'm the Senior Pilot of the Squadron here and the most senior officer on site.'

Rupert frowned. 'Sorry old chap, I wasn't briefed about you. I was told to liaise with the chap in command and anyway I can't really tell him anything as only Lieutenant Hunt here is cleared to the required level.'

'Yes, well that was probably before I arrived,' he blustered. 'You can obviously include me in all the briefings now. After all, this is my squadron and pilot we're talking about.'

Rupert realised this wasn't going the way he needed. 'With respect, I don't think you heard what I just said. There is only one person here on this base who I am authorised to talk to and it's not you. I really don't care who you are or what rank you have. I repeat you are not cleared to know about this operation. Would you kindly leave.'

'You can't speak to me like that, this is a military base and I am the senior officer here. Let's get that absolutely clear.'

Rupert sighed and pulled a sheet of paper out of his briefcase. He thrust it towards the red faced officer. 'Read this.'

He snatched the paper and scanned it becoming more and more red faced in the process. 'Well, we'll see about this. I'll go and talk to my CO. Hunt you come with me.'

Rupert had had enough. 'Jon stay where you are,' and then turning to the Senior Pilot. 'Clearly, you didn't read that instruction properly. Lieutenant Hunt here is now under my command and I have the authority to utilise him and any of the military equipment as I see fit. For goodness sake, surely you must see this is important. We're not doing this for fun but this situation is highly classified and the numbers of those involved must be kept to a minimum. Now, please, just leave us to get on with our business.'

The Senior Pilot looked at them all and realised this was an argument he wasn't going to win. With a grunt he turned round and left, slamming the door in his wake.

For a few seconds there was a startled silence in the room and then Brian broke it. 'Fuck me Jon, is that idiot part of your squadron? Where the hell did they scare him up from?'

Jon shrugged. 'He arrived a few days ago and has already managed to piss off just about everybody up here, so why should you two be any different?'

Rupert broke in. 'Jon, I'll get on the phone about this after we've briefed. Don't worry, he won't be a problem. Now look, we really need to get on with talking over this operation.'

He pulled out some more papers from his briefcase and several photographs. 'First things first. When we last met, I was running Dragonfly, which is of course now all wound up. I was then asked to head up the Scandinavian section of MI6 for which I was pretty grateful as it was promotion apart from anything else. As part of the task, I have a relatively large interface with you lot in the military. And one specific interface is a joint effort we have running a little to the north of here.'

'North?' queried Jon. 'There's nothing but sea and ice north of here.'

'Er, not quite as you will find out.'

Brian joined in. 'Jon this is quite a story and it will also explain why they roped me in.'

'OK, sorry I'll shut up and let Rupert carry on.'

Rupert handed over some photographs that Jon couldn't really interpret. 'Don't worry about those just yet. Now, a question, what is the biggest Soviet threat in naval terms?'

Jon thought for a moment. 'Their submarines I would guess. It's what we all seem to get worked up about these days.'

'And you'd be absolutely correct. It's the biggest submarine fleet in the world by far and there doesn't seem to be any let up in production or development. They have literally hundreds of them and a large number are a based here in their northern fleet. However, they have a couple of problems. The first is that to get into the open Atlantic they have to go past us here or through the Iceland Faeroes gap and that constrains their routes. It wouldn't matter so much if they were difficult to detect but for some reason, they don't seem to have realised how noisy they are. We can track them with passive sonar over quite a distance.'

'Yes, my last ship heard one even though we didn't have a full passive array and I know we have to put noise makers on our own subs to allow them to simulate the Russian ones.'

'That's right, so we've been a bit sneaky and put a listening station up in the ice. We can track just about any submarine that leaves the Kola and heads out. If we know where they start from it's pretty easy to keep track of them thereafter.'

'Hang on a second,' said Jon. 'How on earth did you get something like that up there without the Russians finding out? Oh yes and doesn't the polar ice cap move? Won't the station end up in the wrong place?'

'Two very good questions with one simple answer,' said Brian taking over the brief. 'We got it there by submarine and that's also how we move it.' He hurried on seeing the look on Jon's face. 'It's a fairly small facility and it's actually based on the design of a submarine, with self contained accommodation, stores, a generator and a control room The first photo I gave you shows what it looks like before it's deployed.'

They saw a photograph of what looked like a small truncated submarine, with an odd, very tall, narrow fin and no propeller.

'It's towed behind a submarine with the staff on the mother ship rather like they used to do with the midget submarines in the last war. Submarines can normally break through the ice and then they position it through the hole. It has a fin, as you can see, which is the only part that protrudes above the ice. One of the big problems is the infra red signature which could easily be seen by a satellite, especially from the generator but some clever boffins and a lot of shovelled snow can disguise it pretty well.'

'Alright,' said Jon. 'All good stuff but what's it got do with me?'

Rupert answered. 'Firstly, the clearances you two got for the Dragonfly operation are still extant and so you were immediately available. And we needed people like you to do the mid winter resupply. The only access is through the hatch at the top of the fin. The winter has been unusually harsh and the latest ice depths rule out a submarine being able to break through. This shouldn't have happened but that'll teach us to believe the weather men.'

'You mentioned a joint effort Rupert. What else is there going on that involves MI6? It seems you've accidentally missed out that bit.'

'Ah, yes, well, can't tell you everything old chap. Just take it from me that we have some of our stuff up there as well. Now look, they can last out for another month, even six weeks but that won't be long enough for the spring thaw to start. It's quite simple, we want you to fly up there and take them their stores.'

Jon looked at Brian who replied before Jon could formulate the question. 'It's alright Jon, I've done the calculations and worked out a route. It should be quite straightforward. Oh and Rupert needs to come too although apparently, we don't need to know why.'

'Sorry about that,' said Rupert with an apologetic smile. 'But I have one of my men up there on the team and need to talk to him personally. I can't say anymore I'm afraid.'

'Fair enough, now you said this is not desperately urgent, so have we got a few days to get you some basic arctic survival training? It's really quite important.'

'Yes, we anticipated that. We reckon we would need to leave in about five days will that be enough?'

Jon thought for a second. 'Yes, I'm sure we can work something out in that time frame.'

With the basics covered, they moved on to discuss some more general planning issues, before Jon called time out and forced his unwilling partners to the bar.

Ewan Bailey had left the meeting in a foul mood. It then wasn't helped by SNOB firstly telling him to mind his own business and then going on to make it quite clear who was in charge of what. Grinding his teeth in impotent rage, he went back to his office to think about what to do next. As he sat in his chair, he suddenly realised he could hear voices from the room next door. The walls in this building were clearly quite thin. He realised he could hear the two newcomers and Jon Hunt. They were fairly indistinct but if he moved his chair to the wall, he could make out a fair amount of what was being said. When they had finished, he sat back feeling a little better. From what he could make out, it was actually a fairly routine task. Maybe he shouldn't have worried in the first place, it didn't sound like he was going to be missing out on anything after all. However, that didn't mean he wouldn't be taking that arrogant young Lieutenant down a peg or two when the opportunity arose.

Chapter 7

The Caspian Sea

Yuri was truly happy again. He was sitting behind the controls of an aircraft and flying. What more could he ask for? Well actually it was only a sort of flying as he was only twenty metres up and wasn't likely to get much higher. But this close to the sea and at this speed it was tremendously exhilarating. Concentration levels were necessarily high. It wouldn't take much of a twitch on the controls, to make some part of the machine to hit the sea and at this speed that would be disastrous. At least he had the comfort of knowing that should an engine fail he had an infinitely long runway to land on just below him.

The machine he was flying was considerably smaller than the original he had been shown. It weighed in at a mere one hundred and twenty five tons. However, here he was using only the one massive turboprop on the tail to provide the power. The two jet engines in the nose had been shut down as soon as take off had been achieved.

He had to smile when he first heard the name of this machine. It was called 'Orlyonok' which meant 'Eaglet'. He supposed that was because it was so much smaller than the original designs. However, a small bird she definitely was not. She was still capable of carrying one hundred and fifty troops at four hundred kilometres an hour with an enormous range.

When he started work in earnest, he had found out that the design was quite old but had been subject to several major revisions after two bad crashes. The machine he was testing was due to be the first real production model and the first of one hundred and thirty to be built. It varied quite a deal from the original and that is why the test programme was being resumed. He was quite surprised about how well he had been received by the other flight test crew. There had been some initial resentment from the more experienced pilots, especially those detailed to train him on the vagaries of a machine that was at least part boat. But someone must have leaked something about his past. Secrecy was a way of life in the Soviet Union but pilots had their own way of knowing what was going on. When asked point blank whether it was him who had been the pilot of the Tiger programme who had ejected at over Mach Two, he was at first surprised and then instantly refused to answer. For some reason, this was taken as assent and his stock shot up.

However, now that he was fully in the driving seat of the test programme, he was making new friends and a few enemies. The friends were the flight crews and engineers who had been critical of the programme to date and who relished his fresh new approach. His enemies were those whose methods he had sidelined but even most of them were slowly coming round.

Today's flight was one of the last in a long line of tests to find and explore the limits of the full flight envelope of the machine. Despite being fast and economical, the basic design had a few flaws. Like any machine, it was a compromise and he wanted to minimise as many of those as possible. It was soon discovered that despite the theory, Ekranoplans would fly higher than predicted although this was still only at about 20 metres. Getting any higher would result in an odd shuffling roll as the ground effect cushion started to dissipate. Using the two front engines could reduce this as they were mounted at an angle and their thrust could reinforce the air cushion under the hull but even so, only another ten metres could be achieved and the effect on fuel consumption was terrible.

The reason for needing height was to be able to turn. In a straight line, it was relatively easy to fly and it could cope with any sea state. But to turn, one had to bank the machine and the wing tips could get very close to the sea surface very quickly. Even though they were fitted with reinforced end plates, put one into a wave and there was a good chance the machine would catapult to its destruction. Not surprisingly, pilots were very careful. Yuri had been looking at the problem from a three dimensional pilot's perspective and today he was going to try out a new idea. Normal turns were limited to about eight degrees of bank which gave an enormous radius of turn. One could also use an amount of rudder to skew the turn but today he was going to try to increase the rate of turn significantly with a new technique.

His flight engineer called over the intercom from the seat behind him. 'Starting the jets now.'

Yuri saw the gauges of the two Kuznetsov NK8 turbo fan engines run up to idle speed and he acknowledged the good light up.

'OK, everyone here we go,' he called as he applied power and pulled the nose up.

The effect of the extra forty six thousand pounds of thrust was instantaneous and the machine climbed steadily to over fifty metres. Yuri rolled to twenty degrees of bank and held everything steady. The wing tips should be well clear of the water at this height and his rate of turn was building nicely. However, he now started to encounter the problem he expected. As the angle of bank increased, the ground cushion started to dissipate and despite all the extra thrust at his command, the height started to fall away. He immediately had to reduce bank to compensate and they ended up nose high back at twenty metres again.

'We managed about a forty five degree turn,' his co-pilot observed. 'That's not too bad. If we repeated the manoeuvre we could reverse direction quite quickly compared to using less bank and lots of rudder.'

Yuri agreed and they happily spent the rest of the afternoon refining the technique.

Rostislav looked out of his office window as he heard the roar of the returning Ekranoplan. He watched as the monstrous machine half disappeared in a tumultuous cloud of spray. The two turbo jets in the nose were blasting exhaust gas partly under the wings which were trapping it behind enormous flaps lowered from the trailing edge.

The Caspian Monster

The resultant pressure helped keep the monster off the ground rather like a hovercraft. However, this machine also had wheels it could use on a smooth surface and the lumbering, roaring beast, slowly mounted the slipway before coming to rest like a beached whale. No matter how many times he saw one of his creations in operation he couldn't help feel a twinge of pride. They looked like nothing else on earth but somehow they looked the business. There was a design adage that said if something looked right then it probably was right and by God, his machines looked fantastic. Standing on a boat and watching one roar past at high speed was simply awesome, just as when they manoeuvred at slow speed as he had just witnessed.

The door to the flight compartment opened and he recognised Yuri climbing out. He smiled to himself. Getting that man on the team had been exactly the right thing to do. He had shaken up the whole programme and was now actively seeking new ways to reduce the limitations of the design. It would be interesting to hear how this afternoon's test had gone. Some of his designers had expressed reservations about the feasibility of the idea saying it was just too risky to manoeuvre at high altitude. But Yuri with his typical robustness had pointed out that they wouldn't know unless they tried and his test procedures were clearly designed to incrementally increase the severity of any manoeuvre and so minimise any risk.

He went down to the operations room and sat in on the debrief. Afterwards, he called Yuri to his office.

'Well done Yuri, another nail in the coffin of the sceptics. Do you think that's a manoeuvre an ordinary military pilot can be cleared to do though?'

Yuri responded immediately. 'Absolutely, although I wouldn't allow them to go to quite the extremes that we did today. But it should allow a great deal more operational flexibility, especially in a combat situation.'

'Good, we should be able to tell Moscow that we'll soon be ready to start initial operational training for military crews.'

Yuri laughed, 'Yes, as soon as the navy decide whether they want to assign pilots or ships captains to the job. If you ask me, they should have one of each. The hardest part of this job for me has been learning the maritime collision avoidance rules.'

'Well, that's their problem. Now, although the Eaglet meets its military specification, indeed it exceeds it in many ways, we both know there is one major problem to solve. I've been working on this for some time but before I tell you my thoughts, I would be interested if you have any ideas?'

Chapter 8

Bardufoss town

Jon Hunt desperately needed the loo. He had been lying quietly for some time but biology was winning. He slipped as quietly as he could from beneath the duvet and padded to the room next door. Minutes later and much relieved, he tiptoed back and slipped carefully back into bed. As he lifted the sheet he couldn't resist looking at the cute, smooth, sexy ass of Inga, as she lay on her side.

'*What a gorgeous, sexy girl, what a lovely bum,*' he thought, just as she rolled over, opened one eye and stretched luxuriously. The wan, pale light from the snowy scene outside was filtering through the light curtains. It silhouetted her profile and made her blonde hair seem almost white. '*The archetypal Snow Queen and she's all mine.*'

She smiled at him, seeing his eyes lock onto her breasts. 'Morning Jon, is there something there of interest to you?' she giggled.

'Silly question you raving nymphomaniac.'

Inga had needed the word explaining to her when Jon first said it but now she was quite proud when he used it about her. She reached her hand down. 'Seems I'm not the only one around here mad about sex.' She slid down the bed and confirmed his interest with her warm lips and tongue.

Later as they lay back in the tangled sheets, Inga looked over at the clock. 'Don't you have to be back at base this morning Jon?'

'No, as I said last night, if you remember, I'm working all over the weekend, so I've got the day off. Well at least until this evening.'

'Good, we can have breakfast and then spend all day in bed.'

Jon laughed slightly nervously, quite prepared to believe she really meant it. 'No, we agreed to go skiing remember. You seem to have a very selective memory this morning.'

She pouted back at him but made no reply as she jumped out of bed and headed to the shower. Jon lay back knowing he would have to wait at least five minutes or even more before he could use the room himself. Inga was a shower hog. He reached over and pulled back the curtain. It was almost pitch black outside, even though it was past nine in the morning. It wouldn't get fully light until eleven thirty and would be dark again by two. Luckily, the ski slopes in Tromso were well floodlit like most ski areas in this part of the world. He could see the heaped snow outside although it didn't seem to be snowing at the moment. He wondered what the weather would be like for his trip this weekend. The forecasts were good but you never knew. If the wind came from the east, it got cold very fast but the slightest shift to the west brought much warmer air as, this close to the sea, the remnants of the warm Gulf Stream would then have a major effect.

Sighing, he looked back into the room. The contrast to the dark black and white world outside was stark. Like most Norwegian houses, it was made of wood and all the walls were dark overlaid planks of spruce or pine. But on top were pictures, tapestries and decorations of the most vivid colours. It took some getting used to but was quite understandable. It didn't take long stuck outside to crave colour of any sort to relieve the monotony. It was unusual for a single girl to have a house like this but she had explained that both her parents had died some years before in a road accident. The one good thing to come of the tragedy was that she had inherited the house and he had the use of it and its owner so he wasn't complaining.

A damp and delightfully naked Inga broke his reverie. 'Come on lazybones, if you want to go skiing, you have to get out of bed you know.'

As he walked past the naked girl who was now towling herself vigorously, he was tempted to make a grab which he knew would probably not be resisted. However, he didn't get the chance to go downhill skiing too often, so he successfully fought off the temptation.

While Jon was in the shower, Inga went into the kitchen and started to make breakfast. She put the coffee on and got some meat and bread out of the fridge. She shuddered to remember the day at Christmas when Jon had decided to treat her to the British version of breakfast. How could anyone start the day with such a turgid mass of fried food? She remembered his disappointed response when she offered her opinion. It hadn't stopped him polishing off the lot though. There again, she was surprised at his opinion of pickled herrings. She had to point out that they were a refined taste. Clearly, the cultural divide was quite large in some areas. She sighed to herself. She was starting to get too fond of the good looking dark haired Englishman. She found that, all too often these days, she was having to remind herself of her real job.

Because Inga Thorsenn was not Norwegian. She had been born Inga Pochenko, in a small village on the Russian steppes. Her early life had been a classic Soviet story. The collective farm that provided her family with sustenance was a ramshackle affair, highly inefficient and over managed. Yet, much of what they produced disappeared into other people's pockets. However, none of that mattered to her because of her father. Her mother had died in childbirth when Inga was three and left behind a family of four brothers and herself. From a surprisingly early age, she had taken on or rather had been given the role of the woman of the house which mainly consisted of looking after her younger baby brother and doing the men's washing, cooking and cleaning. None of this mattered because of the stories her father told her. He had been a tank commander in one of the famous T34s and had taken part in several of the epic tank battles of the war. The stories he told of those confrontations could keep all his children enthralled for hours as could the tales of Nazi brutality and oppression. He explained that the current Soviet system was not perfect but was so much better than what they had before. Inga grew up hard working and extremely patriotic. At her local school she also stood out for another reason, top in class in all subjects, her teachers soon realised they would never be able to do her full justice. When she reached fourteen, her headmaster contacted an organisation specifically set up to take the best of the country's talent. What the headmaster didn't know was that it was run by the KGB.

She also developed into a beauty. Her mother had been attractive and she had inherited her blonde hair and clear skin but she also had her father's piercing blue eyes and strong features. By the time she was in her teens, her father was having to mount almost permanent guard over her from the hordes of local boys attempting to abuse her virtue.

One Sunday morning, everything changed. Prompted by the headmaster's letter, a man appeared at the door and asked to talk to Inga. He saw a delightfully pretty young girl but also one that he already knew had an excellent brain. He set her some special tests and then went to talk to her father. He took him to one side and explained what he wanted. He kept the details vague but made it clear that it was the patriotic thing to do. Although her father disliked the idea of losing his housemaid, he loved his daughter and wanted the best for her. He eventually agreed and suddenly Inga found herself on a train with a small suitcase of her possessions and absolutely no idea where she was going.

The next few years had been frightening and exhilarating at the same time. The school she found herself in was exclusively for bright children. Long lessons in history, social philosophy and politics reinforced her patriotism. Not only that, she had proved adept in languages and was top of her class in mathematics and science. A tough physical regime kept her trim and fit. When she reached seventeen, she finally worked out why she and her compatriots had been singled out. She was immensely proud to discover that they were to be part of the next generation of the Soviet elite. They would have to prove themselves in various ways but for them the future was golden.

By now, Inga had grown into a stunning teenager. Her looks had not been lost on her male colleagues and she had discovered the delights of sex some years earlier. She wasn't surprised then when one of her tutors approached her and made a suggestion as to how she could help the motherland.

He had made it quite clear that the state wasn't asking her to become a prostitute. It was a simple patriotic function that only pretty young girls could do and their country would be forever grateful. It helped enormously that Inga had enjoyed all her sexual encounters so far. She knew that as a slim young girl, she would not be much use in the Army but this way she could still do her duty, still strike a blow for the motherland, against the tyrannical West. She hoped fervently that her father would approve but of course, she no longer lived in that world and he would never know.

Her first job after graduation had been to seduce a French diplomat from their Embassy in Moscow. It had proved simplicity itself and the photographs were devastating. Unfortunately, the man in question had not proved that amenable to the pressure they should have been able to generate and threats to tell his wife were just met with laughter. However, Inga had done her job well and several more assignments followed. Her handlers kept a close eye on her during this phase. They needed to know how she would react as she learnt more about the western world. Would her head be turned as she found out the weaknesses and limits of the Soviet system? They needn't have worried. Much of what she was told, she dismissed as propaganda and even when she found it wasn't, her patriotism was so strong it overruled all other considerations. Although he would never know it, her father had done an excellent job.

After a couple of years, the first phase of Inga's employment was coming to an end. At twenty years old, she was rapidly losing the youth that middle aged, jaded diplomats seemed to enjoy most.

More importantly, she was becoming too well known. It was time for her to be redeployed somewhere less visible.

Her language skills made her suitable for a job overseas. Her Slavic looks made her suitable for a Scandinavian deployment. She was taken off operations and for a year learnt Norwegian until she was fluent. She also brushed up on her English but only to the level that a Norwegian girl might know. When ready, she was set up in a house in northern Norway. Her new job was to watch the military forces deployed around Bardufoss, particularly the British who had a large presence there with their aircraft and Royal Marines.

She had been there for a year now and had easily integrated into the local society. She tentatively started to make contact with military personnel. It was hardly difficult as there were very few social outlets in the local area and young single girls were at a premium. Then she had met Jon at the cocktail party when they all came over from England in the autumn. Immediately attracted to the slim, confident young man with dark good looks and striking blue eyes, she soon found that mixing business with pleasure was perfectly feasible. That's not to say that she didn't find him infuriating. Despite all the skills she had been taught, he had never let anything drop about his work apart from what was already well known. He wasn't married and so there was little she could do in terms of blackmail. She had considered trying to get him involved in something illegal, maybe involving drugs and had even less success, partly because she had to admit to herself she actually liked him too much. Luckily, he was going to be away for a while, although he was very tight mouthed about what it was he would be doing. So be it, she would look for more suitable prey while he was away.

Chapter 9

Bardufoss base

A tired but happy Jon met his two team mates in the mess at six in the evening. Mind you, his day of skiing and sex were nothing to the efforts Brian and Rupert had been expending. A shortened two and a half day survival course had, of necessity, been quite intense.

'Hiya guys,' he called as he entered the bar. The two of them were drinking their beer with a look of simple delight. 'Looks like you need that.'

Brian looked at his old friend over his glass. 'It was a close thing between bed and a beer but we decided that the beer won. Don't expect us to be awake much longer.'

Rupert looked even more worn out. 'I've never felt so exhausted in my life,' he said with a wan grin. 'When we left the accommodation hut after a hot shower, it was like walking into treacle, every muscle in my body is about to give up.'

Jon smiled back sympathetically. 'I know the feeling but you probably realise now why we needed to give you the training. The Arctic can be bloody unforgiving. How's the leg by the way?'

'Actually, it's not too bad, the Royals didn't make us walk too much just seemed to take delight in ensuring we got no sleep.'

'Well, it's about the only way of simulating how you might feel for real after an accident.'

'Mind you,' said Brian. 'We were with the rest for the squadron for the last day and your Senior Pilot didn't seem to be taking it too well. He tried to pull rank on one of the trainers at one stage. It didn't get him very far though. I suspect he may have come off far worse than us.'

Jon grinned conspiratorially. 'Well, I might just have had a word with some of my marine chums over that but for God's sake don't mention it. It seems I am in enough shit with the bloody man over your presence here as it is. Right, changing the subject, I suggest you two get your heads down. We'll have a full operational sortie brief tomorrow. While you've been on your Arctic snow holiday some of us have actually been doing some work. A Crab Hercules is due in tomorrow at fourteen hundred with the stores. I've arranged for it to be unloaded in our hangar. Apparently, everything is in unmarked crates. Our Sea King has had some extra servicing and is all ready to go.' and then looking at Rupert. 'I just need the last details from you old chap and we can finalise the route.'

Rupert nodded and a few minutes later Jon's friends retired to their beds. As they were leaving, the bar was suddenly invaded by the rest of the Squadron, who had also just finished the survival course. Diehards to a man, it was clear they weren't going to bed soon, however tired they might be. Jon saw the Senior Pilot enter and managed to make his escape before he was collared over some new, imagined grievance.

The next morning, things got busy. The first important decision was their departure day and time. This was heavily weather dependent. Jon and Brian spent an hour with the forecasters over on the main airfield site and it all looked good for that evening. They then went into a huddle with Rupert back in Jon's office.

'OK Guys,' said Jon, 'I've been looking at the route while you were away surviving and it looks workable but pretty tight. Our refuelling stop is absolutely critical, so I hope the ship is actually there as promised. Because if it isn't, we ain't going to make it.'

Brian replied. 'I spent a day at Fleet before we came out. They know how important it is and will give final confirmation by signal at noon today.'

'Good, now Rupert is there anything more from your side we need to know?'

Rupert shook his head. 'Only that I will need a minimum of half an hour and a maximum of one hour on the ground, otherwise it's all yours.'

'Right then,' Jon said pointing to his aviation map. 'This is the general route we'll take. Brian, you need to study the navigation. We've no radar or much else, if it comes to it, to navigate with in a Mark Four, so it's back to basics for this one.'

Brian looked thoughtful. 'I've been brushing up on my dead reckoning and all that stuff. It's a shame we can't take one your aircrewmen with us, they do it all the time.'

'There was no time to get the clearances but if we do this again I think we should try to get the Chief Aircrewman on the team.' Brian looked enquiringly at Rupert.

'Agreed, but hopefully, this is a one off.'

'Alright, we should plan on leaving at five tonight assuming the RAF arrive on time today. Rupert, I've arranged a full aircraft briefing for you next. Go down to the hangar and they'll look after you. Brian, we need to do the same. The aircraft is cleared for single front crew operation but if you're going to sit next to me, then I need you to know how to operate at least some of the switches.'

The time shot by and at five o'clock, the heavily laden Sea King lifted into the hover, its blades coning up steeply as they took the weight. As it transitioned away, it took a westerly heading until well clear of the airfield just in case anyone was interested in where it was going. Once it reached the coast, it turned north staying low and hugging the land. It was going to be a long night.

Ewan Bailey ached in every muscle. The survival course had been a killer. He was not amused by the attitude of the Royal Marines. When he had pointed out that he outranked them all by a considerable margin, it had been of no help at all. If he didn't know better he would think they were deliberately, even maliciously, making life more difficult for him than the others. If he could prove that then they had better watch out. However, they had been quite clever and he felt sure he would never be able to actually prove anything.

He shrugged off his concerns. It was a Saturday and they all had the weekend off. He had been down to the flight line to see Lieutenant Hunt and his odd team off on their precious secret mission and so there was nothing on the radar now until Monday when Arctic flying training would begin. Time to let his hair down, although this time he absolutely promised himself he would not get carried away, not like the last time and the many times before that.

Later that evening, he found himself in the only night spot for miles around, the disco in the Bardufoss Hotel. He had forgotten his vow and was feeling really good in the glow of the beer which had followed the several drinks he had indulged in at the bar before coming ashore. The rest of the squadron were also here and letting their hair down with the local girls.

One particular female kept catching his eye and he was pretty sure she was also sizing him up. He was sure he had seen her with Jon Hunt before but so what. Full of alcoholic bonhomie, he went boldly up to her and asked for a dance. Wouldn't it be good if he managed to get one over on that smug bastard's girlfriend? To his mild surprise, she agreed readily and they spent the evening together. Her name was Inga and she lived just down the road. He discovered she worked in the local hospital as an auxiliary helper and had her own house. The more he drank, the prettier she got and the more he lusted after her delightful curves. What was even better was that she seemed to reciprocate his feelings. In their conversation, he managed to conceal that he was actually married. Mind you, from what he had heard of the local girls, that wouldn't have made too much difference. He suspected he would feel guilty in the morning and when she suggested they move back to her place, he had just enough sense left to propose that they leave separately. If the squadron boys saw them leaving together, he would never live it down.

The Caspian Monster

Later that evening, Inga looked down at the sleeping form of her new conquest with mild disgust. He was not her idea of a good bed partner. She had spotted him as a newcomer as soon as he walked into the disco and he was clearly a senior officer as most of the other pilots seemed to want to keep clear of him. Definitely a good target. When she had managed to get him home, firstly he had been full of rutting aggression which hadn't lasted long before it was all prematurely over. But that didn't matter because afterwards, with the application of a little more of her precious store of scotch, she had got what she wanted. It was amazing how much people would open up after sex and this guy wouldn't stop once he started. It had all poured out; all the times others had conspired against him, how often he had done amazing things that others just hadn't appreciated. He had finished by explaining how he was going to sort things out up here and how a certain Lieutenant Hunt was the object of his wrath. He had then let slip what Jon was up to, at least how much he knew about it and that was it, the Jackpot. She felt slightly guilty that it involved Jon because she was really beginning to like him but this was too important. She had kept plying Ewan with booze until he was finally sick. She didn't care, the state he was in there was no chance he would remember what he had said and that was almost as important as getting this information to her superiors as soon as she could.

Chapter 10

200 feet above the Norwegian Sea

Flying at two hundred feet in the dark, just off the coast, even with the help of night vision goggles was hard work. But after an hour, the novelty was inevitably beginning to wear off. All the gauges in a strip in the centre of the instrument panel were stuck firmly, vertically, in the green. The Flight Control system was doggedly holding their height and heading accurately using the radar altimeter under the aircraft's belly and the highly accurate compass. It was cold outside but there was no sign of cloud or rain at this height, so icing shouldn't be a problem. For the moment, the navigation was straightforward as there were enough features along the rugged coast for Brian to be able to constantly update their position. Slowly, they all relaxed.

'So, Brian, when did you last fly in one of these old tubs?' asked Jon. 'They're a bit different to our Lynx aren't they?'

'Oh, I did a tour on a Pinger squadron straight after training, so it's not that strange. Mind you it is odd sitting up here in the front. In a Pinger, we sat in the back and always in the dark with blinds on the windows, so we could see the bloody radar.'

'Excuse me you WAFU's but once again you're talking in bloody code. What the hell is a Pinger?' Rupert was standing between the two seats and looking out. He had been furnished with his own set of night goggles and was thoroughly enjoying seeing where he was actually going, unlike the last time he had flown in a naval helicopter.

Jon laughed. 'Sorry mate, let's have another language lesson. A Pinger is an anti-submarine helicopter. They go into a high hover and have a sonar they lower out of the helicopter on a winch. It pings away looking for submarines, hence the name.'

Brian cut in. 'And this lot are known as Junglies. Apparently, it goes back to the days when they were operating in the Borneo jungles. The first time that helicopters were used that way. Or of course, it could be because they're all a load of apes who just swing from tree to tree.'

'Ignore him,' responded Jon. 'He's just jealous that we don't normally have talking ballast in the Jungly fleet.'

Before Rupert could ask, Brian riposted. 'By talking ballast he means us Observers. You know it's funny how they're not so bloody rude when they need someone to tell them how to get home.'

Rupert had to chuckle at the good natured banter even though he had heard its sort before. 'So what rude term do they use for the Lynx lot then?'

The question was met with a moments silence, eventually Jon answered. 'Good question, I don't think there is a rude epithet yet, maybe we should think of one.'

Brian forced himself back to the job in hand. 'Right, everyone, that headland ahead is our last point of land. It's all wetness after that until we hit the ice.' He told Jon the heading they needed from where they now to find their refuel stop and Jon turned the aircraft. After that, it was all eyes out to spot the tiny light in the darkness that would mean their ship was where she should be. Unlike the Lynx, they had no radar in this machine and so were relying on the helicopter controller in the ship seeing them when they got in range.

A tense hour passed and then suddenly the VHF radio broke the silence. 'Victor Tango, this is Echo Bravo, I hold you on my One Seven Zero. Turn to Three Five Zero, range twenty miles, out.'

A sigh of relief went around the cockpit. Brian's course had been dead on. Soon they would be able to top up the tanks. It wasn't long before Jon picked up the green light of the ships Glide Path Indicator and bought the aircraft to a hover alongside the stern of the ship.

'Hang on a second,' said Rupert. 'Isn't that a Leander Frigate like your old Prometheus? Surely you're not going to land this bloody great big machine on that tiny flight deck?'

Jon laughed. 'Nope, although I suppose it could be done in an emergency. We're going to do a thing called Helicopter In Flight Refuelling or HIFR for short. Brian's about to go down aft and do the business. You can go down and watch if you like, just don't fall out of the bloody door.'

'It's all right Rupert,' said Brian as he unstrapped and climbed out his seat. 'I've got a waist harness you can wear. It will keep you safe just as long as this hamfisted pilot can keep a steady hover.'

'Noted sunshine, you do your job I'll do mine.'

Brian walked down to the big cabin door. He put on a waist harness and gave one to Rupert. They clipped on and then he pulled the large sliding door open. The blast of arctic air made their eyes water immediately. Brian pulled on a lever by the door and the rescue winch dropped its hook into his hands. He then started up a continual verbal con to Jon up front to keep the aircraft in position. Attaching a weighted bag to the hook, to stop it blowing around in the downwash, he then lowered it to the waiting team on the Frigate's flight deck. The deck crew clipped the hook to a hose and Brian raised the whole thing up until it was at the same height as the cabin floor. The hook had been attached well down from the nozzle of the hose, leaving a long free end. He then lay down on the floor and undid the fuel filler cap from the tank filler and pulled the hose over.

'This is always the bloody awkward bit,' he grunted as he manhandled the heavy hose over the filler. With another grunt, he managed to fit it on and give it a securing twist. He then gave a thumbs up to the flightdeck crew.

'OK Jon, fuel should be coming in now.'

In the cockpit, Jon saw the two fuel gauges start to register as the contents slowly increased. He felt a great deal of tension ease. If this hadn't worked, they would have been forced to turn back. It was not unknown for a Frigate's equipment to be faulty. It wasn't used very often. He didn't know what he had feared more, aborting the mission or the sarcastic remarks bound to be supplied by the Senior Pilot if they got back early. Soon, the tanks were full and Brian returned the hose to the deck before he and Rupert gratefully slid the door shut and they made their way back up to the front of the aircraft.

As they transitioned away from the little ship without any thanks for a successful mission due to the need to minimise radio transmissions, Brian gave Jon a new heading to fly and they all settled down again.

'We've about two hours to go,' said Brian. 'The ship will steam north at max chat to meet us on the way back. Next thing to look out for is the ice and then the base. Let's just hope we can find it.'

They droned north for an hour, then suddenly the ice appeared. Now, somehow, they were going to have to find an exact spot in this vast wilderness.

'Anyone know how fast the ice is actually moving?' asked Jon in a worried voice. 'Because the position we were given could have moved.'

'It's alright Jon,' replied Brian. 'At this time year, it gets anchored to the various landmasses and slows down. The position should be pretty accurate. Only fifteen minutes to go.'

They all put down their night vision goggles which had been of little use this far away from any ambient light. However, now they would be invaluable in spotting the light beacon the base should have switched on by now.

Suddenly, all the goggles blanked out.

'What the fuck?' shouted Jon and he desperately pulled his goggles away from his face, as did the other two. He looked out and realised he could see quite well. But that wasn't what took his breath away. Looking up, he could see shimmering, moving, curtains of gold and purple.

'Bloody hell, it's the Northern Lights,' said Brian with awe in his voice. 'Will you just look at that? What did the met man say back at Bardufoss? Oh yes, there would be too much low cloud for them to be seen.'

'Never mind that,' said Jon, who was focusing back on flying the helicopter. 'We've got to find this bloody base and with all that powerful ambient light the goggles won't work, so how are we going to see their beacon?'

'Shit, you're right,' said Rupert. 'And we daren't use radio up here. The commies could easily hear it.'

'Right,' said Jon. 'Brian, take us to the datum position and we'll do an expanding square search until we find them or have to turn back for fuel.'

'Look on the bright side,' said Rupert. 'With the lack of cloud cover promised by that bloody met man at least the lights will stop any Soviet satellites seeing us.'

Jon just grunted. He would far rather have a dark night and the beacon standing out like a dog's bollocks, clear in the goggles.

They arrived at the designated position and Jon slowed down to sixty knots. Flying in short right angled legs, they started to search.

'Shit, this is useless.' said Rupert after a few minutes. 'There's absolutely nothing to see.'

'You're right,' said Jon. 'Brian take us back to the datum. We'll land on and wait for the light show to stop otherwise we're going to run out of fuel.'

When they got to the right place, Jon picked out the shadow of a hump in the ice and made his approach. He would need that visual reference when the recirculating snow cloud caused by their downwash caught them up. With Brian back at the cabin door looking out at the tail, he brought the large machine down to a smooth landing and stopped the rotors.

They all clambered out into the still night. Jon breathed in, squeezed his nostrils and was rewarded with a crunching feeling. 'Temperature's below minus eighteen.'

'How on earth do you know that?' asked Rupert.

Jon chuckled. 'It varies a little from person to person but my nose hairs freeze at that temperature or lower.'

Rupert tried it and was rewarded with the same response.

They were well dressed for the conditions, so were safe from the cold for a while. None the less Brian passed around a thermos of hot chocolate and they all took grateful swigs. After an hour, the spectacular light show started to diminish. Jon tried his goggles and could see the cloud cover re-establishing itself.

'Hold on guys,' he said and he climbed up the side of the aircraft and looked around thought the goggles from the higher vantage point. He was rewarded with a flashing light not far off and dead ahead of them.

Fifteen minutes later, they landed safely by the light and shut down once again. Climbing out, they were met by several white suited figures. Conversation was limited. Jon directed the newcomers to the back of the aircraft and they all started to unload the stores. Rupert excused himself and disappeared with one of the men, promising to return as soon as he could. Try as he might Jon couldn't see any sign of a base where men might live. He turned to one of the white clad men and asked where it was. The stranger chuckled and suggested he take one of the crates. They walked together down the snowy path trodden down by the men ahead. Suddenly, Jon could make out the oblong shape of the access fin but as it was the same white as the snow around it and was almost totally buried, he would probably have walked straight by without seeing it. No wonder they had seen nothing from the air. The stores were being loaded through the hatch.

'*Rather them than me,*' he thought. '*I'd go barmy cooped up in there for months on end.*'

The aircraft was soon unloaded and it wasn't much longer before a satisfied looking Rupert reappeared.

'Right guys, we can go. The boss here asked me to pass on their thanks. They were getting pretty fed up with basic rations and apparently we've delivered all their Christmas presents as well, so they're gearing up for a party.'

'Best of luck,' said Brian echoing Jon's earlier thoughts. 'You wouldn't get me staying in such conditions.'

Soon, they were airborne again and heading south.

Rupert was in a relieved mood. 'Well done guys, apart from the light show that went just about according to plan.'

'Only one problem left to solve,' said a tight lipped Jon. 'With all that farting about back there, we're very low on fuel. If the ship is out of position, we could be out of gas before we find her.'

That cut through any euphoria and they droned on feeling very lonely out in the black darkness.

About forty five minutes later they cleared the ice and headed out to sea. The ship should be about fifty miles away and Brian was checking and rechecking his calculations. Unlike last time, the radio stayed stubbornly quiet. When they reached the estimated ship's position, there was nothing to see, either with the goggles or the naked eye. Jon slowed down again and started to do another square search.

'I've got a fucking feeling of Déjà bloody Vu,' he muttered to Brian. 'It's like that time we came back from Rio Grande during the Falklands. Why can't the bloody Fisheads ever be in the right place at the right time?'

'Yeah, well most people think the biggest lie in the world is 'I promise not to come in your mouth' of course we know it's really 'the ship's position is.''

Rupert snorted with laughter but then, as if on cue, the radio broke in. 'Victor Tango this is Echo Bravo, believe I hold you on my three five five at seventy five miles.'

Brian looked at Jon. 'Shit, that's a long way out. Have we got the fuel to get that far?'

Jon was already calculating it in his head as Brian spoke, 'Just, maybe, it rather depends on this headwind. Let's get down and speed up.' He then called the ship and explained the problem asking them to turn towards them as fast as they could go.

As they headed towards the Frigate at maximum speed, Jon explained what they were doing to Rupert. 'Listen mate, we're going low and fast to minimise the effects of this headwind and we actually get more range out of her the faster we go. Also, if we run out of gas then we can land in the sea and our naval chums can pick us up out of the liferaft.'

'Thanks for that,' replied an anxious Rupert who was suddenly feeling quite scared. He knew how cold the sea was.

Half an hour later and Jon was definitely getting worried. The fuel gauges were getting very low. Once they reached one hundred and sixty pounds he was technically out of fuel and either or both engines could then flame out at any time.

They saw the ship's Glide Path Indicator just as the fuel read two hundred pounds a side. Jon realised there was enough to get to the ship but definitely not enough to hover alongside and pick up the fuel hose. They would have to ditch.

'Bollocks,' he thought furiously. *'I'm buggered if I'm going to lose the aircraft having got this far.'*

'Rupert, remember asking me if we were going to land on that tiny deck?'

'Er yes,' said Rupert who had already guessed what was coming.

'Well, we're about to make history. Brian, pop down aft and watch the tail please.'

Brian just nodded tight lipped and climbed out of his seat again. Jon indicated for Rupert to take his place. He would be safer strapped in the seat than anywhere else.

Jon called the ship with his intentions. There was a stunned silence over the radio before the ship's Captain came on and queried what Jon had said.

'Echo Bravo, I have no choice,' said Jon tightly. 'It's either that or ditch and I have no time to argue. For God's sake, give me a wind across the port side and clear the flight deck.'

The Captain must have realised from Jon's strained voice that he had no option and the ship started to turn across the wind.

With his heart in his mouth, Jon slowly approached from starboard until he was over the deck. He knew that technically his wheels should fit but it gave him absolutely no margin for error and the ship was rolling as well. But he was dreading the sound of his engines winding down and knew he had no time left. It was this or swim. Even with the protection afforded by the dry suits they were wearing, their survival time would be measured in minutes and he doubted the ship's ability to get to them in such a short time. By craning his neck back he could just see the front wheels under the sponsons, so was able to judge when they were in position. Brian called out confirmation when the tail wheel was also over the deck edge. Muttering imprecations to every deity he could think of, he gently lowered the aircraft down. With enormous relief, he felt, rather than saw the wheels touch. This far ahead of the undercarriage, the cockpit was actually out over the sea which he could see rushing past him below his feet through the small side windows. It was quite disorientating. He didn't dare look and see how close the tips of the rotor blades were to the hangar.

He called the ship. 'Victor Tango safely down, can we get fuel urgently please?'

The hangar door opened up and the hose was run quickly out to them. Jon was still half flying the helicopter as it rolled with the ship to stop it sliding and he prayed fervently that the fuelling wouldn't take too long. There was no way lashings could be attached to help secure them. Apart from anything else, the deck crew couldn't get past the aircraft to attach them to the far side. The gauges seemed to creep upwards with an almost malicious slowness. Eventually, they showed full and the hose was disconnected. With an enormous feeling of relief and without even requesting clearance from the ship, Jon pulled up on the collective lever and transitioned away.

Chapter 11

Oslo

Inga looked out of the train window at the white landscape flashing past. Not long now and they would arrive in Oslo. She was never quite sure why she had to travel so far to meet her controller but she was far from unhappy with the arrangement. An opportunity to get away from Bardufoss, especially in winter was not to be missed. Even the days were longer this much further south. She was also looking forward to a little retail therapy in addition to her visit to the Embassy. Shopping opportunities were extremely limited up north and she had little to spend her allowances on. As the lights of the houses on the outskirts of the town started to appear, once again she started to wonder about her commitment to her home country. She was immensely proud of its achievements and still deeply suspicious of the western world. But how was it she never saw any queues here? Why were all the shops completely full of food and produce? When she was tucked away up in bleak Bardufoss it wasn't so apparent but whenever she came here, she was almost overwhelmed by the plenty she saw everywhere. Brought up from childhood to believe in the efficiencies of the Soviet system where everyone had a job and no one starved, she found it hard to reconcile that view of life with the reality of the bustling city. She was intelligent enough and had enough experience by now to realise that much of what she had been taught was propaganda and her love of her country was still her overwhelming motivation but she couldn't help but feel slightly aggrieved at the deception. It didn't help that she was starting to miss Jon which was very unprofessional of her. She knew he would be back at base once she returned. Her musings were broken as the train pulled into the station and she grabbed her bag and joined the queue of people to get off the train. Once clear of the bustling concourse, she pulled the collar of her coat up and decided to walk to her hotel. It wasn't far and she was looking forward to a good night's sleep before her meeting in the morning.

Michael Burton was sitting in the same hotel in the dining room and almost missed seeing Inga walk in. However, a noise from the kitchens broke his reverie and as he looked up he saw her in profile as she made her way to reception. It was a shock to see that face here. Surely it couldn't be her? Being careful not to be seen himself, he made his way to the toilets and managed to get a proper look at her face. Yes, it was that bitch Inga, the bloody girl who had ruined his career. The person responsible for the second rate job he now had in this shit hole of a country. What the fucking hell was she doing in Oslo?

Two years ago, Michael had been an up and coming diplomat in the Embassy in Moscow. He strongly felt he was destined for a high position in time. Then one evening he met this beautiful young girl in a bar. He knew he should have known better. He had been regularly warned of Soviet espionage techniques but surely this pretty little thing could have nothing to do with the KGB? He fell headlong into the trap, one of the oldest in the book. By the time the photographs arrived, he had convinced himself he was in love and that so was she. They had even spoken about her leaving with him and setting up home in England when he returned. Quite what his wife would have said about that he hadn't actually considered. He was infatuated. The only thing that saved him and the remains of his career was that he went straight to his superiors and confessed it all. His superiors had been angry but agreed to his suggestion to try and use it to advantage and feed her misinformation. However, he soon found out he was one of the world's worst liars and she quickly saw through him and realised what was going on. His wife had received a copy of the photographs and his career and marriage were over. The only things that kept him in the service were his original honesty and the fact that he couldn't think of anything else he could do. So here he was, stuck in a backwater country, in a backwater job. Now suddenly, by one of life's staggering coincidences, there was an opportunity to erase some of the black marks from his past. He would keep watch on the beautiful, deceptive Inga and find out what she was doing here and then his superiors would have to take notice.

The next morning, Inga made her way to the Embassy. She didn't go inside, that would be far too dangerous. As she sauntered past the entrance she saw her man and they made eye contact. She kept on walking until she came to the park. On the far side, there was a cafe. She made herself comfortable at a vacant table well away from other early customers and out of view from the window.

Sergei came in minutes later and sat down next to her.

'Inga my darling, so nice to see you.'

She smiled at him. They had only met three times in the last year but she made it look to any watcher as if they were old friends.

Quietly, 'Sergei, I have some very interesting news.'

'Go on.'

'This weekend, the British sent one of their helicopters on a secret mission to the north of Bardufoss. I don't know where it went but it had to meet up with a ship to refuel. It was one of their Sea Kings and it was full of packing crates.'

'Why do you think this is so important? They fly all over the area.'

'My source made it clear it was very important and very secret, so it must have been something unusual. With a refuel, they could go very far, well up into the ice for example.'

Sergei thought for a moment, 'You're right, this is something new. I'll report it back urgently. Is there anything else?'

She considered how much more to say. 'I'm working on a relationship with the pilot who flew the mission but he is very tight mouthed. I actually got the information from his superior officer while the pilot was away. But personally, I think it would be better for me to concentrate on the pilot as he'll have all the detail. I don't think I can work both of them at the same time.' She didn't add that the senior man gave her the creeps whereas a reason to stick with Jon would be far more personally rewarding.

Sergei nodded. 'That makes sense Inga. You've done well so far, I will trust your judgement. Now, while I've got you, what about any general issues?'

They talked for another ten minutes over their coffee and then went their separate ways. Inga had a whole day to kill and made full use of it before catching her train the next morning.

Michael Burton cursed the Russian girl as she finally left on the train. She had led him a merry dance all the previous day and his feet were killing him. He didn't dare let her out his sight but soon realised that she was bound to eventually spot him even though he had done as much as he could to change his appearance. He managed to ring into the Embassy while she was in a dress shop and told them what he was doing. They assigned two more men to help him. With the pressure eased, they were able to keep track of her all day. It soon became clear that she was just visiting and lived somewhere else in the country. They had managed to distract the receptionist at the hotel and take a look at the register. If it was to be believed, she lived in Bardufoss, way up in the north but where there was a big military presence. That made a sort of sense and it was confirmed when one his men stood behind her in the ticket queue at the station and overheard her destination as she bought a ticket. It was decided to let her go without a tail at this stage. She wouldn't be hard to find now.

Once she had gone, a meeting was called to discuss what to do. Michael was congratulated on his initiative but clearly, once his involvement was explained, he couldn't take any further part in the investigation. However, he was able to identify the man she had met in the cafe who was a known KGB operative. All in all, a good day's work and one that would look good on his record. The priority now was to get someone up to Bardufoss and find out what she was up to and what she had reported to her man here in Oslo.

Chapter 12

The Pentagon

The 'monster' team as they liked to call themselves now had been called out again. Over the years, they had tracked the ongoing programme in the Caspian Sea with a great deal of interest. The original machine had been seen on several occasions and they now had a pretty good idea of its performance and more importantly how it actually worked. They had been puzzled for a while when it disappeared from view but the general conclusion was that it must have crashed. This theory had been supported by the fact that they had spotted some frantic salvage activity soon after it had disappeared and had never seen it again thereafter.

The emergence of the much smaller machine had caused considerable interest and once again it had been pretty well analysed. They understood the concept. While the West had concentrated on the use of ground cushion vehicles, such as hovercraft, the clever Russian engineers had gone in a totally different direction. However, in many ways, the tactical question they were trying to answer was the same. How to get troops ashore, quickly and at a time and place of your own choosing without allowing the enemy to see you and so anticipate where you might arrive. The big weakness of the Russian concept seemed to be that, although the beasts could operate over flat terrain, landing on anything other than water would be a real problem. However, they were undeniably fast, much faster than anything their opponents had and therefore the cause of much worry in the higher echelons of the NATO military. If they wanted to get around the defensive lines in northern Norway for example, these would be the machines to do it. The tacticians had also pointed out that to protect the machines in an assault you would need conventional aircraft, nothing else was fast enough and if you were trying to be stealthy, that could give the game away, especially as the Soviets had no real aircraft carriers. All that said, if you needed a rapid way of outflanking your enemy from the sea, these machines were the perfect solution.

And now they seemed to have come up with an answer to the force protection problem. The team were poring over the latest photographs.

'Jesus,' exclaimed the Boss. 'It's almost as big as the original monster but what the hell are the lumps all over it.'

The senior analyst spoke up. 'As we said in our digest Sir, we're pretty sure the six canisters on the back are SSN 22, Sunburn missile canisters. As you know, it's the latest Soviet maritime surface to surface missile. We still haven't got a handle on its performance but it is estimated to be pretty effective. The bulges on the nose and tail will be the targeting radars. We are also pretty sure they've got gun turrets as well. So it looks like they're working on an armed escort for the smaller troop carriers, a sort of Ekranoplan battleship.'

'Hmm, I guess the real question is why they're spending all the money on these damned things. What are they really up to?' mused the Boss. 'Thank the Lord we have a President now who is prepared to stand up to these bastards. OK guys, finish off the technical report and I'll alert the higher ups that the commies have come up with yet another scary achievement.'

Astrakhan

Yuri and Rostislav had been discussing the results of the latest tests with the new machine. Having learnt the lessons from the earlier prototype and the Eaglet development programme, the new Lun class Ekranoplan was proving to be much more capable. They had dispensed with the tail engine and the eight turbo jets mounted by the nose could be swivelled down to improve takeoff performance. Once in flight, the machine only needed two operating engines, to sustain a speed of almost four hundred and fifty kilometres per hour. They had even solved one of the biggest problems with all Ekranoplans to date, that of accurate navigation. On Yuri's initiative, they had installed a Doppler radar system as well as 'borrowing' an inertial navigation system from a submarine. The two systems working in tandem had proved to be more than sufficiently accurate. Unfortunately, it was too costly to consider fitting it to the smaller Eaglets but at least one machine could now navigate with pin point accuracy.

'So Yuri, we're ready now for the next phase, is that correct?'

Yuri nodded. 'Yes Boss and it should be pretty interesting. No one has fired a naval missile from a machine going so fast before but we will take it in stages. If all is well, we'll have proved how incredibly capable the Lun really is.'

'That's good news and I'm afraid we going to need as much of that as possible.'

'Don't tell me, you've been to Moscow again?'

'I'm afraid so. Yuri, you know I spend more time playing politics these days than managing this bureau. There's so much pressure on budgets now, everything is under intense scrutiny. I'm not sure we're going to get the go ahead to finish off the second machine.'

Yuri grimaced. 'But we've already finished the fuselage.'

'I know but Yuri I need to tell you what's going on. I probably shouldn't but I think it's only fair that you know. Several days ago there was a briefing at the Kremlin. All the design bureau heads were there as well as many others. It was all about the Americans and their new President.'

Yuri snorted contemptuously. 'You mean that old film star. Only the Americans could elect such a man.'

'Don't underestimate him. He's causing us great concern. Since he came to power, the Americans seemed to have changed tactics. Comrade Andropov of the KGB, is so worried, he has initiated a major intelligence gathering exercise to try and discover whether they are really preparing for a first strike because that is what it looks like to many in power. The NATO military have been conducting all sorts of exercises and testing our defences over the last few years. Why would they do that if they are not gearing up for war? They harass our submarines. Their Air Force flies right up to our borders and only turn away at the last moment. What you probably also don't know is that they are going to deploy their Pershing missiles to our borders. These can be made ready, literally in minutes and so, if they wanted to hit us with a first strike we would be defenceless.'

Yuri almost blurted out that he already knew about the missiles but that would mean admitting that he listened to the western radio stations and he wasn't sure how his boss would take that, it was illegal after all.

Rostislav continued. 'It doesn't help that comrade Brezhnev's health is starting to fail. Many expect we will need to elect a new leader soon.'

Yuri considered his superior's words. In some ways they were nothing new. He been brought up to fear and despise the western world. However, this seemed to be a new development. Maybe NATO was at last feeling strong enough to wipe out the Soviet Union and avoid reprisals. But surely they wouldn't be that mad? He said as much to Rostislav.

'Some feel that maybe we might appear the same to them but mutual paranoia could start a war as much as anything else. Too many people remember what Hitler did only a few decades ago you know.'

'Fine, Boss, I understand all that but in the end, I expect any decisions will way above our pay grade. What I don't understand is that if we're so worried, why would we be looking at reducing spending on projects like ours?'

'Hm, Yuri, I think you have to look at what our leaders want. Years ago, when we started this programme, Russia was a new world power and wanted to flex its muscles. Ekranoplans are a very good offensive weapon if you want to land troops quickly where an enemy is least expecting it. But look at us now. Our leaders are old men. Our borders have been static for decades. We even have to fight to keep our Union together. The cost of our military is enormous and is slowly crippling the economy. The West seems to be able to spend as much as they want and that means they can outspend us whenever they want. I'll be honest with you Yuri, this programme has run for many years and although we have proved we can do everything we said we could, as you already know there are many who would like to shut us down. We need to prove that the concept is worthwhile, we need some form of mission that only an Ekranoplan can accomplish, otherwise I fear for us all.'

Chapter 13

Bardufoss

They made it back to Bardufoss by ten in the morning. It was still dark. Jon handed the aircraft over to the engineers and followed his comrades back towards the mess building. They had a hurried debrief and then headed to their cabins for some well deserved sleep. The Senior Pilot accosted Jon as he was on his way but Jon gave him short thrift. Splot didn't make an issue of it. Although Jon suspected he would suffer for it at a later date.

Despite or maybe because of the adrenalin expenditure of the last twenty four hours, Jon fell asleep as soon as his head touched the pillow and he was dead to the world for a solid eight hours. When he awoke, he realised there was just time for a shower while still being able to make the mess for the evening meal. He knocked on Brian and Rupert's doors as he passed but it seemed they were already ahead of him. When he entered the mess, he saw them seated and eating.

'Bloody hell mate, so your bed rejected you then?' quipped Brian.

'Looks that way but boy did I need that sleep.'

Rupert looked over sympathetically. 'You probably had the hardest work to do but well done, that could have gone badly but you got us home.'

'Ah, now Rupert, I've got a question for you. There's something you forgot to tell us.'

Rupert looked puzzled.

'You know all these operations have a code name, normally a really naff one. So what was this one called then? You never mentioned it.'

'Oh, yes you're right. Well, the whole thing is called 'Pickwick' and before you say anything, I didn't select it, just another randomly generated one I guess.'

That got a sarcastic grunt from Jon. 'Thanks for that but what happens now?'

Rupert looked surprised. 'Well, nothing really. Hopefully, that was a one off mission and they should be fine now until the ice retreats and we can use our normal resupply system.'

Brian cut in. 'And I'm guessing we can't say a thing about it, including landing a Sea King on the deck of a Frigate?'

'Fraid so, sorry guys but that mission never happened. And the Frigate will be under strict instructions to keep quiet as well.'

'Don't worry Brian,' said Jon. 'Look on the bright side, we're all in one piece and we know what we did. So, I suppose you're both off back to Blighty now Rupert?'

'Yes, the plane should pick us up tomorrow. How about we hit the bar for a beerio or ten?'

There was no dissent.

The next morning Jon waved a slightly hung over goodbye to his two colleagues and then made his way back to his side of the airfield. He groaned when he saw the Senior Pilot approaching with a sour look on his face. *'Here we go,'* he thought. *'I wonder what the bloody man has cooked up now.'* Still, there was always Inga waiting for him. He would phone her as soon as he could. At least he had that to look forward to.

Back in Oslo, investigations quickly discovered the exact whereabouts of a certain Inga Thorsenn. It hadn't proved hard to get her address and from there build up a comprehensive picture of her life. Detailed examination of her past soon showed up anomalies. The KGB had been quite clever but clearly never expected there would ever be such a detailed look into her background. The main aim now was to discover what she was up to and how much if anything she knew. A decision would then be made about what action to take. There were several options, from a quick arrest to trying to get her to defect. No decision would be made until more was known. To this end, an agent was despatched to the area to start surveillance and a report sent urgently to the head of the head of the Scandinavian section of MI6.

Jamie Davidson was the man detailed to travel up to Bardufoss and start the investigations on site. He felt thrilled with the task. An honours graduate from Oxford, he had been recruited into the service during the second year of his degree. Full of patriotic fervour, he had sailed through his training and then landed with a resounding, boring thump in the Embassy in Oslo where for the first year of his employment he had done nothing but shuffle paper. At last, they were giving him an assignment and what an assignment it was. Travel to the northern part of the country and put a beautiful Russian spy under surveillance. He couldn't wait and despite all the careful briefings he had received, he knew that this was his chance to show his bosses what he could really do.

After arriving in Bardufoss, he booked into the only hotel and set about checking out Inga's address. It was easily found and it wasn't long before he saw the girl herself. She was every bit as pretty as her photographs had indicated. He wondered if he should try and establish a relationship with her? After all, that's what James Bond would have done. However, the strict instructions he had received made it quite clear what he was required to do. He put that fantasy quickly aside. Within a few days, he had established her routine and it appeared to be pretty banal. She worked in the local hospital during the day and spent most evenings at home. Apart from shopping and the occasional walk in the surrounding area, she seemed to live a monastic life. Then, on the third evening, she changed her routine. She had an old beaten up Volkswagen Beetle and when she finished work, instead of going home, she drove to the main gate of the British side of the military airfield. When she pulled up, a young man came out of the main gate and they drove off together back to her house. By midnight he was frozen stiff and bored out of his mind sitting in his rented car. Apart from the lights coming on behind the windows of the house, absolutely nothing had happened. He couldn't stay here all night. It was time to go to bed as well. He would find out who the young man was in the morning. He was probably one of the naval staff on the base. Maybe this was what she was up to?

Suddenly the front door opened and the young man appeared. He looked over the road to where Jamie was parked and started striding angrily towards him. Desperate to avoid a confrontation, he started the car and pulled away fast, too fast. The car barely moved but skidded sideways as the rear wheels spun in the snow. The young man was shouting now although he couldn't be heard over the roaring of the engine. Suddenly, the tyres cut through the ice and hit tarmac obtaining instant grip and the car shot forward. The man hit the bonnet and for a second his face was hard against the windscreen. Both men got a clear view of each other before he slipped sideways off the front of the car and into a snow drift to the side of the road. As he slithered away, Jamie saw the man pick himself out of the snow and shake his fist at the retreating car.

He cursed his luck. Clearly, they had been observing him as much as he had been doing the same to them. So much for being James bloody Bond. Now, how the hell was he going to report this without making a complete idiot of himself?

Chapter 14

Bardufoss

Jon lay on his bed and tried to concentrate on the tape recording he was listening to and the book in front of him. He had always been good at languages and had decided to try and teach himself the basics of Russian as a way of passing the time. He knew from previous experience that four months in Bardufoss would include plenty of spare hours and he had promised himself that he would use it productively rather than in the bar. That was until Inga came along. She managed to fill up his spare time quite usefully in various and far more interesting ways. Unfortunately, the girl had disappeared into thin air. He had been round to her house several times now but the doors were locked and her car was missing.

His mind wandered back to when he had last seen her. She had picked him up from the main gate and they had gone back to her place where she had prepared supper. They had even managed to get round to eating it some hours after originally planned. For some reason, other things had managed to get in the way. He smiled at the memory. Over the delayed meal, she mentioned that she thought someone was watching her. Over the last few days a strange man had kept on appearing and she was pretty sure she had seen him parked up the road as they drove past when they arrived that evening. Jon thought she was being paranoid but peeked out of the curtains and sure enough, a car was parked about fifty yards away down the road. When the machine was still there at midnight, he had had enough and decided to do something about it. But as he approached it the driver had started up and apparently tried to run him over as he drove away. Luckily for Jon, the conditions saved him and the worst he suffered was a great deal of snow rammed into various parts of his clothing and anatomy.

When he went back inside, Inga looked terrified. At the time he put it down to the shock of seeing him almost run over but on later reflection, he wondered if there hadn't been something more to it. He stayed with her for the night but in the morning, when he said goodbye, it was almost as if they were parting forever. After that, she never answered his calls and when he went to her house, she seemed to have just disappeared. That was several weeks ago now. Maybe he should just forget her. Bloody Norwegian females, they all seemed to be odd, not surprising living up here in the dark for half the year but he did miss her.

His reverie was interrupted by the door opening and with an inward groan, he saw the head of the Senior Pilot appear.

'Hunt, you're wanted. My office now.' And before Jon could respond he disappeared.

'Oh fuck, what did the bloody man want now?' he wondered wearily as he clambered off his bed and removed his earphones. Only one way to find out, so he put on his jacket and headed off to the Administration building.

Knocking on Splots door, he deliberately opened it and went in without waiting for an answer. To his surprise, there were two men in the room. The Senior Pilot had an odd smirk on his face.

'Lieutenant Hunt, this is Mr Robertson from the SIB. He wants to talk to you. I'll leave you two alone.' And without saying anything more he got up and left the room.

Jon turned to the newcomer and held out his hand, 'Jonathon Hunt, Mr Robertson but I'm sorry, I've no idea what SIB is.'

The stranger gave a very firm handshake and indicated that Jon should sit. Jon appraised him as he did so. The man had a very stiff, almost formal bearing and the dark suit he was wearing was definitely not typical attire for this part of the world. If Jon didn't know better, he would have said that he looked like some sort of policeman.

'SIB Sir, stands for Special Investigation Branch. We're a section of the MOD police.'

'*Well I was spot on with that deduction,*' thought Jon. '*But what the hell do they want with me?*'

'Sir, I have to ask you formally, do you know a local girl who goes by the name of Inga Thorsenn?'

Nonplussed, Jon looked back at the serious faced man. '*What on earth was this about? Could it have anything to do with that man in the car and Inga's disappearance?*' Anyway, he would have to be honest. What did he have to hide?

'Yes, until about two weeks ago. But now she seems to have disappeared. Why? Do you know where she is? Is she alright?'

The man nodded as if this was an important revelation. 'In that case Sir, I also have to ask if you attacked a British subject in a car on the night of the eleventh?'

'What? No hang on, yes, there was a man watching us that night but he tried to run me over. I ended up in a bloody snow drift actually.'

'Sorry Sir, that's not what I've been told. I'm afraid to say that from your replies I am going to have to ask you to accompany me back to the UK to answer more questions.'

Jon was starting to get worried and angry at the same time. 'Now hang on a minute, Mr bloody Robertson, you can't just come in here and demand things like that. I've got a job to do up here. Are you arresting me or something? What the fuck is going on?'

Robertson sighed. 'Firstly Sir, your Senior Pilot has confirmed that you can actually be spared and secondly, this is a very serious matter that involves national security.'

'Oh, for fuck's sake, be serious. What can my relationship with a local Norwegian girl have to do with national bloody security?'

'If that was the truth of the matter, the answer would be nothing Sir. The problem with this case is that you were actually having a relationship with a Russian girl, not a Norwegian one and a girl who was almost certainly working for the KGB. By telling you that I've probably exceeded my authority.'

The Caspian Monster

Cold water ran down Jon's spine. My God, could that be true? Jesus, he could be in serious trouble. But hang on a second, he still hadn't done anything wrong. All he could do was be totally honest.

'OK, I can see how that would be a problem. You're sure of that I suppose?'

Mr Robertson simply nodded. 'Now Sir, I need to accompany you while you pack. We have an aircraft waiting on the airfield.'

Jon realised he wasn't even trusted enough to pack on his own. God how much trouble was he in?

A disorientating eight hours later, he was back in England. The jet looked to be the same one that Rupert and Brian had used. It landed at RAF Northolt just outside London. Once they landed, they were met by a car but to Jon's surprise headed north and entered the naval headquarters at Northwood. He was escorted into an office in what was called the 'hole', a massive underground bunker designed to withstand a nuclear blast, not that he really registered what he was seeing. The shock and worry of what he had been told, coupled with almost no sleep, had rendered him into an almost zombie state.

The room had a desk and several chairs. Once inside, the taciturn Mr Robertson left without a word of parting. Jon looked around at his surroundings. The room was pretty bare but it had the air of an office rather than a prison. With a sigh, he sat down and attempted to catch up on some sleep. He had no idea how long he would be here, so he might as well try to rest.

Some indeterminate time later, the door opened and several people filed in. To his surprise, Jon recognised the naval Captain who entered first. They had met after the Falklands War. He had been the secretary to the Admiral. Jon jumped to his feet, conscious that he was wearing slightly shabby field clothing. The Captain made no sign of recognition and just indicated for Jon to sit again. The next man looked familiar but before he could work out why, Rupert walked through the door.

'Jesus Rupert, am I glad to see you. Maybe someone will now tell me what the hell this all about.'

'Sorry, Lieutenant Hunt,' replied Rupert in a neutral tone. 'This is an initial formal interview to see what damage has been done to Pickwick and we need your total cooperation is that clear?'

'Oh come on. Yes alright. I understand but I've nothing to hide, fire away.'

'First, we need to sort out something fairly simple. Do you recognise this man?' and Rupert indicate the younger man who had come in second.

Jon looked carefully back at the stranger. Suddenly, it came back to him. That was the bastard who had tried to run him over that night.

'Yes, I think I do,' he replied grimly. 'That's the shit who tried to kill me a couple of weeks ago. I recognise his face. I saw it through the windscreen of his bloody car as he tried to run me over.'

Rupert turned to look at the man, who looked slightly discomforted with Jon's response. 'Well, that's not what he says. This is Mr Davidson and he works for me. Several weeks ago he was tasked to investigate a certain lady who lives in Bardufoss. He says he saw you enter her house for the evening and later that night you came out and attempted to attack him. He tried to drive away and you continued to attack him until he got clear.'

Jon burst out laughing. 'What a load of bollocks. How could I attack him if he was inside a car? Yes, I went outside to ask what the hell he was doing. He'd been parked up outside the house in pretty much plain view for hours and it was giving Inga the creeps. I was simply going to ask what the hell he was playing at. I thought he might be some kind pervert or stalker or something. As soon as he saw me, he started the car and if I didn't know better, tried to run me down. In retrospect maybe he's just a crap driver. If that's how you teach your guys to do surveillance then God help us. Look, if he was meant to be watching us, how come he was in such a plain view that I could simply walk out and confront him?'

The newcomer was looking even more discomforted when Rupert spoke. 'Right, I think that probably is all I need to hear about that matter. Jamie, you may leave now. I'll call for you when I'm ready.'

Looking as though he wanted to protest but realising it was probably not worthwhile, the man left and shut the door hard behind him.

'Sorry about that Jon but now we've got to get to the serious matter. What do you know about Inga Thorsenn?'

Rupert quizzed Jon for hours. He managed to get some coffee and sandwiches but the questions never let up. Jon was as truthful as he could be. He had nothing to hide. Eventually Rupert explained how Inga had been spotted in Oslo talking to a known KGB operative and how her so called Norwegian past had proved to be a fake. The fact that this had happened literally as they were returning from the Pickwick mission, was the real problem. Absolutely nothing out of the ordinary had taken place over that period except the Pickwick flight, so why had she gone to Oslo, unless someone had told her something about what was going on? Was she seeing anyone else on the base? Jon was adamant there was no one else and so the questions kept coming back, had he let anything slip? Jon was sure he hadn't said anything but the fatigue and continual questioning was starting to wear him down. He started to question his own memory. Had he maybe said something after one of the parties when they had all got horribly pissed? But no there hadn't been any parties after Rupert and Brian had arrived.

He stuck to his guns and managed to get a few questions of his own in as well. He also pointed out that maybe Inga wouldn't have done a runner if the MI6 operative had been a little more subtle in his surveillance. There was no answer to that. He also wanted to know why they assumed that her trip to Oslo was a result of finding something out. Couldn't it have been just a routine meeting? The point was accepted but as it couldn't be proved either way there had to be an assumption that the worst case had occurred.

Eventually, the interrogation stopped and they let Jon go to the wardroom where there was a cabin for him. He was to remain on the base until further notice.

Rupert sighed and turned to his naval colleague. 'That man saved my life a few weeks ago and did something really heroic for me during the Falklands War. I'm pretty sure he's telling us everything. No, I'm certain of it. The problem is that I'm almost as certain that the bloody Russians have discovered something about Pickwick. God, what a mess.'

The Captain didn't look much happier. 'Yes, we had him picked out as a high flyer and almost certain for early promotion especially after his Falklands performance.'

'So, what will happen to him now?'

'Well, if you say you've no more questions then that's that. I'll speak to his appointer tomorrow. That's the officer who manages officer's career appointments. We'll find something for him in the wings to keep him out of circulation for while. He'll probably get the message and resign but whatever happens, I'm afraid his career is over.'

Chapter 15

Russia, Matchenkov

Inga sighed as she looked out of the grimy window. Her backside was going slowly numb as she sat on the hard wooden seat. She couldn't get up and walk about as the train carriage was far too crowded. It was packed with grey, stoic looking people, all numbly passing the time, the same as her. She had finished her book several hours ago and didn't even have that solace left to help the hours to go by. They should be there by now but the train had suffered numerous stoppages. No one explained why and none of the passengers seemed surprised. Her time in the West had clearly changed her attitude. No one there would put up with such an appalling service. Outside the window, the endless Russian plains sped by, flat and featureless. Her mind turned to her return to Moscow.

When she had telephoned her controller after Jon had left that morning she had been surprised by his reaction. He ordered her to conduct an immediate evacuation and drive to Oslo. When she arrived, she was taken straight to the Embassy and quizzed for hours. It hadn't been a pleasant experience. However, in the end, they concluded that she hadn't been at fault. The man who had almost run down Jon wasn't one of theirs, so he must have been from the opposition even if his actions had seemed odd at the time. That could only mean that Inga's cover was blown. The consensus was that she must have been seen by someone who recognised her when she had visited Oslo. They showed her photographs of current personnel from the UK and US embassies and it didn't take long for her to recognise one all too familiar face. Once it had all been cleared up she was ordered back to Moscow. In a surprisingly short time, she was back in the capital, undergoing yet another debrief. It quickly became very clear that they were having trouble thinking of what to do with her. The last thing she wanted was to be returned to her family but it appeared that was exactly what was being contemplated. It was made quite plain that she could never be used overseas again. Once an agent's cover was blown that was it. The anonymous man who gave her, her final interview was quite adamant about that. He also made it clear that she would do as she was told. Inga desperately pointed out her qualifications in languages and science and the man agreed that they would be useful but it would take some time to find her a new job. However, until they came up with more work for her she was expected to travel back to her home and wait for a call.

So here she was, just hours from going full circle, back to the collective farm and her father and brothers. She groaned at the thought. What would she find once she arrived?

Despite all her misgiving, she wasn't prepared for what she did find when the train eventually pulled in to the shabby old station. With her suitcase in hand, she walked up the streets she vaguely recollected from a distant childhood. Distant both in time and experience and all too soon she was standing in front of her old home. The weather was grey and damp, and the long day was coming to an end but that didn't excuse her depression. The house was always scruffy but she remembered an air of bustle and purpose. Now, it was just small and run down. Slates from the roof had fallen off and hadn't been repaired. The yard at the front was overgrown with weeds. With mounting trepidation, she walked up the rough path and knocked on the door. It was opened by Gregori her oldest brother.

She recognised him instantly although he looked much older than he ought to. 'Yes can I help?' he asked and then realising how pretty the girl was looking up at him, followed his words with a frank appraising stare.

'Gregori, don't you recognise me?' asked Inga both surprised by his non recognition and upset by his stare.

The Caspian Monster

Inga could see the tumblers turning in Gregori's mind.

'Sister Inga, is that you?' and he enveloped her in an all embracing and more than smelly hug. His breath stank of vodka. 'Come in, I didn't know you were coming, come in, come in.'

She was ushered into the living room and reunited with her family home. She immediately realised they were the only two people in the room.

'Gregori, where are my other brothers? Where is Father?'

A shadow crossed Gregori's face. 'Your brothers have all left Inga. There is little to keep anyone here now. They've gone to look for better work somewhere and we don't speak. Father is still here but he isn't well, not well at all.'

Sensing that something was hiding behind her brother's words, Inga looked hard at him. 'Gregori, take me to him. He is here I assume?'

Her brother nodded but didn't speak. He led her up the corridor past the dirty kitchen to the bedroom. He opened the door but didn't make any effort to go in.

Inga pushed past him and went up to the bed. She was appalled. The first thing that hit her was the smell but before she could fully react to it, she saw the shrunken figure under the dirty blankets. No, this wasn't the strong powerful man of her memories, not the man who had single handedly won the Second World War for Russia in his tank and then brought her and her brothers up on his own. It couldn't be.

But she realised that of course, it was. Age and hard work had taken their toll. He was breathing slowly and his eyes were shut. She gently went to the bed and touched his forehead. His eyes opened. At least they were the same piercing blue that she remembered. Unlike Gregori, he recognised her instantly.

'Inga, you came back,' he half whispered in a frail voice.

'Yes Papa, I'm here now. I will look after you.' His face was blurring through her tears.

'Good, I am so tired these days,' and he drifted off to sleep again.

She turned around and this time took proper stock of the room and then started to get angry.

Leaving her father asleep, she stormed out and confronted Gregori who had gone back to the living room and was staring morosely at the old stove and drinking more vodka.

'What's going on?' she demanded. 'Who is looking after him? What is wrong with him? How could you let him get into such a state?'

Gregori looked up. 'Sit sister, I understand your anger but maybe if you had stayed with us things would have been different.'

The words hit her like a blow and she sat down on the only other chair. 'I had no choice,' she said weakly. 'I was taken away. No one asked me if I wanted to go.'

Gregori grunted in acknowledgement. 'Well, you seem to have done well for yourself. Just looking at your clothing tells me that.'

'Oh shut up, give and me a vodka before you drink it all.'

Slightly surprised, Gregori filled a glass for her and watched it disappear in classic Russian fashion.

'Now, tell me everything.'

They talked for several hours although the story was pretty simple. The collective farm had slowly deteriorated as people took more for themselves just to survive. The officials continued in their self centred greed and for the last few years it had almost become open warfare between them and the people they were meant to be representing and supporting. Inga's other three brothers had slipped away one by one. Gregori suspected that they had headed to the cities but hadn't heard from them for several years now. Father had become ill last year. The doctors had said cancer and because they had no cure, had simply told him to go home. Any help that the state should have provided was never forthcoming. The local officials weren't interested and so Gregori did what he could which even he admitted was not very much.

The Caspian Monster

Even though it was now late in the evening, Inga forced her brother to get up and help her clean up the old man. She couldn't bear the thought of leaving him as she had found him. She managed to find some reasonably clean sheets and blankets and was able to give him quick bed wash as well. Finally, she was able to curl up on her old bed which was still where it had been when she left and sink into an exhausted sleep.

The next morning, after managing to make a rudimentary breakfast for all three of them, she asked the way to the collective manager's office. She strode down the rutted tracks until she came to the only building that appeared to have been maintained in recent years. She went straight in and asked the tired looking old woman who was sitting behind a shabby counter to see the manager. She was told curtly that he wasn't in and she would have to make an appointment. This was clearly a blatant lie as Inga could see the man in question through an open door. He was sitting behind his desk. Ignoring the woman, she marched into the office and kicked the door shut behind her. The man she confronted looked up at her. Middle aged, balding and running to fat, he was the best fed person she had seen since she arrived.

'And you are?' he asked with a lascivious grin as his eyes travelled up and down her body.

'My name is Inga Pochenko and I want to know why my father has been so neglected by the collective. You're meant to look after sick people.'

He spread his hands. 'My dear, our resources are limited and he has an incurable disease. What are we meant to do?'

'How about providing some decent food and someone to help care for him for a start?'

The official just shrugged. 'My dear as I just said, we are limited in what we can do you must understand that.' He stood up and came round his desk to her. 'Of course, a grateful daughter could do much to help things.' He smiled and tried to put his hand round Inga to touch her bottom.

Inga smiled at him and moved closer to allow his hand to grope the better. Consequently, it came as quite a surprise when her knee came up hard into his testicles. With a groan, he clutched himself and sank to the floor.

'You fucking bitch, if you wanted help for your father, you're definitely not getting it now.'

Inga just smiled. 'Is that so? Well, you weren't here when I left to go to Moscow but let me tell you that I went to work for an organisation that is probably the most powerful in this country. Do you understand?'

He looked at her again through tears of pain and realised what she meant. Everything from her bearing to her clothes confirmed her claim. Suddenly, the pain in his groin was secondary to the cold shiver that went down his spine.

'Now, you will arrange for some decent food to be sent over straight away. I suggest you look in your own larder. It must be pretty well stocked seeing how fat you are. Then I will want you to arrange some nursing care from the hospital in the town to come and help me out. Is that clear?'

He nodded miserably while attempting to stand and make his way back to his chair.

'And in case you think I am bluffing, here is a telephone number you can ring if you want to verify my story with my employer.'

She handed him a slip of paper and walked out confident that he would do no such thing. Fear of the KGB was endemic in this country. She left feeling elated and cheap at the same time. What were things coming to when you had to put the fear of God into someone just to get some basic human rights?

For two weeks she stayed and nursed her father. Better food helped, as did getting him into a clean and healthy environment. Gregori was of no help but she didn't mind. She felt fulfilled in a way she never expected to be. They didn't speak much. Father found it too difficult but the look of love and gratitude in his eyes was sometimes almost too much to bear. It wasn't to last. One morning, on going to his room, she realised he wasn't breathing. His face was grey. He must have slipped away in the night. She felt guilty that she hadn't been there for him but she had to sleep sometime. The same day, she got a call from Moscow ordering her back. They had found a job for her as an intelligence analyst. Yes, she could have time for the funeral but after that she must return as soon as possible.

As she stood by the grave and watched the earth being shovelled over the cheap coffin, she finally gave in to her grief and tears flooded down her cheeks. Her brother held her tight, as she sobbed. What she couldn't understand was whether she was crying for the loss of her lovely father or the loss of her belief in her country.

Chapter 16

London

Jon sat on a park bench in St James Park. He was wearing a suit which didn't fit too well. Not surprising as he hadn't worn it for several years. It felt odd in other ways. He hadn't been out of uniform for quite some time and civilian clothes just felt strange. He looked around at the view. The park was full of early daffodils and pretty girls walking in the spring sunshine. Through the trees, in one direction, he could see the Mall and a bit of Buckingham Palace. The last time he had been there it had been for a very different reason. The Queen had given him a bloody medal. In the other direction was Whitehall with the white stone buildings of government. One of which he would have to go into in the next few minutes. Despite the spring air and promise of warmer days, he felt numb and indecisive. They had let him leave Northwood after a couple of days with stern admonishments to say nothing about the events in Norway. He was no longer on the squadron that was made clear. The navy would find something else for him to do. He was pretty sure that his career was over and in one way he could understand why. But he also felt it was bitterly unfair. There wasn't even any direct evidence that Pickwick had been compromised, at least none that Rupert would share.

Part of him was saying, just go in and hand in your notice but the other part was digging in its toes. Why should he be treated so shabbily just why the fucking hell should he lie down and take it? He decided to keep his powder dry and see what was on offer. Looking at his watch he realised it was time. He picked up his briefcase which despite looking quite formal, only contained a copy of Private Eye and some sandwiches and made his way over the gravel parade ground of Horse Guards parade and into Whitehall. He turned left, up the wide street until he came to the little stone arch and courtyard

The Caspian Monster

of the Old Admiralty Building. How many naval officers had walked through here to learn of their fate over the centuries he wondered? The place dripped history. The dark suited man at the desk consulted a list when he told him his name and indicated where he should sit. However, he wasn't even able to get his Private Eye out of his brief case before the friendly face of Lieutenant Commander Brown, the aircrew appointing officer, appeared around the corner of the corridor and beckoned Jon to follow.

Once the door to the appointer's office closed, Jon was offered a seat in front of the old oak desk.

'Jon, good to see you, I'm just sorry it's not in better circumstances.'

'Yes Sir, so am I,' replied Jon. 'I guess I have to ask you what you know and what it means for me?'

'Ah, now that's a very good question,' the appointer said with a puzzled look. 'All I've been told is that something happened up in snowy old Norway and you need another job. Also, I've been told that it can't be front line or even on a training squadron I'm afraid.'

'What, you mean I can't fly?'

'Sorry old chap. You didn't fall foul of that wanker of a Senior Pilot of yours, did you? I reckon I would have lasted five whole minutes with him myself. I trained with him. It's bad enough being his contemporary. Sorry, shouldn't have said that about a colleague but I don't suppose I'm the only one that feels that way.'

Jon realised he was being put at his ease at the same time as a subtle bit of fishing was being undertaken to try and discover what sort of black he had really put up.

'Sorry Sir, I really can't tell you anything. But look, if you can't give me a flying job what is there for me?' He almost added that in that case, he might as well just hand in his notice but at the last moment couldn't make himself do it. Dammit, he loved the navy and the life just too much.

'Well, we could send you to sea as a bridge watchkeeper or some admin job at one of the naval bases.' He saw the look on Jon's face. 'OK then, I guess not, have you any ideas?'

Jon had a brain wave. 'How about a Russian interpreter's course? I'm good at languages as you probably know and I've just started a linguaphone course, so have some of the rudiments.'

The appointer looked thoughtful. Getting Jon out of the mainstream had been his aim in the first place. A full course would take nine months which wasn't quite as much as he wanted but it would mean he might be of more use to the navy once it was finished. Although he had been given strict instructions about what to do with Jon, he had some leeway and anyway he just couldn't believe that he really deserved such bad treatment. His past performance was just too good. He had been given a DSO for his Falklands work for goodness sake and they weren't given away with the cornflakes.

'You know, that seems like quite a good idea, just give me a moment,' and he got up and went out of the office. Jon looked around while he waited. From the window, he could see the bustle of people going up and down Whitehall. Why hadn't he resigned? He could be one them out there. Not beholden to a thankless system and free to do whatever he wanted. Before he could finish the thought, the appointer came back.

'Right Jon, the Boss agrees. These tend to be one off courses. You do a concentrated month down at HMS Excellent, then we farm you out to a family, where you speak nothing but the lingo all the time. Of course, normally that would be in the relevant country but strangely not many Russian speaking countries would be prepared to host you. However, we have several of the right sort of family here. So by Christmas, you should be fluent. Is that OK?'

Jon nodded and that was that. He was given a couple of days leave which he spent awkwardly with his parents. He had broken up with his last girlfriend some months earlier, so really had nowhere else to go. He found it very difficult to keep his counsel, especially with his father who, with almost prescient parental skill, spotted a problem immediately Jon arrived. It was almost with relief that he escaped their loving but cloying presence and immersed himself in the course at the school in HMS Excellent in Portsmouth. It was a very concentrated period of instruction but he found that he loved it. Languages had always been easy for him even though Russian was a very different one from those he was familiar with. All too soon, the course was over and he was given an address to report to.

To his surprise, it was in Scotland, just outside Edinburgh. He drove up in his old Triumph sports car and found the house. It was quite a large Victorian manse in a row of similar ones in a suburban street. Mentally rehearsing a Russian greeting, he knocked on the door. It was opened by a ruddy faced, jovial looking man, with a very firm handshake.

Before Jon could speak, he welcomed Jon in Russian. He didn't have too much trouble understanding the man but was startled by what he thought he had heard.

'Ah my friend, you must be the lodger we were expecting, I am Victor from the KGB.'

Chapter 17

200 metres below the Arctic Ice

Captain Orlov was on what was probably his last patrol. Sadly, he knew he was getting too old and too senior to command a submarine for much longer but this time his mission was different, this time he could really make a difference. He was getting thoroughly fed up with being harassed by British and American submarines. His previous patrol had been typical and he spent most of the time fruitlessly trying to disappear from their grasp. When he returned to base, he had had a long talk with his superiors. They had passed on a snippet of information from the KGB. Apparently, earlier that winter, the British had flown some sort of helicopter mission way to the north of their normal operating area. It may have been nothing but it gave him enough ammunition to start to convince them that his idea was worth pursuing. He was sure there was some form of detection base up here in the ice. The problem was that there had been rigorous surveys from orbit, by naval reconnaissance aircraft, even the new Tiger super plane but nothing had been detected. So, convincing them that his idea was worthwhile had taken some time.

In the end, it was the KGB again who had come to his aid. Not only had they provided the information about the British flight but their concern over NATO intentions was intensifying and now under Operation Ryan, the military were to be included in their intelligence gathering. Anything that could provide information was to be pursued vigorously.

This time, instead of leaving the ice to patrol the northern Atlantic, he was going to spend his first three weeks surveying the ice from below. If NATO did have something up here it could only be in a certain area. Three weeks should be enough. At least that's what he thought when he started. He only had a few days left and so far they had drawn a complete blank. The two special weapons in his arsenal were a very sensitive infra red sensor on his attack periscope and some especially sensitive hydrophones. His theory was simple. If they were here and couldn't be detected from above then he would detect them from below. They had to generate some heat and would almost certainly make some noise. The beauty of infra red thermal detectors was that they didn't really detect heat. They detected differences of temperature and it so it didn't really matter whether it was freezing or boiling as long as the target was at a different temperature. Unfortunately, the visual range of his periscope underwater was very limited, so he was also hoping that whatever generator they were using would make enough noise for them to hear it. The final problem he had was that he didn't want to alert them that they had been found. If he was right, then they would be tracking him the whole time. To this end, the KGB had deliberately leaked that the navy was conducting under ice geographical surveys. Hopefully, they would think he was looking down at the bottom rather than up at the surface.

Suddenly, the quiet of the control room was broken. 'Captain you are requested to come to the sonar room.'

He shot down the corridor and looked at the sonar operator who took off his headphones and handed them to him. He closed his eyes and listened. At first, he couldn't hear anything just the background hiss and clicks of the Arctic sea. However, he knew how good his sonar operator was and he wouldn't have alerted him for no reason. And there it was, a very distant, very faint hum. It was fading in and out but definitely there.

'Bearing two nine five Captain.'

He nodded his thanks and handed back the headphones. On returning to the control room, he ordered a course change to track down the bearing and crossed his fingers. Sonar kept updating the bearing and the noise level slowly increased. Had they not been specifically looking for it, they would probably have never even noticed it but now they were on the hunt. Soon, he was glued to the periscope, looking, hoping and praying he would see something. Just as the sonar room reported no further increase in noise level, he saw it. It wasn't much, just a lighter patch in the ice only a few degrees warmer than the rest. But it was enough. He didn't dare stop. He mustn't give the game away but he had the evidence. The bastards were here and now he knew exactly where they were.

Three hundred feet up, the sonar operator had to take off his earphones. Despite turning the gain down as far as he could, the noise of the Soviet submarine was just too loud.

'Jesus, Boss, he's passed right below us. Bloody hell, does he know we're here?'

'What's he doing now?' asked the supervisor.

'Hang on,' the operator put his earphones back on. 'Just keeping on the same track. No change to bearing or propeller count, so he hasn't altered course or speed.'

'No, I don't think he knows. Intelligence has said they're surveying the whole area. It's something they do quite often. Anyway, if the Defence Research boffins are to be believed, Soviet submarines don't have any equipment sensitive enough to pick us up. No, they had to pass close sometime. They treat this area like their own back yard after all. I'll let home know in the next SITREP signal but let's get back to work guys.'

The supervisor's confident words belied his true feelings. That had been a very close call. The bloody Russians always seemed to come up with new developments. What if they had been detected? They were in international waters but that might not put them off trying something. He would pass his concerns on as well as the information.

Moscow

The Caspian Monster

A week after returning from patrol, Captain Orlov was called to naval headquarters in Moscow. His report had been read and that along with several other issues were going to be discussed at the highest level. He found himself in a large oak lined room almost filled with a green felt covered table and surrounded by chairs, all filled with senior officers. Before he was asked to speak, a briefing was given on the observations of the American fleet in the Pacific. They had just completed Fleetex 83. It had been the largest naval exercise in the area since the last war. Everyone was worried about the Americans intentions. Why where they sabre rattling like this? Common thought in the Kremlin was that if they were going to strike it would be under the guise of a major exercise. That way they could have all their forces on alert under the pretence of a peacetime operation. Luckily, it seemed that all the naval units involved were now dispersing but it had been a tense few weeks.

Orlov then got up and took over the lectern at the front of the room to speak to a charged and tense atmosphere. He knew what he was going to say wouldn't help calm things down. He started by outlining his original suspicions and how they had led to the search he had successfully conducted on his last patrol. He then showed the photographs he had taken through the periscope. These had been enhanced by the shore side scientists and showed a little more detail. He pointed out the main heat source, explaining how it indicated some form of habitation, probably for up to a dozen people. He then pointed out the faint traces of dots radiating out on several bearings from the base and attached to under side of the ice.

'We think these are sensors. The most obvious types to use would be hydrophones but they would have to be more sensitive than any we have. However, there is speculation that they could also be Magnetic Anomaly Detectors or even devices that can detect nucleid particles from our reactors. We are a working on those technologies ourselves. However, they could also be something else entirely. They have been at such pains to disguise this base who knows what they might be so desperate to hide?'

He answered questions for some time and then was allowed to return to his seat.

The debate initially centred around how submarines could avoid the base but it soon became clear that that was going to be difficult. It was very well positioned to cover all approaches out into the Atlantic. Someone then suggested an alternative. Could not Special Forces go in and neutralise the base? Surprisingly, no one was against the idea probably because of the atmosphere in the room after the earlier briefing. The idea was even more popular when it was suggested that not only could it be neutralised but the technologies they were using could also be retrieved for study. However, some cooler heads pointed out that the base was in international waters and a covert raid during the summer months, when it was almost always daylight, would be nigh impossible. If they waited until the darkness of winter, the ice could probably be too thick to force a submarine up through it. So how could they get there? One thing was certain, if they did do this, it had to be in such a way that they could deny any liability.

The senior Admiral looked over to Orlov. 'Captain, thank you for all your efforts and all you have done to bring this to our attention. And now that you have done so, I think it only right that we give you the honour of coming up with a plan to stop NATO and preferably retrieve the equipment they are using for our own evaluation. I will give you full authority. Work on the problem and then come back to me. You have six weeks to present some initial findings.'

Orlov nodded, this was a great responsibility but also a fantastic opportunity. However, his insides turned over. He remained looking confident while realising he didn't have a clue how he was going to come up with a solution.

Chapter 18

Edinburgh

Jon had decided he loved learning Russian. He and his friend Victor from the KGB were indulging in some Russian culture. He was slowly realising that many things he had been brought up to believe in were at the best half truths and quite often complete fabrications. The last few months he had spent with Victor and his delightful family were fascinating and instructive. One thing he had definitely learnt was that they liked their vodka.

'Za lyoo bof' called Victor as he threw yet another shot straight down. He was teaching Jon the various Russian toasts. 'That, my friend means. 'To Love'. A wonderful sentiment, no?'

Jon repeated the toast and polished off his glass. 'Indeed my friend, if only I had some.' And they both started giggling like silly children. At that point, Natasha, Victor's wife, came in and took in the scene.

'Right, you two that's enough vodka. I seem to remember you promising to take the children to the football tomorrow. Any more of that and you will never get out of bed.' She looked at Jon reproachfully. 'I thought you would be a good influence. It seems I was mistaken.'

'Sorry Natty,' said Jon in a slightly slurred voice as he got up from the arm chair. 'But I need to learn all about you lovely Russians you know, it's my job,' and he gave her a warm hug not noticing the sour look on her face when called her Natty.

She gracefully steered him towards the stairs and his bedroom before turning to start berating her husband. Jon had to smile as he heard her start to lay into Victor. It was a daily occurrence and seemed to be part of the way their marriage worked. He wasn't concerned. He just wished he could find someone to love enough that they could argue so hard and then forgive each other so often. He briefly thought back to Inga. For a while there he had harboured a thought that they might have made something of a couple. So much for that, the bitch was probably back in Moscow laughing her head off at the thought of him.

He made it back to his room and gratefully sank back onto his bed. He supposed he should really get undressed. He managed to kick off both shoes but that was as far as he got before the room went blank.

Sometime in the early hours he woke up and threw off his clothes before crawling properly under the sheets. He lay looking at the ceiling, feeling the dull ache of yet another vodka inspired thick head but couldn't seem to find any refuge in sleep. The last few months had been a revelation and most of the time he had been able to forget about the recent incidents in Norway as he concentrated on the present. His language skills were certainly developing well. He wasn't even sure what language he was thinking in now. But what was even more fascinating was what he was learning from Victor and to a lesser extent his family.

Victor was indeed from the KGB. He was a defector and although he refused to answer any questions about his direct role or how he and his family had managed to get out of the Soviet Union he was a fount of information about the country. Once Victor had been debriefed by MI6, he and the family had been put in the security services protection programme. Part of the deal was that they would look after the occasional language student. Jon was extremely surprised by this. Surely if MI6 thought that he was a security risk then this was the last place they should have put him? But then he saw the cleverness of the idea. He was pretty sure that Victor had a brief to watch him and see if he let anything slip. Jon wasn't worried, he knew he had nothing to hide but even so, he was careful to avoid any discussions that might be considered dangerous.

But the things he had learnt. Probably the most basic thing was that Russians were really nice people. A somewhat stupid thing to discover in some ways but the whole of western culture seemed to want to depict the Russians as a mass of ignorant and rather savage monsters rather than just ordinary people. For his part, Victor explained that he had undergone a similar process of enlightenment. He had expected to see beggars on every corner and the rich flying past in their expensive cars. Where were the dirty industrial valleys full of exploited workers? When they had first taken him to a supermarket he was convinced it was a setup. He simply couldn't believe the quantity and variety of goods on offer. But it was the same everywhere and there were no queues. Mind you, he found the endless advertising and consumerism quite grating.

Jon was also beginning to understand the deep paranoia that was embedded in the Russian psyche. The revolution of nineteen seventeen had been a popular uprising against the endless repression and excesses of the Czarist system. It wasn't borne out of a desire for communism at all but as that seemed a good alternative at the time, they had taken to it gladly. That they had then saddled themselves with yet another oppressive system had taken many years to sink in. Indeed, many never saw it that way. The common peasant had at least benefited. But it was the Russian view of the Second World War and its aftermath which really surprised Jon. When Jon mentioned the Battle of Britain, Victor didn't know what he was talking about. When he explained, he merely shrugged it off as a sideline, probably one of the many things Hitler had done to keep everyone's eyes off his real intention which was to renege on his treaty with Stalin as soon as he felt it was feasible. That betrayal still hurt to this day. Funnily enough once Jon thought about it that way he started to query his own views. As Victor pointed out, could an invasion of England really have happened? Even with total air supremacy and ninety per cent of the Royal Navy destroyed? Britain would still have had enough warships left to decimate any landings especially as the German navy was so weak. And that took the discussion on to the opposite invasions. When D Day occurred in France, the Russians were fighting their enormous tank battles on the plains and starting to roll the Germans back while taking enormous losses. An order of magnitude more losses than occurred on the beaches of Normandy. As far as Victor was concerned, D Day was just a diversion which helped pin down some German troops away from Russia. Not only that, many Russians felt that the Allies had deliberately delayed the invasion to ensure that their forces were weakened as a tactic for the forthcoming peace. Jon had scoffed openly at such a ludicrous idea but had realised that Victor saw things very differently. But when Victor described some of the atrocities committed by the Germans he couldn't help feel deep sympathy.

When Jon then pointed out that the Russian and then Soviet governments were reputed to have been just as vicious with their own people on occasions, Victor nodded sadly. That was one of the reasons he had decided to leave his country. Initially, he wouldn't say any more on the subject but when pressed he gave Jon a view of the present state of Soviet Russia. Many there felt the government was losing touch with reality. Although Victor still believed that their system was inherently fairer to all it was clear to him that stagnation and paranoia were doing their part to slowly destroy the system from within. Sections of society were slowly polarising into the rich and poor once again. Victor could see the possibility of another revolution if things didn't change. Either that or his leaders would lead them into some form of disastrous military confrontation just to save their skins. Wasn't that what the Argentinians had tried to do just last year in the Falklands? The difference, of course, was that an East-West confrontation would be catastrophic for the whole planet. It didn't help that the Americans, in particular, were being so belligerent. At this point, Jon had to protest. He had been hassled by Soviet aircraft himself in the past and knew many stories from others about how belligerent they could be. Victor had to agree, he acknowledged that maybe it was time both sides try rapprochement rather than confrontation. Jon reflected that he would never think about the current world situation in such black and white terms again.

Victor then went on to outline the Soviet view of recent years and in particular the current situation. Scared that the West would use tactical nuclear strikes to circumvent the Soviet numerical superiority in Europe, they had produced the SS20 missile. Being medium range, it circumvented the SALT treaty and was accurate enough to target moving military headquarters. Now, some years later, the Americans were countering them with the Pershing missiles. In the Soviet view, this meant a further shift of the established balance.

'And now, my friend,' said Victor grimly. 'We have just had the announcement of this Strategic Defence Initiative, what do you say? 'Star Wars.''

Jon had to interject. 'Victor, it's purely defensive. Surely you can see that?'

'It's being sold to you that way my friend and to be frank I probably agree. However, I absolutely guarantee that my former masters won't see it that way. It is largely space based is it not? I would bet that they think it is just a ruse to extend the American nuclear arsenal into orbit. And don't forget that although the Americans are asking you and the rest of Europe to participate, you get virtually no protection from it. That's a pretty one sided deal in my view.'

Jon could only nod.

Victor talked a great deal more about the Soviet leadership. He reminded Jon that President Brezhnev had died recently. The period of uncertainty hadn't lasted long although Victor was dismayed when he learnt who his successor was to be. Yuri Andropov had been head of the KGB and very much one of the old guard. According to Victor, he was just about the worst choice that could have been made. It was Andropov who had instigated Operation Ryan to try and discover the true intentions of the Reagan administration. He was hardly the most balanced character to lead a nuclear superpower. Apparently, he was also quite old and not in good health, so the only good thing was that he probably wouldn't last long. As long as it wasn't long enough to drag the world into nuclear war of course. When Jon asked how on earth these men were selected and how the process could be justified to the population, Victor wasn't able to give an answer that Jon could either understand or accept. However, it did start him thinking about how his own system worked.

As he reflected on Victor's Russian history lessons he realised that until now he had been too busy enjoying himself, playing the warrior and believing all that his masters told him. He decided he was going to do some serious reading on these subjects as soon as he could.

'Yes it had been quite a wakeup call,' he thought as he finally drifted off to sleep.

The next day he and Victor took the two kids to the football. It wasn't Jon's sport but he loved the atmosphere in the stadium and even more, he loved the look on the children's faces. Just ordinary kids having fun and enjoying life. Why did anything need to be more complicated?

Chapter 19

Caspian Sea

Yuri was elated but in some ways quite sad. This time he was flying the massive Lun. Once again he was at the controls of an Ekranoplan and once again he was about to make history. The only problem was that this could easily be the last time he did any real test flying. The successful outcome of this trip meant the successful culmination of the main test programme. After this, it would be routine production work or even worse, nothing at all. He had already been offered a more senior management role in the bureau and that was good but he still wanted to fly, to be in control of these ridiculous, savage, flying monsters.

Reigning in his wandering thoughts, he forced himself to concentrate on the job in hand. The navigator called out that the first range boat was due to appear soon and sure enough there it was in the distance just to the right of the nose. God knew what they looked like to the personnel on the boat. Yuri knew it was packed with senior brass and politicians. It was a final attempt by Rostislav to convince them that these machines were something special, something worth continued investment. Frankly, if they weren't convinced today they never would be. At first, Yuri had protested that conducting a test flight in front of these people was too much of a risk. What would be the result if something went wrong? He was overruled and in his heart, he understood why. He just prayed that everything went well.

The giant machine was travelling absolutely flat out with all eight engines howling. Normally, all but two would be shut down but for this flight, maximum speed would be needed. They were a mere twenty metres above the sea. Although he couldn't see it, he knew the machine would be spraying a massive rooster tail of water into the air behind it. He was having to concentrate on his flying very carefully. At this speed, she could easily become directionally unstable with disastrous consequences. This was the biggest and heaviest flying machine ever to take to the skies and it would not look good if he smeared it all over the sea in front of all those influential people. Someone had said that the American Spruce Goose was bigger but Yuri had laughed derisively. That museum piece had only flown once and that was by accident. He was doing almost seven hundred kilometres an hour and was about to do something even more astounding.

His missile officer called over the intercom. 'Range targets acquired Captain, all weapons are fully armed. Permission to fire?'

Yuri felt a small tug of relief. That was the last link in the chain. They were now all ready. 'Permission granted but wait to fire on my call.' He wanted this display to be the most effective he could manage. He waited until the range boat was a mile ahead of them.

'Fire.'

On the range boat, they had heard the machine long before they saw it. Then the Lun appeared over the horizon like some massive prehistoric beast travelling at a ludicrously high speed and trailing a massive wake of spray. Its tiny wings seemed too small for what it was actually doing. Its nose and tail bulged with the radomes of its targeting radars and its back was covered in serried ranks of giant missile tubes. Shortly before it reached them, there was a massive gout of flame and blast of smoke as the first missile left its canister on the back of the monster. Seconds later, the second missile launched, followed by four more. The noise was so loud it was felt rather than heard. As a demonstration of raw savage power, it had no equal. Eyes on the boat and the machine then tracked the missiles as they sped away towards their targets many miles ahead. The Ekranoplan roared onward as the missiles disappeared over the horizon. On board, Yuri and his crew were counting down.

'First impact,' called the missile officer and then five more calls of successful missile strikes. The last was met by cheers from the whole crew.

Yuri gently throttled back six of the engines and slowed down to normal cruising speed.

'OK everyone, that was well done. We will loiter here while the range boat gets back to shore. Navigator, where are the Eaglets?'

'In position,' called the navigator from his radar display. 'Turn to two seven zero to join up.'

This part of the test was pure theatre. The missile firing was the culmination of a lengthy series of tests to prove the machine's weapon capability. The next bit was for show.

Within minutes, they had joined the other two smaller Ekranoplans and flying in loose formation, headed for the marshy beach, a couple of miles to the west of their base. With confirmation that the range boat was in position, they manoeuvred to approach directly from seaward. Two kilometres away, they started to decelerate. By the time they reached the beach they were back in the water surrounded by spray as they roared up onto the sand. With the two Eaglets either side, they ground to a halt several hundred metres from the shoreline.

Pouring from the side of the Lun two hundred naval marines ran onto the sand and took up defensive positions. The complete nose sections of both Eaglets swung to one side and opened up the holds of both machines. Roaring out of one came a tank followed by a second and then fifty more marines. Simultaneously, out of the other came two mobile artillery batteries and a further fifty marines. The engines of the Ekranoplans wound down and silence descended over the scene. It had taken less than nine minutes to land and deploy a full marine assault regiment with their equipment and two tanks.

'Let them say that wasn't bloody impressive,' thought Yuri with enormous pride. *'Bloody hell it impressed the crap out of me and I knew what was coming.'*

The Caspian Monster

Moscow

Inga had arrived back in Moscow and reported to her new boss. Although she had tried to shake off the effects of the previous weeks, it hadn't been easy. She felt grief over the loss of her father and guilt that she should have been there more for him. In the end, she found herself confessing to the man even though she barely knew him. Surprisingly, he had been quite understanding especially when she said how her father had been treated. However, she kept quiet about her deeper thoughts about the system she was starting to despise. That would definitely not be a good revelation to make. She found him strange in many ways, firstly, he hadn't stared at her or her body and secondly, he treated her as an equal. She just wished his eyes weren't so cold. He had explained that he had asked for her because of her academic record and because of her previous experience in Norway. That was what his section was responsible for. If he told her his surname she never remembered it. He was simply Mikhael and he always called her Inga. She was put to work straight away. Her role was to analyse intelligence from the field to try and separate the useful from the dross. She soon settled in and within weeks Mikhael was using her for more and more important tasks. The work was hard and she rarely got back to the small flat she been allocated before late evening but she found that she was really enjoying herself. In part, she realised it was because she was so busy she could put her past behind her and concentrate on the now. But also for the first time in her life, she was being respected for her intellect rather than her sexuality. She found that she still occasionally missed Jon but had to accept that they would never meet again. She firmly put that part of her life behind her.

At first, she looked at the information coming over her desk purely as data and used the analytical part of her mind to sort it out but soon she started to read and understand it as well. As her experience built up, so did her concerns. Eventually, after several months she asked to see Mikhael.

He welcomed her into his office and asked her to sit. 'Yes, Inga what is it?'

She wasn't quite sure how to start, so decided to take the bull by the horns. 'Mikhael, what is going on? We're getting all these reports from our people in Scandinavia and I assume the same is happening around the world. It's all part of Comrade Andropov's Operation Ryan to try and discover what the American's intentions really are. I understand that. What worries me is that we're not forwarding on the personal assessments of the people on the ground, just the facts that they're reporting.'

'So, what's wrong with that? That's exactly what we've been told to do.'

'But surely their local knowledge should be put to more use?'

'I'm sorry, what do you mean?'

'Look, here's an example. There's a report here from my successor in Bardufoss. It talks of a major build up of Royal Navy and Norwegian forces. Taken on face value that sounds quite worrying. But I know, because I was there, that it is almost certainly only their end of season exercise and they will all disperse in a few weeks. Isn't there a risk we could be seeing danger where none exists?'

'Sorry Inga, we've been told quite specifically to do it this way. The higher ups want information, not opinion.'

'Well, it looks like a mistake to me.'

Mikhael looked shrewdly at her. He had a disconcerting direct gaze that sometimes made her feel uncomfortable even though she couldn't really say why. 'Actually, Inga I agree with you. We will keep our own analysis going just in case. Now, was there something else?'

Slightly flustered by his stare but grateful that he had taken her point she shook her head and went back to work.

As she sat back at her desk, she wondered whether there were hidden depths to Mikhael. His continued lack of interest in her as a woman was beginning to pique her curiosity. The only other men she had encountered that treated her in such a way were homosexuals and she was pretty sure he wasn't that way inclined. Sometimes his eyes were very cold. She shivered, maybe she should keep her curiosity to herself.

Chapter 20

35,000 feet above the Sea of Japan

The Boeing 747 had just taken off from Anchorage Alaska. It wasn't full, only two hundred and forty six passengers, although one was a US congressman and twenty two were children. It was bound for Seoul in South Korea. It climbed to its cruising height of thirty five thousand feet and headed to the west to travel through the night along its designate airway, 'Romeo Twenty'. Once established in the cruise, one of two things happened. Either the co-pilot reached over and switched the autopilot INS switch to inertial navigation mode, confident that it would take them all the way to their destination. He should know, he had pre-programmed the waypoints before takeoff. Or he mis-selected the switch and selected heading mode. If he had gone to INS, what he didn't notice was that the system didn't accept his input because the aircraft was already just over seven and a half miles off its programmed track and so the INS couldn't work out where it was to start navigating. Whatever the reason, the autopilot just stayed on a fixed heading and for the next five and half hours the giant aircraft slowly deviated from its track to the north. By the time it reached Russian airspace, it was over one hundred and sixty miles off course. The North Pacific Ocean is a big place and communication is not always easy. Radar coverage is minimal. So, no one on the ground was alerted to the fact that the aircraft was getting seriously out of position. Used to flying the route, there was a breakdown in situational awareness in the cockpit, which wasn't helped by the ethos in the airline at the time that the 'Captain was always right'. At any time, a simple navigational check would have revealed the problem. The reason it wasn't done will never be known.

The Caspian Monster

While it travelled blithely on its way with little going on in the cockpit, all hell slowly started breaking out below.

The Russian peninsula of Kamchatka is a fairly desolate place which is why it was popular with the military. A test missile firing was due to take place and with so much overt observations from the Americans, they were on high alert. Initially, when radar picked up the 747 it wasn't clear what it was but as soon as it entered restricted airspace one Mig 23 and three SU 15 fighters were scrambled to intercept it. Frustratingly, it proved hard to find probably because one of the main tracking and intercept radars had been badly damaged in a storm some days before.

The 747 sailed serenely on and out of Soviet airspace. However, the Russians were now getting frantic and the senior command were seriously worried about what the hell it actually was. A furious debate raged over whether it should be shot down. As it had already flown through restricted Soviet airspace the consensus was that it should be but some argued that it should be identified first in case it was a civilian airliner.

Continuing on in the wrong direction, the 747 then entered Soviet airspace again over the Island of Sakhalin just to the North of Japan. This time, the intercepting fighters caught it up. At least one of the pilots identified it as a Boeing but it was dark and he couldn't make out the civilian markings and anyway they all knew the Americans used civilian airliner types as surveillance planes. The pilot of the lead SU 15 started firing warning shots but as they were high explosive and not tracer nobody in the 747 even noticed.

Suddenly, the nose of the 747 came up and it slowed down as it climbed to a higher altitude as directed by Tokyo air traffic control. The fighters almost stalled as they slowed down trying to keep station. They took it as a deliberate evasive manoeuvre. The General in command of Sukol Air Base ordered the fighters to shoot before the 747 left Soviet airspace for a second time. An SU 15 having overshot the 747 when it slowed down engaged his afterburner and turned hard below the big machine and managed to get missile lock.

He fired two, Kalingrad A8, Air to Air missiles. The first exploded in the proximity of the tail and the second near the left wing. Shrapnel from the first missile punctured the tail area causing an immediate explosive decompression in the plane. It also severed control cables and three out of four hydraulic systems pipes.

To the Russians amazement, it didn't die straight away. The pilots maintained limited control. It levelled off twice at sixteen and then ten thousand feet. Eventually, it impacted the sea and all aboard died. It was in international airspace when the missiles were fired.

For eight days the Soviets denied anything had happened. The US Navy took charge of search and salvage operations and were continually harassed and interfered with by the Russian Navy often in blatant violation of international law. Meanwhile, the Russians had already located the wreckage inside their territorial waters and recovered the aircraft's flight data recorders. For some reason, the Kremlin decided not to declare that they had them. They kept the fact secret until they were released by Boris Yeltsin in 1991.

Edinburgh

'Jesus, Victor, come and look at this,' Jon was in front of the television. He shouldn't really be watching English language programmes but he allowed himself one session of news a day.

Victor came out of the kitchen. 'What is it Jon?'

'Your old lot have apparently shot down a commercial 747 airliner near Japan. What on earth are they playing at?'

The two of them watched the piece in stunned silence and then the talking heads analysis afterwards. It was clear that much was unknown but one thing was confirmed by air traffic records, it had really happened and the Soviets appeared to be in denial. Initial reports that the aircraft had been forced to land were definitely untrue. The American fleet were mounting an enormous search effort but the Russian fleet was posturing and even apparently interfering.

'What the fucking hell are they thinking of?' asked Jon. 'They shoot down an unarmed civilian airliner and then try to hamper the rescue. Jesus, are they trying to start World War Three?'

Victor was as nonplussed as his guest but felt he had a better understanding of what could have prompted it.

'Jon, the Soviet Government is getting terrified that the Americans are really planning a first strike. When Reagan announced the Star Wars thing back in March I had just come over here. I'm sure no one in Moscow believes it's anything other than a cover for an arms build up. Frankly, I'm not sure that I don't agree.'

'Oh come on Victor, we've had this conversation already. Star Wars is pure self-defence. Surely you can see that?'

'OK, so you become invulnerable to ballistic missile attack. What's to stop you then going on the offensive? President Reagan's policies seem pretty belligerent to many people.'

'Alright, so what's that got to do with murdering civilians?'

'Don't be so black and white Jon. If the Soviet Government is worried you can bet that the military are even more so. It looks like that airliner was near or even actually over Russian territory and it was a dark night. We may never hear the full story but they are not complete idiots you know. Mind you, this isn't going to help ease tension is it?'

Moscow

Inga and Mikhael were discussing the intelligence digest over the same incident. There had been virtually nothing in the Russian press about the affair but they were party to the internal KGB information briefings.

'Oh my goodness,' said Inga. 'All those poor people, why on earth didn't the pilots respond to the warnings our fighters gave?'

Mikhael was far from sympathetic. 'Who knows, it may not have been a civilian aircraft you know. We were about to do a missile test and there was at least one other American spy plane in the area. Just because the Americans claim it was full of civilians doesn't mean that it really was.'

'I suppose so but the evidence seems pretty strong. Surely they wouldn't be so stupid as to fly a military aircraft into our internationally recognised airspace?'

'But that's the point, maybe by putting airline markings on it they were gambling that we wouldn't shoot it down. Of course, with it being so dark, no one saw the markings and so we effectively called their bluff. Come on, how could a commercial airliner just get lost like that? Those machines are full of navigation computers and radios. Put yourself in the position of our commanders. I know I would have shot the bloody thing down. What worries me is that that they can now use this as yet another excuse to vilify us internationally. So, even if we were in the right and I think we were, as a propaganda mistake it's up there with the best of them.'

Inga frowned, she hadn't thought of it that way. 'Goodness you're right, they'll certainly try to take the moral high ground once again. Why on earth don't our government come clean and tell the world what really happened? They're still officially denying it aren't they?'

'Yes, that does seem rather short sighted. I'm afraid the old men in the Kremlin don't seem to be that in touch with the modern world do they?'

She realised it was yet another symptom of what she was seeing every day around her even in the capital city. The crumbling buildings and queues everywhere for even the most basic things like bread and shoes. And yet, special lanes on the roads were kept solely for the use of senior politicians. They even had their own shops and there were no shortages there. How long would they bury their heads in the sand and ignore what was clearly going on around them, while at the same time ranting about the dangers of the aggressive and decadent West? She was starting to get seriously worried. Where was this all going to end?

Mikhael broke into her thoughts. 'Now, we must move on. Have you prepared that information I asked you to compile for our meeting with this naval Captain Orlov?'

Chapter 21

Moscow

Andrei Orlov needed somewhere to start. The task he had been given was not going to be easy. He realised that but in the end, it was his idea to instigate the search for the hidden NATO facility, so he appreciated the irony of being given the job of neutralising it. When he started to work out a plan of action he remembered being told that the KGB had originally gained the information about the British navy conducting some form of supply flight. He would start there. Finding out the original source of the information had been straightforward and he made an appointment for the next day.

When he arrived at the anonymous KGB office block and showed his identity card he was sent up to the second floor. He knocked on the numbered door he was looking for and an absolutely stunning blonde girl answered it and ushered him in. The sight of her was so unexpected it almost took his breath away. She introduced him to her superior and they all sat around a table inside the inner office. He was even more surprised when Inga, the blonde girl, was introduced as the person who had been in Norway and delivered the original report. Clearly not just the dumb office blonde then. Gathering himself up and berating himself for being unprofessional he briefed them on the situation.

Inga, in particular, wasn't surprised when she heard the results of Andrei's under ice search. She had been pretty certain there must have been something well hidden otherwise she would have heard about it during her year in Norway. With the notable exception of Jon, most naval officers could be easily relieved of their secrets.

Andrei produced a map from his briefcase and showed them the exact position he had discovered. He also gave them an outline of possible ideas he had been toying with. Anything they did had to fulfil two critical criteria. Firstly, they had to take the place intact enough to discover what technology was being used and preferably be able to take it back with them. Secondly, they had to be able to deny they had done it. A bomb or missile strike was clearly out of the question. The delivery mechanism, be it aircraft or rocket would be easily traced and the technology they wanted to discover would end up being destroyed. They really needed good darkness and preferably cloud cover and it had to be fast. That meant a winter operation but it also meant that the ice would be more extensive and thicker. Helicopters didn't have the range. Landing a transport plane on the ice in the dark was far too dangerous and they couldn't guarantee they could come up from below because the ice could be too thick. All he could think of was a small team of Special Forces and a careful overland trip. It would mean a covert two way journey of hundreds of kilometres with the return leg carrying God knows what equipment. Another complicating factor was that he couldn't work out how the base was communicating with their shore side link. No HF or any other radio transmissions had been intercepted. Underwater sonar communication would not work either as its range was far too short and anyway it would have been heard. So, ensuring that they didn't get out a distress call was going to be another problem.

'So, my friends, we need to get in and out in a matter of hours. We need a degree of load carrying capacity and aircraft and helicopters are not feasible. Sorry, I know that's not your problem but as I continue to talk to people about the project I want to brainstorm any ideas no matter how unusual.'

Inga looked thoughtful. 'Mikhael, do you remember the last but one digest that came around? The one with that weird missile machine on it?'

Mikhael looked back at her quizzically, immediately remembering the report. It had been quite extraordinary. 'But that was a seaplane wasn't it?'

'Yes but out of curiosity, I read up a bit more and apparently it can travel over flat land. Hang on, I've still got a copy.' She went to her desk and retrieved it before handing it over to Mikhael.

'Hmm, I see what you mean. Captain Orlov, have a look at this. Could one of these do the job?'

Orlov studied the paper for several minutes. 'Good God,' he muttered under his breath. 'The things some of our engineers come up with. That's amazing but it looks a bit big and over engineered for what I want.'

Inga cut in excitedly. 'Yes Captain but look at the end of the article they mention using them as land assault craft and that there is another smaller version.'

'Oh yes, so they do. I wonder whether there is any merit in talking to these people. Do you know where they're based?'

'Yes,' said Inga. 'Near Astrakhan, on the coast of the Caspian Sea.'

He read the whole report with mounting excitement. This could be just what he needed. With the authority he had been given he should have no problem commandeering one these machines. It was definitely worth a try. 'Right, I can't thank you enough. I think I need to go and talk to them.'

Mikhael thought for a second. 'Captain, if this mission goes ahead you realise that the government will almost certainly insist on a KGB member going along. It would be standard procedure.'

Andrei nodded, he suspected he knew what was coming and when normally having a spook along would be a royal pain in the ass, this time he probably wouldn't argue.

He was strangely disappointed then, when Mikhael said, 'Inga, you've been here long enough to look after the section for a few days. I will accompany the Captain to Astrakhan, if that is acceptable?' He looked queryingly at Andrei.

Andrei had no choice but to smile and agree.

Caspian Sea

Three days later, Andrei and Mikhael were sitting with Yuri in the main office of the Soviet Central Hydrofoil Design Bureau. Rostislav had asked him to host the visit. They were getting plenty of them these days after their demonstration and he was sharing out the load. Yuri was amused by the look on both of the men's faces.

'*I guess that's what I looked like the day I arrived,*' he thought. The tour could be pretty overwhelming especially with the enormous form of the Lun parked on the slipway just outside the window. The meeting had been set up at very short notice and he still hadn't been briefed on its purpose. The naval Captain had done most of the questioning as the tour progressed. The other man had kept in the background. Yuri still wasn't sure exactly who he was but suspected something a little more sinister than the military. Despite the impressive Lun, the Captain seemed most interested in the Eaglet, asking a great deal of questions about its performance.

'So, gentlemen,' said Yuri. 'You've seen what we can do. May I ask what's your exact interest in our machines?'

'One final question before I answer that,' responded the Captain. 'Could a machine like the Eaglet fly over ice, say at the northern polar area?'

The question caught Yuri by surprise but a glimmer of excitement ran through him. 'Well, as I've said, they fly at a nominal twenty metres. We can push that up to about thirty or even forty at a pinch before they become too difficult to fly. If the ice is smooth and has no obstructions above about half that, then yes, an Ekranoplan doesn't really care what it's flying over. Now please gentlemen, what on earth is this all about? You're clearly not on a normal fact finding mission. You've something specific in mind, have you not?'

For the first time, the other man spoke more than two words. 'Mr Alexeyev, as I understand it you hold the rank of Major in the naval Special Forces. Is that correct?'

Taken aback, Yuri had to think for a second. 'Well, that's how I started out. I then went on to flying training and became a pilot but that was many years ago and no one has ever rescinded my commission. So I guess you're correct. Mind you, I am sure that's an administrative oversight more than anything else.'

'Why do you say that?'

Yuri tapped his lower leg with his knuckles. It made a hollow metallic sound. 'You may have noticed I have a slight limp courtesy of a small accident a few years back. I don't think I would be much use in a Special Forces role now. This leg below the knee is just tin.'

The Captain looked surprised but the other man just frowned. 'Well two things, firstly it doesn't seem to have impeded your ability to fly these machines and secondly as you still hold the commission you are still subject to its restrictions if you follow me.'

Yuri understood exactly and rather resented the inference. 'I assume you mean that I am subject to military law as regards security issues. Of course, I understand that but this whole project is classified anyway. If you looked at my record you will also see that the previous project I worked on was even more highly classified.'

'Gentlemen,' interrupted the Captain. 'I think we can take it that we can discuss this within these four walls. I am confident that Major Alexeyev here knows how to keep a secret.' He went on to explain the situation to Yuri. He refrained from going into much of the technical detail, keeping the briefing to the issues of transport and logistics. Once the problem had been outlined, he sat back and waited for a response.

Yuri stood up and looked out of the window trying to hide his excitement. This could be what they had been waiting for, an operation that would finally justify the Ekranoplan and silence their critics. It was also risky and there were going to be several issues to overcome.

'Captain Orlov. First things first, could an Eaglet travel over the ranges required, the terrain you describe, carry the necessary loads and land on the ice? The answer to all those questions is a qualified yes. Not only that, it could do so at speeds that would have you easily in and out in a matter of hours.' He saw the smiles start to appear on both men's faces. 'But, before you get too excited, I said it was a qualified answer. There will be two problems. The first is logistics. We have to get a machine up to the Kola. It isn't really feasible to fly it there around the various coasts. I think our NATO friends might be rather interested, would they not? So, we're going to have to transport it overland. That means partially dismantling it and shipping it by train. That will take several months by the time it's reassembled.'

The Captain nodded. 'That shouldn't be a problem. We don't want to move on this until the nights are at their longest. That should give you the time you need. And what's the other issue?'

Yuri decided to be totally honest. 'The Ekranoplan concept has always been dogged by the problem of accurate navigation. The machines are very fast and can cover a great deal of ground, so even small inaccuracies can multiply very quickly. We now have a rather expensive and cumbersome system in the Lun which we could transplant into an Eaglet but it will take up some of the internal space. I reckon it's accurate to within about half a per cent of the distance flown. So, we could be up to several kilometres out by the time we arrive. If, as you say, the base is well camouflaged, how are we going to find it?'

'Actually, that's better than what I was hoping for,' replied the Captain. 'And you're right about the navigation problem but in fact, it's worse than that because the position we have will be well out of date by the time we move as the ice is in continual motion. Actually, I think I know how to overcome that problem, so we can leave that until later. Right, I think I have heard enough. I will head back to Moscow and hopefully, you will receive instructions in the next few days to start preparing an Eaglet.'

Chapter 22

Hog Island Grenada

The air was hot and still. October in the Caribbean was the height of the hurricane season but what that meant was that unless a tropical storm was brewing, then the weather was settled and roasting. It also meant that cruising boats were few and far between. Most yachtsmen hauled out for the summer months or headed to less dangerous waters.

Despite that, Roger and his friend Lou were restocking the beer cooler at his beach bar. Actually, that was a rather loose description as it was really just a palm shack set back from the beach. He opened it on Sundays only but always kept a cooler full of beer available for visiting crews along with an honesty box which never seemed to be abused.

'Hey man, what you hear about what they did to Maurice Bishop?' asked Lou. He, like the whole island, was getting worried about what the hell was going on in the capital St Georges over the last few days. Bishop had taken power four years ago and led the countries socialist government but recently one of his ministers had rebelled and deposed him. He had managed to escape but not for long and he had just been recaptured.

'Well, I heard that they caught him again and that he and some of his ministers were shot by the military and now the soldiers are taking charge.' replied Roger. 'You know, I was never sure about his politics but I could get really angry about that.'

'But I heard on the radio that the Americans are getting all upset. They're saying that the work on the airport is all military as we've got Cubans helping us and they gonna do something about it.'

'Hey that's crazy man, they working on the airport so we can get more tourists in and make more money, everyone knows that. The airport up north is just too small. Anyway, the Queen of England is our boss, so what are the Americans doing?' It's none of their damn business.'

'Yeah, well you know what the Yanks are like. I guess, with all this trouble we've had since the revolution in seventy nine people are getting worried. They say they got their people here in the university and they're now at risk. Load of rubbish of course.'

He was interrupted by a roaring noise as an American Huey Attack Helicopter flew low overhead and headed off in the direction of the new airport only a few miles to the west. Out to sea, around the headland there appeared the massive menacing shape of an aircraft carrier.

'Oh well,' said Roger. 'Guess it's all too late now. I wonder if they'll have time to stop here for a beer.'

London, No 10 Downing Street

Prime Minister Margret Thatcher was livid. She had just come back from Buckingham Palace where she had had the embarrassment of having to explain to the Queen that a sovereign country, of which she was officially still Head of State and a member of the British Commonwealth, had been invaded by the United States with no prior warning or even consultation. At the same time that the action had already started, Ronald bloody Reagan had denied that anything was going on.

She called her private secretary to her office to take a letter. 'Write this down please; *'this action will be seen as intervention by a western country in the internal affairs of a small independent nation, however unattractive its regime. I ask you to consider this in the context of our wider East-West relations and of the fact that we will be having in the next few days to present to our Parliament and people, the siting of Cruise Missiles in this country. I cannot conceal that I am deeply disturbed by your latest communication.'*

There, she couldn't put it any plainer than that. Some members of her cabinet were talking of a United Nations Security Council resolution condemning the invasion. Much bloody good that would do. Since when did the US take any notice of the UN? Dammit Britain was meant to be their closest ally and Reagan had lied to her. It was all down to paranoia again. Yes, there were some Cubans helping to build a long runway at the new airport but half of the contractors were British as well and yes there had been a very nasty coup but what possible threat could there be to the US? Cuba five times the size and already hostile was much closer. Was the world going mad?

Edinburgh

Jon and Victor were sitting in front of the television again. This time, the boot was on the other foot and it was Victor questioning what the hell the West was doing.

'Well, from what I can tell,' said Jon. 'The British Government are as surprised as anyone else. Jesus, I'm not even sure where Grenada is.'

'Hang on,' replied Victor. He got up and found his young daughter's atlas and turned to the page on the Caribbean. 'Ah, here it is. It's this little island down the bottom just next to Trinidad. I can't see how much of a threat it could be.'

'Well, one report is saying that the airfield is being built by Cuban and Russian contractors and is for military use and another is saying the Americans themselves concluded it was for commercial use only a year ago.'

'Actually, it gets better than that,' chuckled Victor. 'You know those Russian technicians they said were putting in a military radar system? Well, it appears they actually work for the British company Plessey and were under a joint US, UK contract.'

'Well, one thing about the US, like everything they do, when they fuck up, they do it really big. I heard from another report, that their maps were so out of date they didn't even know where the airport was. Some of their maps had it drawn on in pencil and in the wrong place.'

Victor looked unsurprised. 'You know Jon, I've got a rather cynical theory about the whole thing.'

'Go on.'

'Well last year, you lot travelled eight thousand miles and retook the Falklands. The whole world thought it was impossible and you showed what a tough nation you really are. It's one of the reasons I wanted to come over to you, not the Americans. You know, I wonder if their military was so annoyed at being upstaged they needed to find an excuse to show they could do it too?'

'Bloody hell, that's pretty cynical Victor and anyway if you're right its backfired big time, hasn't it? A tiny, unarmed island, in their own back yard and they make a complete pig's ear of it.'

'Yes, well I guess they're as rusty as the rest of us. No doubt they'll learn a lot of really useful lessons from it. But what really worries me is what it says about the US government's attitude. If they are prepared to take military action over such a trifling threat purely because they could see the possibility of an increase in Cuban influence, what sort of a hair trigger are they on with the rest of the world? This President of theirs seems to be the most aggressive one they've ever had. I wonder what Moscow are making of it?'

Moscow

Inga shook the water from her coat as she got into the office. It was covered in flecks of sleet. Winter was coming early to Moscow again. She was surprised to see that Mikhael was already in. Normally, she had time to put on the kettle, make tea and read the summaries before he arrived.

'Morning Inga,' he called from his desk. 'You need to look at the latest digest.'

'Is it something to do with the news report I just heard about the Americans doing something?'

'That's right. They seem to have invaded a small Caribbean island for some reason. Have a read and we'll have a chat.'

Inga did just that and then with a cup of tea for Mikhael they sat down to talk. 'They seem to think the Cubans were up to something. Do we know if they really were?'

'No, as far as we know it was purely commercial. There is one worrying aspect though.'

'What's that?'

'Well, for the last couple of days we've been monitoring an enormous increase in encrypted communications between the Americans and British. Of course, this invasion may be the reason. The only problem is that the British seem to have been caught by as much surprise as the rest of us. So, there is a serious concern that this is just a smokescreen for something far more serious. You have to remember that it's only a month since that Korean airliner was shot down and the Americans are still making a fuss about that even now. I tell you Inga, the government are really getting worried about American policy intentions. It wouldn't take much to tip the whole situation over the edge.'

'So, is our little mission to the Arctic going to be cancelled?'

'On the contrary my dear, if things do get out of hand, one thing we must have is unrestricted access to the Atlantic for our ballistic submarines. If anything, this reinforces the need to do something. No, the reason I am here early this morning is that I was called in to be given the green light. Captain Orlov has convinced the higher ups that the idea is feasible and we're to go ahead as fast as we can. It will be a joint navy and KGB operation with him and myself running it. I don't need to say that if we succeed we all stand to do personally very well out of it and that of course includes you my dear.'

She knew his words were meant to be reassuring. Somehow they achieved the exact opposite.

Chapter 23

Royal Naval Air Station, Yeovilton, Somerset

Lieutenant Commander Ewan Bailey had never felt so low in his life. He was in his office looking out over the vast concrete hardstanding and staring blindly into the distance. Sitting on his desk before him was a brown envelope. No, it was THE brown envelope. Inside it was the infamous letter that everyone dreaded receiving. The one that dashed every last hope they had ever had. He knew he'd left it late but was convinced his recent performance had been good enough. Now he had the stigma of 'passed over for promotion' attached to him. It was the dreaded phrase that meant that he was going no further in his chosen career. Not for him a Commander's 'Brass hat' and more important roles in the MOD, even ship command. No, he would be relegated to sidelined jobs. That's if he had the balls to stay in. He knew the whole bloody squadron would find out soon enough and they would all be laughing at him. Facing them was not going to be easy. Dammit, that's why he had given everyone such a hard time over recent months. He had to show them how tough and uncompromising he could be. Surely they must see that? But it hadn't been enough. Five years in the promotion zone was all the bloody navy gave you and it just hadn't been enough.

The door of his office opened and he was just about to snarl something at whoever it was when he realised it was the Commanding Officer.

'Splot, I'm so sorry. I've just seen the promotion list and realised that your name wasn't on it. That was your last shot wasn't it?'

Ewan waved him in and showed him the envelope.

'Come on, cheer up old chap. It's not the end of the world. At least this way you can keep flying. There are no Commander pilots jobs in the navy you know. Everyone knows all the fun jobs go to those who aren't fighting each other for promotion.'

Ewan almost felt like saying what he really thought about that. Although he scarcely admitted it to himself, deep inside, he actually hated flying. Most of the time he found it boring and all too often he was scared stiff not that he'd ever admit that to anyone.

'Sorry Boss, yes you're right. It's just such a blow to the ego I guess. God knows what I'm going to do. I guess I'll let it sink in a bit first.'

'Good man, anyway its lunchtime and in case you've forgotten we're all needed over in the mess for the Wardroom Christmas lunch. Come on, I'll buy you the first one.'

Several hours later, he was feeling better. He could almost say he was feeling fine. Almost certainly it had everything to do with the large amount of booze he had drunk but as everyone else he could see was as seriously pissed as he was, that wasn't a problem. Wardroom Christmas lunches were rather notorious in the Fleet Air Arm. Squadron rivalry, the imminence of several weeks of holiday and the end of a strenuous term of flying often became a lethal mix that could lead to quite outrageous behaviour. He remembered last year when a contemporary had driven his little 2CV car into the mess. It had been quite impressive and drawn roars of appreciation from the throng, mainly because the double doors to the mess had been shut at the time. The fact that he had promptly paid the enormous repair bill had also increased his stock. Pianos also had a habit of bursting into flames. The local fire brigade had issued dire warnings about the consequences of being called out yet again to put out another patch of burning tarmac outside the mess. However, the new mess president, the station Commander, had impressed everyone with his approach. Rather than call the Squadron COs and other miscreants in for a post lunch bollocking and presentation of repair bills he had tried to be more proactive and it appeared to be working. He had issued a challenge to all station units who wanted to take part and it seemed to be working in channelling the worst of the end of term aggressiveness. His boys were going to have a go as were all the other squadrons. He staggered outside onto the lawn to watch the Christmas pudding ballista competition.

Brian Pearce was missing his old mate Jon. Christmas was coming up and somehow they had always managed at least one good piss up together before the break. Here he was in the mess for the Christmas lunch and Jon was God knows where up in Scotland learning to speak Russian for fuck's sake. He also went outside unsteadily to watch the fun and games. The rules were very simple. Each unit was given a two pound Christmas pudding. They had to make a device to project said pudding over twenty yards at a Father Christmas target of their own making. The only hard rule was that explosives of any sort were absolutely not allowed. Somehow Brian knew that someone would ignore that because someone always did. Marks were going to be given for range, accuracy and style, the Commander's decision being final. When people complained about that he simply pointed out the mess was a democracy with one man and one vote. He was that one man and it was his vote and if anyone wanted to argue about it, tough luck.

Brian found himself standing next to Ewan Bailey, the guy who had given Jon so much stick up in Norway. He decided to ignore the man.

The first few competitors drew drunken applause or derision as their performance dictated. The Air Engineering Department produced a fantastic device clearly made up in the mechanical workshops. It was incredibly powerful but also hopelessly inaccurate. When the pudding actually went through a glass window several hundred yards away the cheers were deafening. Then the inevitable happened. One of the squadrons had decided to use explosives despite the ban. Everyone was amazed at how far a Christmas pudding could spread out when blown to bits. The Commander blew his whistle and waved a red card.

The Caspian Monster

Ewan turned to look blearily at Brian. 'Ah hello, I know you, you're a friend of that Hunt chappy. Well watch this, it's my lots turn now, believe me, there's no way we're going to lose.'

Coming onto the lawn now were Ewan's squadron team. They didn't look very impressive and drew hoots of derision from the watchers. A real Father Christmas heavily cloaked in red with a great bushy beard stood in the appointed place. Three chaps loaded the pudding into a rather poor looking device. Clearly, it had been knocked up at the last minute. When the Commander dropped his flag, the device fired and the pudding flew a pathetic couple of feet and rolled to a stop. Even louder jeers greeted the performance coupled with some quite obscene suggestions about Jungly pilots. One of the team held up his hand and waited for the noise to subside. The target joined them. As soon as it was reasonably quiet, a signal was given and some music started. It was the tune of the 'stripper'. The target threw off her red cloak and beard to reveal a very shapely young blonde, wearing some festive suspenders, a large smile and nothing else. The jeering immediately changed to cheering and became extremely enthusiastic. Before he could react, she went up to the Commander, grabbed hold of him and slapped an enormous 'lip lock' on his surprised but strangely, not very upset face. The cheering if anything grew louder. Ewan's squadron had clearly won hands down.

Turning again to Brian he said, 'You know that tart looks just like the girl I shagged up in Bardufoss. You know the one your mate Hunt was shagging as well.' He turned back drunkenly to watch the goings on.

The words took a few seconds to sink in and then Brian reacted. He grabbed Ewan's arm. 'What the fuck did you just say Sir?'

'I said, I shagged your mate Jon's bird. You know while you lot were off on your secret resupply mission thing. Don't think I didn't know what it was all about. Take more than that to get round me you know. ' He tapped his nose knowingly.

Suddenly, Brian felt stone cold sober. 'Did you know why Jon was sent home?' asked Brian with menace in his voice.

'Not a fucking clue old son, not a clue.'

'Did you tell her anything about what we were doing?'

Suddenly Ewan realised this was more than drunken banter. He pulled his arm away.

'Course not, now just sod off,' and walked over to the rest of the squadron leaving Brian thinking furiously. He watched Ewan's retreating form and wondered what on earth he should do. No one on the Air Station knew anything about Pickwick and although there must be senior officers involved, probably at Fleet, he didn't have a clue who they were. So he couldn't talk to anyone without potentially and grossly compromising his security clearance. There was only one person he could turn to and again he had no idea how to get hold of him. What the hell could he do?

London

The next day, Brian went on leave. Instead of going home he told his wife he had an urgent meeting in London and didn't quite know how or when he would be back. She was getting used to the odd hours he sometimes kept and just made him promise he would be back in a few days. He then jumped on the train from Yeovil Junction heading for Waterloo. On the way, he formulated his plan. It should be quite simple.

Once in the throng of crowds on Waterloo station, he set out to start his search. It really would help if the government even acknowledged the existence of the bloody organisation but secrecy and deniability seemed to be the priority. He knew what road he needed but not where the building was and finding it was going to be the problem. He bought an A to Z and it only took him minutes to find the road. Strangely enough, it started at Westminster Bridge with the iconic tower of Big Ben on the far side. He turned in the opposite direction and walked the half mile of Westminster Bridge

Road looking at all the building on both sides. In the end, he reckoned there were about three candidates, all within sight of each other, so he found a place to sit and decided to park himself for a while and study them. The biggest building directly opposite soon became the prime candidate. The other two really were too small. This one had the look of a government building even though there were no signs to identify it. He wondered what to do. Should he just go into the lobby and make a complete prat of himself when he found out it belonged to an Insurance company. Mind you, that's probably what they would say it was anyway.

Suddenly, his problem solved itself. Two burly men left the building. Brian watched them idly until he realised they were walking straight towards him. *'Oh bugger,'* he thought. *'I must have attracted some attention. I have been sitting here for over an hour after all.'*

Before he could decide what to do, they reached him.

'Excuse me Sir,' said one of the men. 'Can I ask you your business?'

Brian was very tempted to tell him to sod off, after all he was committing no crime but then common sense re-established itself. This was why he was here after all.

'Yes, are you two spies? If you're not, then can you take me to one I know please?'

They put him in a small bare room and locked the door. Despite showing them his identity card, they were clearly taking no chances. He explained that he urgently needed to talk to the head of the Scandinavian section. The fact that he knew such a thing existed at all seemed to worry them as much as his loitering with intent outside. He just prayed that Rupert was in and hadn't gone on seasonal holiday already. He had visions of being kept here until he got back. His wife and kids would never forgive him. The door opened and relief flooded through him as Rupert's friendly face appeared.

'Brian, it is you, I got some garbled story about a naval officer casing the building. How did you find us and what on earth do you want?'

'Finding you was quite simple really old chap,' replied Brian smiling. 'You mentioned Westminster Bridge Road once and finding the building wasn't exactly rocket science.'

Rupert grimaced. 'Yes, well we're hardly a secret, despite what the government would like. Anyway, this must be important so what's up?'

Brian explained what had transpired at Yeovilton the day before. He was primarily focused on helping his friend and Rupert was sympathetic promising to do what he could for Jon.

'Alright Brian, I'll talk to my contacts in Fleet who know about this and I'm sure Jon will get the apology he deserves. But good God, I need to know what this man has said and fast. The last thing we need is Pickwick compromised at the moment. Can't say anything more, I'm sure you understand but this could be much more serious than I originally thought.'

Chapter 24

Edinburgh

Jon was leaving his friends. He was quite sad as he knew he would probably never be able to see them again. Over the months, he felt he had become part of the family and was strangely reluctant to go especially as his future was so uncertain. His final parting was at Edinburgh train station. He gave the kids two wrapped boxes with admonishments not to open them until Christmas Day and then turning to Natasha, he gave her a great big hug and noted there was the start of tears in her eyes. She thanked him for the kid's presents. He replied that if she looked in the top drawer of his bedroom cabinet she might find something for her and Victor as well.

Victor pummelled his hand and handed him a final bottle of vodka that he had been hiding in the car.

'Bloody hell Victor, you obviously want to turn me into a real Russian. Not just the language but the drinking habits as well. Not sure my liver agrees.'

'Goodbye my friend. Yes, your language is just about perfect but you still need to work on those toasts I taught you. Good luck and good fortune.'

The last he saw of them was a waving smiling family group on the platform as the train pulled out of the station into the grey, raining town.

'What now?' wondered Jon as the train gathered speed out into the Scottish countryside. He had passed his interpreters exam only the previous week at the university. Languages had always been easy for him and fluency in the enemy's language could only be a great help. Maybe a job in one of the foreign embassies could be arranged? At least it would keep him away from the Fleet Air Arm. He wasn't sure he could look many of his old friends in the eye,

even now. God knows what stories had been doing the rounds while he had been away. It was a fairly small club and after his Falkland's exploits he was hardly unknown.

During the last few months, he had been able to shelve all these thoughts as he wrestled with the challenge of learning Russian and living with Victor and his family. But now they all came flooding back. Maybe he should just resign and go and fly for some bloody North Sea oil company. There was plenty of good money to be made there even if the work looked horribly boring. He had a visit to the appointer booked for ten tomorrow morning. He would keep his powder dry until then.

London

All too soon, he was walking into Old Admiralty Building again. He had spent the night at the 'In and Out' otherwise known as the Naval and Military Club, on Piccadilly. Luckily, there was no one he knew there that night and he retired early with Victor's bottle of vodka. He promised himself that once it was empty he would have a serious drying out session.

The weather had cleared up. It was bright and sunny if a bit cold. Unlike his mood which was grey, gloomy and full of trepidation. Once again he was shown into the office looking out over Whitehall. To his surprise, the appointer wasn't the only man in the room. Seated to one side and standing as he entered, was the same Captain who had interviewed him at Fleet all those months ago.

The Captain took a pace forward and held out his hand. 'Jonathon, good to see you again,' and seeing the look on Jon's face he continued. 'You're probably surprised to see me but I have some good news and only felt it right to come and tell you myself.' He turned to the appointer. 'If you could just give us a few minutes old chap.'

When they were alone he turned back to Jon. 'Look, this is actually by way of an apology. We have had some new information

The Caspian Monster

regarding the occurrences in Norway. I can't go into too much detail but it appears you were not the only person who spent some time with that Russian girl. It's also absolutely clear that the other person involved was the source of the leak. He has been interviewed and we are certain now that you did nothing wrong. In fact, the only reason he escaped a court martial was because of the need for absolute secrecy about the whole affair. However, he is no longer a serving member of the armed forces.'

Jon didn't know what to think. The enormous burden of guilt and worry was suddenly gone. The weight on his shoulders just melted away. He hadn't even realised it was there until it went. For a second, he wondered whether he ought to get angry over the way he had been treated but on reflection couldn't really see why. The navy had done nothing wrong.

'How on earth did you find out about him Sir?'

'Sorry old chap that's not for me to say and please don't ask me who it was. If you work out his name that's fine but you won't get it from me. Sometimes you just have to accept things. As you know, this whole thing is all cloak and dagger, so let's just put it behind us.'

'Yes Sir and thank you very much for coming to tell me in person but what happens now?'

'Your appointer has a few ideas on that score. One in particular, I would like you to consider but he will go through the details with you.' And he got up and opened the door for the appointer to come back in. 'I'll leave you two to get on with it. Oh, and have a good Christmas won't you?'

Jon nodded, still bemused, as the Captain left the room.

'So Jon, it seems the little misunderstanding, whatever it was, has been cleared up? And getting another language, especially Russian, will do you no harm believe me.'

Jon was still in a daze. He didn't know what to say and so just nodded again.

The appointer reached into his drawer and produced a bottle and two glasses.

'Against all the rules Jon but it is Christmas. Care for a tot?'

Jon accepted a glass with far more than a tot in it. It was brimming with what looked like a rather good single malt. '*So much for going on the wagon,*' he thought ruefully, '*but bollocks to it, this was just fantastic.*'

They sipped in silence until Jon broke the spell. 'My God, that feels good even if it is only just past ten in the morning. So come on, what have you got for me? The Captain hinted at something.'

'Well, you could go straight back to a squadron, even another Lynx Flight as you're so footloose. There is a Frigate Squadron Aviation job about to come free. I could probably swing just about anything but Fleet and some other people have asked if you might consider something else. Not a flying job as such but closely related. It will only be for about six months and then you can take your pick of something else.'

'Sounds interesting, go on.'

'Right, seeing as you will have your security clearances back, what I am going to tell you is the normal eat before reading stuff OK?'

Jon nodded, took another swig and sat back, intrigued.

'As you know, at the end of each winter period, we have a major exercise. However, this time it's going to be a bit different. Firstly, we're going to use the Carrier Illustrious in a new role. Instead of jets and anti-submarine Sea Kings, we are going to use her in the assault role and embark nine of your old squadron's Mark Four Sea Kings instead and a load of Royal Marines. It's never been tried before. Everyone says that it should work but we need to prove the concept. We want you on board as the ship's Jungly expert. You will be appointed to the ship in that role. OK so far?'

'Fine, but that doesn't sound exactly eat before reading stuff. What's so secret about that?'

'Two things actually. On top of the normal Royal Marines running around and shouting a lot in the snow stuff, there's going to be a secret, top level NATO exercise to practice our defence mobilisation procedures. With all these scares this year and concerns over the way the Soviets are behaving it was deemed a good idea. It will go right to the top and include several NATO country leaders. We want you to be the ship's coordinator for their input. Only you, the Captain, the Executive Officer and one other will know about it. You will do the donkey work.'

Jon was getting interested and said so.

'Right, then finally there is one extra thing and you will need to come back to London after the holiday for a detailed brief. I'm not allowed to know anything about it except to say that it involves something called Pickwick and you and only one other person will have that responsibility when up near the ice. Not even the Captain will know.'

Jon felt a shiver of excitement. He felt the hand of a certain person in all this and he was pretty sure he knew who would be providing the brief.

He didn't have to think about it for long. It was only short term. He could go back to a proper flying job once it was all over and it sounded both exciting and rewarding. He accepted.

'Excellent, then there is only other thing I need give you.' The appointer reached into his desk and pulled out two cloth Lieutenant Commander's shoulder badges. 'You'll need these for the role. We can't have a mere Lieutenant in such an important position.'

'But I'm not due my half stripe until the summer,' Jon protested. 'Surely, the system doesn't allow early promotion like that?'

'No but it does allow us to give you acting rank until the automatic promotion system kicks in.'

Dazed, Jon sat back and took yet another pull at his glass which was almost empty now. It was all going too fast. Only a few minutes ago he was seriously considering his future outside the navy and now here he was effectively being given early promotion and a really important job to go with it.

'Hang on a second, you mentioned one other person. Who's that going to be?'

'Oh yes,' the appointer laughed. 'He got you into this mess, so we only thought it fair that he goes with you to hold your hand. Hang on a second.' He put his head around the door and called down the corridor.

A few seconds later, a grinning familiar face appeared around the door.

'Well, it's about time we had a decent run ashore old mate. I hope you've got your drinking hat on?' asked Brian.

Later that evening, the last London train rolled into Yeovil Junction station where it terminated. The conductor was walking down the carriages and checking for any passengers still on board when he was alerted by what sounded like snoring. The old fashioned design of individual compartments for eight people meant it was a time consuming business but he didn't want to lock anyone in for the night. It was cold enough that they would probably freeze to death. He looked into the compartment where the noise had come from and saw two fully dressed and rather dishevelled Father Christmases, fast asleep on opposing benches.

'Come on gents time to wake up,' he called and then looking out of the window he could see a young lady with a child in a push chair walking anxiously up and down the platform. Putting two and two together, he called again. 'Come on now wake up. I suspect someone is waiting for you and I expect you're going to need a really good explanation for this one.'

Chapter 25

Russian Northern Fleet Base, Murmansk

Yuri was finally satisfied but it had all taken so long, in fact far too long. The preceding months had been nothing but a nightmare. At first, things had gone surprisingly well. Taking one of the Eaglets to pieces had been relatively straightforward although finding railway wagons that could take the sections had initially proved problematic. That was until someone had the bright idea to contact the space people who often had to move large sections of rocket about and had the necessary rolling stock. With sanction for the project from the highest levels of government, getting other bureaus to support them had been relatively easy.

However, once they reached Murmansk things slowly became more and more difficult. If it wasn't technical issues it was the bloody weather. Firstly, they couldn't find an enclosed space big enough for their machine and ended up having to rebuild her in the open, which made life very difficult, especially when the snow started. Even the jury rigged tarpaulins only slowed the weather down rather than actually stopping it. However, they worked double shifts and despite the weather, she was reassembled in good time. The navigation system that had been ripped out of the Lun then had to be fitted and the sensitive electronics definitely didn't like the cold and damp. In the end, they had to fit it all inside a specially heated casing to keep the humidity and cold away. Just as soon as they were ready for trials one of the turbo jets had failed and they had to wait for a week for another to arrive. At that point, Yuri had stern words with the engineers back at Astrakhan and arranged for a full inventory of spares including engines and a propeller to be sent up to him.

During one particular snowstorm when work continued despite the weather, someone had scrawled the name 'Snezhana' on the nose which meant 'Lady of the Snow' and the name had stuck. Yuri rather liked it and while the whole machine was being repainted white he had it painted on properly in gold letters over the nose.

Luckily, there was a large slipway they could use in the naval base where they were working but it was almost four weeks later than planned before he could take her out for the first test flight. It was then that the real problems started. By now it was December and winter had fully set in. On the shores of the Caspian Sea the winters could be tough but nothing like up here in the Arctic. Quite often the sea froze right up to the shore line. Not that it would affect the Ekranoplan as any flat surface was all she needed. But the cold did strange things to engine oil and control runs. In the end, he put a call in to the local air base and got some of their engineers to come out and help. They brought special heaters and more importantly advice and experience on how to keep operating in temperatures of up to minus forty. All the time this was going on, Moscow were continuing to badger Yuri for results. The plan was to go shortly after Christmas before NATO woke up and got into their winter exercise period.

The first test flight had initially gone quite well. All systems seemed to be working once they had been warmed up and if anything the performance was enhanced in the cold air. Then, after about an hour into the flight, Yuri started experiencing control problems. At first, he thought he was imagining it. Then he realised he was having to put more and more forward control in to keep the nose down and slowly having to increase power to maintain speed and height. Unsure what was going on, he landed in the relatively calm sea. They launched one of their rubber dinghies and rowed around her but could see nothing amiss. Getting airborne again, the problem seemed to have cured itself. He was just about to convince himself that he had been imagining things when it slowly started again. After thinking carefully this time, he got one of the crew to

The Caspian Monster

brave the freezing slipstream and look out of one of the rear doors while they were still airborne. Sure enough, the man reported back that ice was building up on the rear of the hull. The reason Yuri hadn't seen it when they landed was the blast of water when touching down and relative heat of the unfrozen sea had removed it before it could be seen. It was obvious that the rooster tail of wash was producing enough super cooled water to start coating the tail of the machine.

The solution hadn't been easy. In the end, they had scrounged quantities of anti-icing fluid from the local air base and fitted a simple spraying system to the outside of the tail area. It seemed to work most of the time and Yuri always had the option of landing to clear it. Once over the icecap, it wouldn't be a problem. The only other issue they needed to solve then was how to land on the ice rather than the sea. After doing some theoretical calculations, a team of engineers had come up from the home base and fitted some strengthening panels to the bottom of the hull. The small wheel bogeys that they lowered down to taxi up the ramp would not be deployed. Effectively, the hull became one giant sled. Yuri then went off and found a suitably representative area of ice and found that landing on it was actually easier than water. The absence of waves and considerably less friction made all the difference. However, they found it made stopping quite difficult but by putting reverse pitch on the large propeller they could still manage to come to a halt in a reasonable distance. The only other problem came if they tried to taxi too slowly, then the world just went white as they disappeared inside their own private snowstorm.

So, now they were just about ready to go. He limped over to the officer's mess to meet Andrei, leaving Snezhana to the ground crew. We wondered if the next flight would be the real one. Frankly he couldn't wait. He had already missed Christmas with his family and the sooner he was out of this frozen place the better.

Andrei was at the bar as he limped in. He saw Yuri coming and handed him a large vodka which disappeared in one gulp.

'Thank you, I needed that.'

'I see you are limping my friend. Do you have a problem?' asked Andrei with concern in his voice.

Yuri snorted. 'No, not really, it's just that the damned leg is made of aluminium and it shrinks when it gets cold just like every bloody thing else around here. Don't worry I'll be fine.'

Andrei nodded. 'And that was your last proving flight I believe?'

'Yes, it's all good now. The icing problem has been solved, so we're finally ready. I'm just sorry it's taken so long.'

'Well other issues have delayed us as well, so we're not too concerned. In fact, we are now planning our little trip to occur right in the middle of the NATO winter exercise. Rather than go when they are all on holiday. The current thinking is that if we choose our moment, they will be so busy with their own exercise their focus will be on other things and they will have nothing to get in our way.'

Yuri nodded. 'Well, if it goes to plan, we'll be in and out before they know anyway. But there's one detail that worries me a bit.'

'Oh, what's that?'

'Well, there are going to upwards of a dozen people at that base. What happens to them?'

Andrei thought for a moment, wondering how honest he should be. In the end, he decided to prevaricate. 'That my friend is a question that several others are asking but now I can report that you are ready, we are to go to Moscow where we will have the final planning meeting. All that will be discussed there.'

The Pentagon

The monster team had been puzzled for some time now. All indications were that activity at the Caspian Sea base had reduced enormously. They had seen some work going on with one of the smaller machines in the late summer and then just about everything seemed to have stopped. They didn't know that they had missed the

The Caspian Monster

dismantling of the machine as the Russians had done all the loading at night and by the time the parts were on the trains they no longer looked like an Ekranoplan.

Then, one afternoon in late November, one of the other analysts had called to say that he had something odd on the slipway in Murmansk. Sure enough, when the experts looked at it, it was identified as an Ekranoplan. They even knew what the Soviets called it now and it was positively identified as an Orlyonok.

The subject was duly reported at the routine weekly meeting. The Boss asked for an assessment of what the analysts thought it might mean.

His deputy responded first. 'Well Sir, given the timing and all, we reckon they moved it there for cold weather trials. If they're going to deploy these machines to the Northern fleet in due course then that would be a standard prerequisite. They must have disguised its move up north. We never saw it happen but we know how secretive they can be.'

'So, do we flag this up to the hierarchy as a something we need to keep a special eye on?'

'No Sir, we don't think so. It's only one machine after all. What threat could that be? A few dozen or more could be a worry but one Ekranoplan?'

'OK,' said the Boss. 'I agree but put something out in the regular intelligence digest please.'

Chapter 26

Portsmouth Naval Base

The great, grey, slab sides, of HMS Illustrious, towered over Jon and Brian as they got out of their taxi next to the ship. The muted growl of diesel generators could be heard behind the shouts and calls of the sailors taking stores on board via the forward gangway. The much quieter, rear gangway had the name of the ship emblazoned on a large canvas sheet down each side and at the end were two ceremonial lifebelts, again with the ships name proudly picked out in gold leaf.

Brian looked up at the overhanging flight deck way above their heads. 'I know the Yanks have got much bigger ones but seeing these ships always gives me a hard on.'

'Er, yes I think I know what you mean,' laughed Jon. 'Anyway, are you going to stop gawping and help me with these bags? After all, I'm the Senior Officer now.'

'Yes Sir, sorry Sir, can't have a Lieutenant Commander doing physical work now can we?'

'Brian.'

'Yes Sir.'

'Fuck off.'

'Aye, Aye Sir.'

Chuckling, they made their way up the gangway with their grips in hand leaving the big trunks to be taken on board by the mess stewards later.

As they reached the top, they saluted and in turn, the Quartermaster and Officer of the Day saluted back.

Jon announced themselves, 'good morning, Lieutenant Commander Hunt and Lieutenant Pearce joining the ship.' It still sounded odd to hear him give himself that rank. He wondered how long it would be before the novelty wore off.

The young Lieutenant, who was the OOD and had been expecting them, stepped forward.

'Yes Sir, welcome on board, the Captain is expecting you. He asked me to escort you to his cabin as soon as you arrived. Please leave your bags. I'll arrange for them to be taken to your cabins.'

'By the way, who is the Captain these days?' asked Brian. 'We were appointed here at the last minute and I haven't had time to look him up.'

'Oh, he's new as well, he joined just before Christmas. Got a bit of a reputation, his last ship was a Leander in the Falklands. His name is Test.'

Jon and Brian looked at each other and smiled.

When ushered into the Captain's harbour cabin, their old Commanding Officer from their ship during the Falklands War got up from his desk and greeted them warmly.

'When I heard you two were coming back to haunt me I wondered what I'd done wrong with their Lordships. Clearly, they didn't think I would be getting enough excitement, so they decided to send me you two.'

'Sorry about that,' said Jon not looking at all apologetic. 'But it's really nice to see you again Sir.'

'Well, take a seat and I'll get us some coffee and get the Commander to join us. Then we'd better talk about what you're here to do.'

They settled in the Captain's arm chairs and the Commander, who was second in command and also the ship's Executive Officer joined them. Once the Captain's steward was safely out of earshot, Jon briefed them on everything they needed to know. It seemed strange to be withholding things from the Captain but their instructions had been very clear. They had spent the last two days in Fleet Headquarters with Rupert and few other naval experts going over the situation at Pickwick as well as some specifics about the mobilisation exercise which was going to be called 'Good Bowman' for some unfathomable reason.

'Right Sirs, the squadron embark in three days time as you know. I understand the engineers and others have been talking already. Junglies tend to travel fairly self contained, so I don't suppose there will be too many issues with stores or other logistic issues.'

'Yes, I agree,' the Commander said. 'I guess, if you're used to operating out of a muddy field for weeks on end, then a Carrier's got to be pretty luxurious.'

'Spot on Sir, just don't give them too much free time in the bar.'

'Oh, no worries there,' said the Captain with a knowing smile. 'Their CO made it clear that they're all a bit rusty with deck operations, so we have a pretty busy flying programme arranged and then they go straight into the assault for the exercise before heading off ashore to play with the Royals for two weeks. I guess if they want to let their hair down after that we'll be able to cope. They'll probably have earned it by then. Now, you're going to be our ship liaison officer for all this but your secondary role interests me more.'

Brian spoke up for both of them. 'Yes Sir, I'll be taking the lead on all the cryptographic traffic for that. They're going to be trying out some new secure comms procedures and I've been given the training. The cryptographic keymat material should be delivered this afternoon. Once the Jungly assault has gone in, Jon and I will man an operations cell for Good Bowman and liaise with you over the progress of the exercise. To a large extent, it's a paper exercise but there will be times when you will have to provide a command input.'

'Fine, that all makes sense. Look, sorry to ask you to leave me now but I've got a shed load of paperwork to catch up on. Maybe you'd like to meet up for dinner tonight? One of the perks of commanding a ship this size is that I can entertain as much as I want.'

The Caspian Monster

They all got up to leave but as the Commander opened the door, the Captain called out, 'Oh Jon, hang on second would you mind popping back in. I need a word in private.'

When the door had closed the Captain turned to Jon. 'Now look old chap, I thought you ought to know that I've been briefed on the little unpleasantness over the last few months. Frankly, I was pretty disgusted to find out that anyone would doubt your word but then we've known each other through some interesting times have we not?'

'Yes Sir but it's all resolved now.'

'So I've been reliably informed. Oh and one other thing.'

'Sir?'

'When the time comes, you will tell me why you're really here won't you?'

Later that evening, after getting acquainted with the massive ship and even getting lost a couple of times, Jon was getting changed for dinner in his palatial cabin when Brian put his head around the door.

'Hey, these cabins are something else aren't they?'

'Compared to the rabbit hutches we had on a Frigate they are but be careful. Apparently, they can bite.'

'Eh, what do you mean?'

'You see how the bunk folds out of the way to make a sofa in the day?'

'Yes, mine's the same.'

'Apparently, when they're opened up as beds they lock into place. But I've been told that if we hit a big wave, the latch can come undone and the whole poxy thing can then fold away with you inside. Some guy on Invincible is meant to have been stuck in one all night until someone found him the next morning.'

Brian wasn't sure if Jon was bullshitting and said so.

'No it's true. See that thing that looks like a car seat belt? It's meant to be used in rough weather to hold you in but most of the ship's officers use it the other way round to hold the bed open.'

'Well bugger me, we build a beautiful ship like this and can't make the bloody beds work. Mind you that's not the only design fault.'

'Oh?' queried Jon. 'Don't tell me there's something worse than being eaten by your own bed?'

'Yeah, well when they designed these ships they put the two propellers rather close to the hull and then put the wardroom directly above. All I'll say is that if we are doing over thirteen knots, hold onto your G and T otherwise it will shake itself onto the deck. Anyway, what did father want with you after we left this morning?'

Jon thought for a second. 'Not a lot really, he said he had been briefed on the Norway incident but he's such a perceptive bugger. He said he knew we were really here for a third reason but didn't press too hard to find out.'

'What did you tell him?'

'Nothing of course, what could I say? That Fleet and MI6 are worried that one of our most secret installations could be under threat from the Russians. After all, we're only meant to be keeping a watching brief.'

Chapter 27

London

Rupert Thomas continued to gnaw at the problem. Even though he had two people he could trust in a bloody great Aircraft Carrier full of helicopters and Royal Marines as close to Pickwick as it was feasibly possible, he still felt nervous. The debrief with that dreadful naval officer had been frustrating. Once the fear of God had been installed into the man he did his best to answer truthfully. Rupert was quite sure of that. He had conducted enough interviews in the past to be confident in his ability to spot prevarication at any level. The problem was that the man admitted to being so drunk that he really couldn't remember much and Rupert believed him. That said, he did confess to deliberately listening in to the operational briefing although he never managed to overhear where the destination actually was or its function. Nevertheless, Rupert had to act on the assumption that he had told the woman everything that he had discovered and that was bad enough. Then there had been that odd encounter with a Soviet submarine last year. There was no direct evidence that they had located the base but the coincidence seemed too strong to ignore.

What most people didn't know was that the base actually fulfilled two functions. The first was for the navy and used the hydrophone network under the ice for submarine detection. However, MI6 also had an enormous radio array laid out on the top of the ice. It was only a receiver but with so much real estate to play with and as it only consisted of miles of light wire, it covered a vast area. This made it extremely sensitive. The base used satellite communications on a very tight beam to get the information out which was nigh on impossible to intercept. On top of that, they had some very special computers that could compress vast amounts of data into a very short burst. It was the information coming from this system that was now the most worrying. Much of the Soviet's military communications were very heavily encrypted. Despite the successes of the Second World War, things had moved on and very little could be decrypted quickly by GCHQ these days. That said, sometimes they got lucky and there was one word that kept on appearing from the Murmansk HQ. In itself it meant nothing. The word was Orlyonok or Eaglet. It was plainly a code word for an operation but what exactly was the operation? Normally, this time of year, Murmansk was frozen solid. Maritime movements ground to a halt except for a few icebreakers and the submarines that could deploy under the ice. So, if the bloody Russians had located Pickwick, what could they do about it if anything?

Rupert sighed, he would have one more trawl through the latest information but then he really ought to go home and get some sleep.

Moscow

The planning room was crowded and stank of smoke. Inga was sitting at the back taking notes for Mikhael. She was the only female present and was getting fed up with the appraising glances being made at her from just about every male in the room. That was despite the fact that she had deliberately dressed as dowdily as she could and was wearing thick rimmed glasses.

The first part of the briefing covered the political situation. Operation Ryan continued to provide evidence that the Americans were pursuing their policy of aggressive military operations. They had been using their outrage over the incident with the Korean airliner to fuel both military and civilian anger. However, any criticism over their invasion of Grenada was being brushed off with arrogant disdain. That was in the face of a UN resolution deploring the action which was passed by a massive vote of 108 to 9, stating that it was a flagrant violation of international law and of the independence, sovereignty and territorial integrity of Grenada. The arrogance of the American reaction to this was causing outrage around the world. When Reagan was asked to comment on the vote his response had been, 'it didn't upset my breakfast at all.'

With such obvious evidence of American duplicity and aggressiveness the concern was that now, they would use a military exercise, as cover to get their nuclear forces in full readiness for a pre-emptive strike. The atmosphere in the room was very tense and angry.

A KGB expert then got up and showed evidence that they might be planning just such an exercise. Intercepts of NATO communications were showing a slow build up in traffic. Reports from agents in the field seemed to confirm an unusual amount of activity at various headquarters but none at real military bases as of yet. A worldwide alert had been put out for any evidence of physical activity. One particular deployment had been spotted in the Norwegian Sea. The Royal Navy's new Aircraft Carrier, Illustrious, had been seen leaving Portsmouth with one of their Assault ships, Fearless and several escorts. Unusually, it seemed she had embarked assault helicopters rather than her usual outfit of jets. A large number of Royal Marines were also on board her and the accompanying ships. Inga whispered into to Mikhael's ear and said it was probably for their normal annual winter exercise. Mikhael then stood up to make this point which was agreed as the most likely supposition by the other experts there. But that did nothing to help defuse the feelings in the room.

With the general situation covered, most people left the room and the hard core for the raid remained behind. Inga looked around curiously. She recognised Mikhael's boss and the naval Captain but not the other three. They introduced themselves. The man with the limp was Yuri, the pilot of the Ekranoplan, the other fitter looking man, was a Major Baturin from Special Forces who would be leading the soldiers on the raid. Finally, a rather older man who was a specialist scientist, he would be coming along to assess the equipment they found and decide what should be retrieved.

Captain Orlov got up to speak.

'Now we talk specifics. The submarine that will provide the communications jamming and relocate the base for us is ready to go. I will be commanding her and we sail as soon as this meeting is concluded. Yuri tells me the Eaglet is ready to go.' He looked at Yuri expectantly, who nodded his agreement.

'Now, I understand there is plenty of room in the machine for more than enough troops but of course we don't know how much equipment we will be retrieving, so we must keep plenty of space available for that. I understand that we will be taking twelve soldiers?'

The Special Forces Major concurred.

'Fine, then the only thing left to talk about is the timing. It will take me about two to three days to get into position and do my work. Once I have the information we need it will transmitted via HF radio on our agreed schedule. However, we will then have to wait until the British exercise is in the right phase and all their assets are ashore. I will try to get into a tail position behind their Carrier to watch and we will have an intelligence ship on station as well, so we should have plenty of warning. Yuri, what is your estimate for arrival once given the go ahead?'

Yuri had done all his calculations. 'Given permission and the ability to leave around sunset, we can be on site in just under five hours. Assuming three hours to find, capture, investigate and retrieve equipment, we should be back in the Kola in under fourteen hours. There will be at least eighteen hours of darkness this time of year, so we have more than enough time. However, I suggest that we leave earlier, in daylight, to give us even more flexibility. Even if we're spotted, it will only be one of a continuing set of flights. Satellites cannot see inside us and see what we are carrying. The weather forecasts are good for the next ten days or so but even so the weather will have to be very poor to stop us. We can fly in just about anything.'

'That may be alright for you,' said the Major. 'But my guys still need to operate on the ground. But I agree we shouldn't be weather limited.'

'Excellent,' said Andrei. 'Now, as I said before, the final timing will be dictated by the Royal Navy. We don't want that Carrier around and full up with marines and helicopters but once they're ashore they will be toothless, especially with the speed we're planning to achieve. We'll use their exercise against them and they will provide an excellent smokescreen for our activities. As I said previously, there will be an intelligence ship with them the whole time and I've arranged airborne surveillance as well. They will be so focused on that and their own aims that we won't be noticed. Even if we are, it will be far too late for them to do anything about it.'

Yuri then asked the question he had tried to get answered before. 'And what about prisoners?'

Captain Orlov had been ready for this. 'Good point Yuri, another reason for keeping plenty of room in the Eaglet. You will bring them with you. They can then be used as bargaining chips or put on trial as spies. Either way, they will be useful to us back here in Moscow.'

'So gentlemen,' said Andrei, who had forgotten Inga's presence. 'I sail early tomorrow morning. In about five day's time, you should get the signal you need from me. Then if our lords and masters give the final go ahead as soon as the British are ashore, you go.'

With the meeting over they all filed out. Mikhael ensured that he and Major Baturin were last to leave. Once everyone else was out of earshot, he spoke quietly. 'Major just to confirm, the prisoners are not to come back, they're an unnecessary burden. Just make it look like they tried to resist or something.'

The Major nodded but said nothing.

Later the evening, Mikhael let himself out of his apartment and pulled his collar up against the biting wind. Tomorrow morning he would be on the train to Murmansk, so he had this one last evening to indulge in a bit of relaxation. He tried to limit these little forays but tonight was definitely a night for indulgence. Earlier on, he had made a call and then gone down to the storeroom in the KGB building and availed himself of a small amount of a certain substance. He had an arrangement with the storekeeper and nothing would appear on any records.

He decided to walk. It wasn't far. As he strode along the snow covered roads his sense of personal power and well being increased. Being a member of the KGB made him part of the elite of this country. He could and did look down on most of the population with disdain. He had to smile inwardly when Inga had told him of the death of her father. So who cared about the death of another peasant? However, he was a good enough dissembler to hide any reactions and sympathise with her. He had recruited her after looking at her file. Her academic achievements were all he needed but it was her beauty that swayed his decision. Not that he was the slightest interested in her for himself of course but having her with him at meetings was an extremely useful psychological tool. Her effect on the average male was enough to distract them when he needed and inviting Mikhael and his attractive assistant to meetings suddenly became very popular. He was even more pleased when she had shown real aptitude for the job. All in all, the reputation of his little department was definitely on the up. All it needed was this raid to go well and his star would definitely be in the ascendant. Who knows, maybe it would be him in a chauffeured Zil limousine heading off to shop in an exclusive GUM store soon.

Ah, here it was. He had reached the tall tenement block of flats he was looking for. One of so many in this city. He pushed open the rusting lobby doors and immediately took to the stairs. Even if the lifts were working, which he doubted, the smell of urine in them was enough to make walking up the few flights he needed a much better option. On the second floor, he found the door and knocked hard, knowing the occupants would find it hard to hear him.

After several attempts, the door opened partially and a worn, grey faced woman looked out. As soon as she recognised him, she gave a sickening welcoming grin and waved him inside. Mikhael knew she was under thirty. She looked over sixty. Her emaciated body ruined by her habit. The flat was filthy and smelled awful but that didn't take anything away from his mounting excitement. They went into a room which he supposed was the kitchen but that was only because there was an old stove in the corner.

'Hello my dear, how are you?' he asked in a solicitous tone.

'Never mind the pleasantries. Have you brought some as you promised?'

'Of course,' he said placatingly and handed over the little packet which was snatched out of his hand by a claw. The woman retreated to the other side of the room and started preparing her needle. He waited until she had satisfied herself using the hypodermic on an arm that was a mass of puncture marks. She sighed and sat back on an old chair. Her eyes actually seemed to focus properly for a second.

'The bedroom,' was all she said.

He smiled and bowed his thanks. He knew she would be out of it now for several hours. She wouldn't hear any screams. Even if she did, she would be far too stoned to do anything about it as usual. He made his way down the corridor to the room he wanted. The delightful sense of anticipation was almost overwhelming as he pushed the door open.

Back in the kitchen, the woman lay back waiting for the rush, waiting for the world to go right again. This time something seemed wrong, the stuff Mikhael had given her seemed too weak. After the initial hit, nothing seemed to be happening. She couldn't believe it but the bastard must have given something that had been cut. After all the sacrifices she made for him and he couldn't even get her a decent fix. She sat in her chair starting to shake, whether it was disappointment or anger she wasn't sure. But this wasn't fair and after all she did for the fucking man. Her anger grew and she pulled open a drawer, grabbing the kitchen knife inside, the one she kept to ward off the nightmares in the middle of the night.

She heard the first sob of pleading from the bedroom as she approached the door. As she pushed it open she heard the first choked scream and concurrent grunt of pleasure. She had never seen or wanted to see what Mikhael did with her nine year old daughter but now she was confronted with the reality. Anger and sheer, raw rage overwhelmed her. With his trousers round his ankles, Mikhael was effectively hobbled and it was so easy to plunge the knife into his unprotected back. Plunge it in again and again.

Chapter 28

HMS Illustrious, the Norwegian Sea

The weather was grey, dull and cold. A biting, force six, half gale was knocking the tops off the waves in rows of whitecaps which rolled steadily towards the side of Illustrious and her escorts. It was a typical January day off the coast of Norway. The big Carrier hardly noticed the swell but the small ship closely following her was making heavy weather of it. She was rolling heavily and shipping water occasionally over her port side.

The conditions were not stopping her crew from their duty, however. The small rust streaked, scruffy Russian trawler bristled with aerials which had nothing to do with catching fish and everything to do with catching any and all radio transmissions from the British ships. Elsewhere, amongst the force, there was a Kashin class destroyer that had been making a bloody nuisance of itself for the last few days by close manoeuvring with the British ships and generally making its presence felt. However, the little intelligence gatherer or AGI in NATO parlance had doggedly stuck to Illustrious's wake whatever the bigger ship did.

Jon and Brian, along with a large number of ship's officers were watching the little ship from the shelter of the Carrier's quarterdeck, the large open space at the stern immediately below the flight deck. The AGI, who had become used to the big ship's routine over the recent days, had already moved even closer for the next expected evolution.

Suddenly, over the ship's loudspeakers came the anticipated tinny sounding voice. 'D'you hear there, stand down from flying stations, gash may now be ditched for the next half an hour.'

The Caspian Monster

'Well, this should be fun,' said Brian. 'I'm glad it's not me on that skanky old thing. You know they spend ages at sea. Still, at least this morning we might brighten their day just a little bit.'

Jon just grunted as he put his binoculars to his eyes as the first of several large sacks of rubbish streamed past in the ship's wake.

Sure enough, the AGI manoeuvred close to the sacks and a team of sailors started pulling them out of the water with large hooks.

'Which ones are they again?' asked Jon.

'Er, the one from the stoker's mess has a large blue stripe and the porn has a red stripe.'

'Here we go,' Jon called cheerfully. 'They've got the blue one.'

There was a cheer from the assembled officers as the bag was opened and then a slightly disappointed laugh as the bag was thrown back into the sea with some violence after the contents had been identified.

'Now, that wasn't very friendly,' said Jon in a deadpan voice. 'You'd think they would be grateful for a sack of underpants and nice woolly socks.'

'Not sure I'd be that grateful. The stokers have been wearing them continually for the last week after all,' chortled Brian. 'Hang on, they've got the porn now. I hope they show a bit more interest.'

They all held their breath as the second bag was opened. Sure enough, the reaction was very different this time as a vast quantity of British and some Scandinavian pornographic magazines were discovered. The sailors immediately looked animated and stopped reaching for the other sacks streaming by.

'Hang on, what's this then?' asked Jon as a blue suited officer came on the bridge wing of the little ship and looked aft. He must have shouted something as he then shot down the ladder and joined the retrieval crew. With much gesticulation on the officer's part, the magazines were gathered up and placed back in the bag. He was then clearly instructing the men to get back on with their work before he picked up the bag himself and took it inside the ship.

The Caspian Monster

Shouts of 'spoilsport and 'let the lads have a few', were lost in the wind but everyone was chuckling. Being able to have some sport at the expense of the AGI was not a common occurrence and everyone was getting a little fed up with the hassle they had been receiving over the last few days.

'Well that was fun, it's nice to get our own back a bit,' said Brian. 'But I don't think I've ever seen so much Soviet interference before. What the hell was that Bear doing yesterday?'

The previous day a Russian Bear Foxtrot, a giant four propellered surveillance aircraft, had spent several hours flying around and over the fleet. At one point, it flew so close to the flight deck that the ship had been forced to call it on the aviation emergency frequency and tell it to clear off as it was encroaching on the ships flying circuit and so low it was in danger of colliding with one of the Sea Kings. There was no acknowledgement but it did eventually move away.

Jon was thoughtful. 'I guess they feel we're in their back yard and have every right to be here.'

'Fine but we're in international waters. They have to comply with international law don't they?'

'Hmm, can you imagine how the Yanks would react if the Ruskies sent a task force this size to Cuba to do an amphibious exercise? Last time they tried something like that, we almost went to war.'

'Oh come on, that involved nuclear missiles.'

'And have we told them that we aren't carrying anything like that?'

'Bloody hell Jon, that summer of love with the Russian family seems to have made you a sympathiser.'

Coming from anyone other than Brian, Jon would have taken exception to that remark but he knew his old friend far too well to do so.

'Bollocks to you, I'm just trying to see it from their point of view. They are human after all.'

'Well apparently, we've also picked up an underwater tail. Our sub who's been escorting us has reported that there is a Victor Three tailing us now. Hopefully, the Russian doesn't know he's there because without any ASW helicopters in the force, a submarine of our own is the only real defence.'

'That would only be a problem if this was a real war and it's only a poxy exercise after all. Come on Brian, I don't know about you but it's getting bloody cold out here. Fancy a coffee?'

A few hours later, they both attended the major operation briefing. Normally, this would take place in one of the Squadron briefing rooms but with so many participants, a space had been cleared in the rear of the hangar.

The vast space was half empty as several of the Sea Kings were still on deck and would be continuing with their flying training as soon as the brief finished. Chairs had been set out at the aft end next to one of the giant scissor action aircraft lifts.

Jon looked around at his old squadron mates. He had been relieved to find out that no one seemed to know what had happened in Norway last year. Everyone just assumed that Jon had been reappointed for some urgent task. There also seemed to be a lack of information about the absence of a certain Senior Pilot. Jon had managed to get a reluctant Brian to tell him the whole story. It had taken a surprising amount of beer and persuasion as Brian had wanted to keep his role out of it but he had succeeded in the end. Jon knew he would never be able to show his friend the true depth of his gratitude and anyway Brian would just shrug it off in his normal bluff fashion. A new Senior Pilot had arrived now and the squadron seemed a far more relaxed place. However, Jon was starting to get serious aviating withdrawal symptoms and would be calling on the appointer as soon as he could after the exercise was over.

'Right, everyone pay attention please.' Captain Test called from the front. 'I just wanted to say thank you to everyone who has contributed to the success of the operation so far. Using a Carrier in this role was always going to be a voyage of discovery and I'm very pleased with the way it's gone so far. So, there will be final training for flight and deck crews today, then a day of rest. The assault is planned for the day after tomorrow at dawn. I'll let the experts take over and give us the detail.'

He sat down and the Squadron CO followed by other experts, went through the programme in detail. This was going to be the first time a simultaneous two company lift of Royal Marines had been attempted for some time and the first time from one of the new carriers. It would involve eight Sea Kings and a variety of landing craft from the other ships. The aim was to get the troops, their guns and all their equipment ashore, in a dawn assault and surprise the enemy, who were somewhere on the designated section of Norwegian shore line. Hopefully, intelligence would find them somewhere to do so unopposed because to conduct such a landing under hostile fire was not considered feasible. Once established ashore, the Squadron would form two Forward Operating Bases that would leap frog each other as the Royal Marines advanced and thoroughly routed the enemy. They expected to be ashore for at least two weeks and the ships would hover offshore to provide support as needed.

When the brief was over, Jon and Brian went back to the corner of the ships operations room they had been assigned for the conduct of the other exercise they were involved in. A stack of signals was waiting for them and they got stuck in sorting them out and getting ready to prepare a brief for the Captain.

'Right,' said Brian thoughtfully. 'We've gone straight to Defcon 3 which means increased force readiness. As far as the exercise goes we're already there of course, so no action from us is required yet. What's the simulated political condition Jon?'

'Er hang on, right here we go,' he answered holding a long sheaf of paper. 'Orange forces, that's the bad guys, have promised military support for the ousted government of one of their allies. It seems there was a revolution and the people democratically kicked them out. Orange are preparing to send in troops and us lot, that's the Blue forces, have told them not to. No prizes for guessing what happens next. It's not exactly the most original exercise scenario is it?'

'Suppose not but we know it could happen because it did and not that long ago in Prague. The Czechs are still smarting even now.'

'Good point. I wonder how it will escalate from here?'

Chapter 29

One hundred metres below, five hundred metres behind HMS Illustrious

Andrei Orlov was very satisfied. Two days after sailing from Murmansk, he had transited under the ice and done what he had come to do. Because he knew roughly where the NATO base should be and because this time he knew what to look for, he was able to accurately relocate it in one pass. The people up there on the ice would have no reason to suspect his was anything other than a normal deployment. Indeed, it would have probably been more suspicious if a submarine hadn't been detected with such a large NATO force assembling off the Norwegian coast.

He had then moved on, carefully monitoring the depth of the ice above him. After a few miles, he had found what he was looking for. It was a compression fracture caused by the immense pressures generated by the summer movement of the ice.

Bringing his massive submarine to a stop under the ice wasn't easy but he used a technique that had been developed over the years. As the submarine slowly halted, he quietly blew ballast, until the top of the fin was pushing up hard against the ceiling of frozen water. With the fin acting as an anchor, he was then able to keep his propulsor turning slowly, which would give the NATO base the impression that he was still moving. The thickness of the ice was such that had he blown all his ballast he might have been able to breach through and actually reach the surface, which was the normal procedure. But this time he had other plans.

He went forward to give the diving team their final brief. They were already assembled and dressed in their specialist cold water diving equipment. Within minutes they had exited the submarine via the diving lock in the forward torpedo compartment. Their job now was to retrieve the specialist equipment on the hull, which included a massive ice drill and deploy the system that had been prepared in so much secrecy. Half an hour later and they were back on board. The leader debriefed Andrei on a successful mission. As soon as they were in clear water, Andrei deployed the submarine's floating long range HF radio aerial and transmitted a simple code word. Everything was now ready.

Once that task was complete, he then moved on to the next part of his patrol. Despite the fact that there was ongoing surveillance of the British fleet from the air and sea it would do no harm to have eyes under the sea as well. With so many ships churning the sea with their propellers, locating the British Task Force had been simple. It had proved even easier than usual to get into position as the expected screen of ASW helicopters that normally operated ahead of any NATO Task Force was missing. Consequently, he had taken over a day to manoeuvre ahead of them and then let them steam overhead. Identifying the Carrier had been relatively simple and once he was sure which one it was, he turned and settled down in the wake of the large ship. By keeping within the noise and turbulence of its propellers he could mask the presence of his own machine and remain undetected. All he had to do now was wait for the sonar signal from the intelligence ship a few metres above his head to tell him the British aircraft and marines were ashore and he would sneak away and await the signal to activate the system under the ice.

A thousand yards astern of the Victor 3 and undetected by Andrei for the same reason that he was so hard to detect, the British submarine Swiftsure maintained its own position.

London

Rupert's suspicions that the Soviets were up to something seemed to be wrong. He had spent the day at Northwood down the hole with his naval colleagues. The Victor Three that was shadowing the Task Force had come out of the Kola a few days before and conducted a normal transit to the Norwegian Sea and was now doing the expected and shadowing the Illustrious group. He was starting to think that his concerns were going to come to nothing. He also had his part to play in Good Bowman and when he returned to London late that afternoon several of his team briefed him on its progress. By now, hypothetical tensions were increasing and although the Blues had warned Orange not to send in troops, they had mobilised large numbers. At the moment they were still the right side of the hypothetical border but there was every sign that an invasion was imminent. NATO Command were debating whether to go to Defcon 2, which meant a level of readiness just below that for total war. Signal traffic was flying between the NATO countries. They had even called in the German Chancellor to exercise some governmental functions. It was all very realistic and quite scary how fast things could escalate even if it was only an exercise.

He looked at this watch and realised that he had time to catch up on some of his routine paperwork. He didn't really want to but it wasn't going to do itself and he was a firm believer in doing as much work up front as possible. You never knew what might be around the corner. He started in on the routine reports from his people abroad. In the real world, Scandinavia was fairly quiet. With the exception of the NATO winter exercise, there was little military activity elsewhere although, as he had discovered at Northwood that morning, the Soviets were being particularly belligerent with the British Task Force. He next turned to the intelligence summaries covering his area. These were pushed out by all the other intelligence services who shared data. In this case that was primarily the Americans. His eyes were starting to feel gritty. He was surprised at how late it was when he looked at his watch again. He really should go home. And then something caught his eye, just one word. It was in an American summary of activity in the Murmansk naval base. The one word was Orlyonok.

He read further and then yelled at one of his staff to get him everything they had about Ekranoplans. An hour later, all his old suspicions were back. He knew he should consult with his superior but time could be very tight. He would tell him afterwards.

He reached for the phone and when the operator answered, said simply, 'get me the Pentagon.'

Moscow

The Politburo was meeting in emergency session. The KGB had been monitoring NATO signal traffic and had reported on the significant increase of heavily encrypted signals over the last ten days. However, several reports had been received which indicated that a major exercise was underway which could explain it. That was countered, in part, by other reports from the ground which didn't show any significant increase in military activity. However, assessments of how the West would initiate a first strike all pointed towards using an exercise as cover. What was worrying about this situation was that the level of encryption and volume of traffic had never been seen before. There was even a report that the German Chancellor had become involved. As it was his country that would be at most physical risk should a war break out, he would be the first Head of Government to become involved in the decision making process.

At the conclusion of the meeting, there was an agreed consensus. If NATO were gearing up for something, then the Soviet Union would not be caught napping. The order went out for all military units to prepare. Leave was cancelled and all war material reserves were to be made ready. In particular, the ballistic missile silos and deployed ballistic missile submarines were to report their status immediately and be prepared to come to full alert.

Chapter 30

HMS Illustrious, Norwegian Sea

Jon was standing to one side in Flyco, the small aircraft control position grafted onto the side of the Carrier's bridge and trying to keep clear of all the activity. Sitting in their comfortable seats, overseeing all aviation activities, were Commander (Air) commonly known as 'Wings.' and Lieutenant Commander Flying, known as 'Little F'. It was nine in the morning and still pitch black. On the deck below, eight olive green Sea Kings were being manned up by their aircrew. On the deck itself, the various flight deck crews were hurrying about getting ready for the word to go. Invisible in the hangar below, the sticks of Royal Marines were forming up with all their equipment and waiting to go up to the flight deck on the aircraft lifts.

Wings turned his head and saw the visitor. 'Morning Jon, come up to watch the action?'

'Yes Sir, I just can't seem to keep away,' he replied with a slightly wistful smile.

'They're your old squadron, aren't they? Bet you wish you were down there now.'

'I certainly do but with any luck, I'll be getting a flying job again soon.'

'Yes, I heard you were involved in something. Don't worry I've no idea what it was but it must have been OK because you've got your half stripe and got it early by all accounts.'

Jon flinched inwardly at his recollections of the last year but was relieved that even someone as senior as Wings clearly didn't know what had really gone on.

'It's been an interesting year Sir, I can certainly say that,' and then changing the subject. 'When's the first launch Sir?'

Before Wings could answer, the tinny voice of the Squadron CO came over the flight deck intercom system. 'Flyco, this is Green leader, ready to start up.'

'There's your answer Jon,' said Wings before clicking one of the microphones sticking out of the console in front of him and giving the requested permission.

Through the armoured glass of Flyco's windows, Jon could clearly hear the sound of gas turbines starting up. The whole operation was being done under full tactical conditions which meant total radio silence and as few lights as possible. Speaking to the aircraft was done through 'telebrief' a system of plug-in wires to each aircraft. It was quite impressive therefore, when all eight sets of rotor blades started to rotate at the same time. Once they were fully up to speed, the aircraft lifts at the front and rear of the flight deck, descended into the blacked out hangar below and quickly returned. On each were four lines of kneeling soldiers. Once the lifts were fully raised again, signals were exchanged between the pilots and flight deck crews, each line of troops ran in and embarked in their respective aircraft.

One dim light flashed from the cockpit of the CO's aircraft. Wings called to the bridge requesting permission to launch which was quickly granted as the ship was already on a flying course with the wind coming from just to port of ship's head. The flight deck lights came on at their dimmest setting. He called the Flight Deck Officer over the secure flight deck communication system and four of the deck crew ran into each aircraft and released the nylon lashings holding them to the deck. They gathered in front of each Sea King and the aircraft's marshaller visibly counted all four lashings to confirm to the pilots that they were no longer connected to the deck. The flight deck lights went out.

Wings then made a switch and a dimmed light on the side of the island, visible to the helicopter's pilots, turned green. One by one, the heavily laden Sea Kings lifted cumbersomely into the hover, their rotors coning up with the effort of lifting over nine tons of aircraft and payload. The metal panels all along the tails of the aircraft rippled with the torque that the rotors were putting into the airframes. Each aircraft was at its maximum all up weight and needed to transition into forward flight as soon as it could to reduce the need to pull so much power. The one next to Flyco lifted into the hover with its rotor tips seemingly only inches away from the glass. Vortices of moisture could clearly be seen tripping off the end of each blade. They could see the pilot looking at the deck and then at them as he eased the cyclic to the left and gathered speed away into the dark.

Suddenly it was quiet. The last aircraft disappeared from sight.

Wings looked pleased. 'Bloody, hell that went well. Now, we're twelve miles out so we should expect them back in about fifteen to twenty minutes. Time for a cup of coffee before it gets busy again.'

All morning, the deck was busy as a train of Sea Kings returned to collect more troops, stores or equipment. Much of this was in the form of underslung loads which were attached to the underneath of a hovering helicopter with a long strop that itself attached to a special release mechanism fitted to the bottom each aircraft. By the time the loads were despatched, the flight deck crew were almost frozen solid. Having to hook on loads while standing underneath the ferocious downdraft of the massive machine hovering only feet from their heads was not an easy task. The most difficult loads were the One Hundred and Five millimetre artillery guns. The heaviest load a Sea King could carry. It was sometimes unclear who was flying who as the heavily laden helicopter started to sway in flight to the pendulum of the gun below it. By midday, the helicopters returned for the final time. They landed on and refuelled and this time their load was their own people. Each aircraft took seven maintenance staff, known as an Eagle Base, so that if need be they could operate in the field autonomously for a considerable time. And then that was it as far as the Carrier was concerned, unless something went awry with the exercise, her job was effectively over. The troops and aircraft would now take the fight to the enemy ashore and there was little the ship could do unless it was to provide some urgent stores or act as a casualty evacuation facility.

Jon finally pried himself away just as it was all coming to an end and went down to the Ops room to find Brian.

'Ah, glad you could make it old chum some of us have been slaving over hot signals while you've been watching your Jungly chums enjoy themselves.' Brian didn't mean any criticism and he knew Jon also knew that but it didn't stop him doing a little bit of winding up.

Jon ignored the sarcasm. 'Yeah, well it was all pilot shit, so I wouldn't expect you to understand anyway. So what's happening?'

'Quite a lot actually, we are all going to Defcon 2 now for Good Bowman purposes. It appears our Orange protagonists have decided to invade their poor revolting neighbour and us freedom loving Blues have decided to rattle our sabres. You need to help me here with all these bloody signals we've got to send in the next few hours. It's not that we've got anything else to do is it?'

Two hundred feet almost below their feet, Captain Andrei Orlov had just received the underwater signal he was expecting from the intelligence ship. He knew the ship would have also sent a coded message back to Murmansk and so the next part of his task was to get into position back towards the ice ready for the start of the operation. He ordered the submarine to slow down and let the British ships draw ahead. When he was sure they were far enough away, he slowly altered course and then increased speed back towards the ice. He would then loiter in open water, with a receiver aerial towed on the surface above him, waiting for the go ahead, waiting for the chance to at last do something about the despised NATO base that had been hiding in the Arctic ice for far too long.

The Captain of Swiftsure had an urgent decision to make. His brief was to stay and escort the Task Force but the Russian Victor

Three was behaving very strangely. He couldn't communicate by underwater telephone with the surface ships as it would give the game away to the Russian. He didn't want to go to periscope depth to put up a VHF aerial as it might mean losing contact, so he would have to decide what to do and then tell Fleet during his next routine broadcast in a few hours time.

'Come about,' he called to his control room team. 'Let's follow this chap and see what on earth he's up to.'

Chapter 31

London

Rupert Thomas had been up all night but strangely he realised that he didn't feel tired at all. As soon as his suspicions had been confirmed he called the navy at Northwood as well as alerting his superiors. A meeting had been set up there for nine o'clock and shortly he would present his findings.

Luckily, when he got hold of his counterpart in the Pentagon the previous evening, the time difference was in his favour and the day shift were still at work. He had explained his dilemma and to his surprise was very quickly put onto the head of what they called the 'monster team.' The name was soon explained and he found it quite appropriate especially after they faxed through a sheaf of photographs of the various machines the Soviets had been producing over the years. However, what he really needed to know was the performance specifications of the Eaglet machine and also what it had been doing up in Murmansk for the last few months. The Americans had been extremely accommodating and now he probably knew as much as they did. He also suspected that they were quite excited over something they had been watching over for years. At last, it might actually be going to be used on some sort of operation. They even agreed to see if there was any recent satellite or Blackbird information available, to try and discover the current status of the Eaglet in Murmansk.

With a sheaf of photographs and specifications written out on acetate sheets, he entered the conference room on the second floor. Present were his boss, a Captain from C in C Fleet and a scientist from Royal Aircraft Establishment at Farnborough.

Nodding to the men, he made sure they all had a coffee and launched into his brief. He started with the machines themselves.

Unsurprisingly, the RAE boffin already knew about them and was able to confirm much of what the Americans had already sent over. When it came to understanding the limitations of the machines, the scientist was quite disparaging. He explained how their manoeuvrability was limited because they flew so close to the surface and also how they would find it extremely difficult to fly over anything but sea. Rupert got the distinct impression of a 'not invented here' attitude from the man. When he showed him a surveillance photo of the Eaglet over the ice quite far from the sea the man seemed to get quite huffy. It was almost as though Rupert was querying his personal integrity.

'Thank you,' he said to the meeting while trying to maintain a level of calmness that was becoming increasingly difficult. 'If I can sum up then, this machine can fly at about two hundred and fifty miles an hour or more, carry a payload of several hundred tons and land and take off on the water and probably the ice cap as well. Would that be a fair summary?'

The scientist reluctantly agreed and so Rupert then had the pleasure of asking the man to leave as he didn't have the clearances for the next part of the discussion.

With just the three of them present, he then went on to outline his concerns over the safety of Pickwick.

'Gentlemen, I may be paranoid but that's what I'm paid to be after all. Firstly, this Russian female agent legs it back to Moscow a few days after our ad hoc supply flight last year. We now know that the man she managed to snare knew far more than he should have about what went on. That said, we're pretty sure that he knew neither where the actual destination was nor what goes on there. However, later in the year we have this submarine apparently doing an underwater survey and managing to go directly underneath the exact location of the base. Now, our scientists have said that it's extremely unlikely that the base could have been detected but frankly Russian engineering skill seems as good if not better than ours. I'm not a betting man but I wouldn't put money on them not being able to find it, especially once they've been given a bloody great clue.'

The Captain nodded but it was Rupert's boss who spoke. 'Alright Rupert, they may have found Pickwick but you clearly think they're planning to do something about it. So, the first question is why do you think that and secondly what would or even could they do?'

'Good questions and until I saw that Ekranoplan thing I was pretty sure there was nothing they could do even if they wanted to. Pickwick is buried in the ice but is in international waters and far too far away from Russian territory for them to get there with conventional forces, not the least because it would take so long that they would inevitably be spotted. Now look, we know, that they know, that we can track their submarines. What they don't seem to know is how we do it and we certainly don't want them to find out. If they get intelligence that one of our detection stations is so tantalising close, don't you think they might consider a quick deniable raid? That is if they thought they had the means to do it?'

There were nods from the other two. This time the Captain spoke. 'A very good point. NATO has been giving them a very hard time for the last two years or so. If I was one of their submariners I would be getting pretty pissed off if every time I left on patrol, I picked up a tail. So you think this Eaglet machine could be the answer they've been looking for?'

'Yes,' said Rupert firmly. 'Until I stumbled upon the information, I was beginning to think my paranoia had gone too far. This machine has the payload, speed and capability to do the job in less than twelve hours. It could be in and out before we knew what was going on.'

'There are two good reasons why they would still have trouble,' responded the Captain. 'Firstly, the base would be able to get off a message to us even while Ivan was trying to break down the door. If they were able to do that we could prove to the international community that the Soviets were conducting an act of war. Why would they risk that, especially in the current political climate? And secondly, for at least the next few weeks, we should be alright. With all the forces we have up there for this winter exercise they would never risk such an action.'

'Good point,' said Rupert's boss. 'Look old chap, you may have something here but it seems we still have a window to make further detailed assessments. Get on this and let me have a full report which I can send up the chain. We'll arrange some extra surveillance and also get a warning to Pickwick just in case.'

Rupert nodded. At least he was being taken seriously. There was just this nagging suspicion that there was more to this and that there was something he had missed.

Murmansk Naval Base

Inga looked at the enormous white machine that dwarfed everything around it. Emblazoned over its nose in gold letters was its name. She couldn't for the life of her think of anything that looked less like a lady but she understood the sentiment especially as she knew where it was going.

For the umpteenth time, she wondered what the hell she was doing here. Yesterday morning, she had arrived at her desk as usual. For the second day in a row, there was no sign of Mikhael and no one seemed to know where he was. She had asked up the chain but his boss seemed as puzzled as she was. Then later that morning, the man actually came into her office to talk to her. Mikhael had completely disappeared. At first, she was quizzed about what she might know of his afterhour's activities but as she really didn't have a clue, she wasn't able to help. After that, he talked about the training she had received when she was appointed to an overseas KGB surveillance job. Yes, she had done all the basic weapon handling and field training work but had never used it since. Yes, she knew all the details of the mission. As Mikhael's deputy, she had been party to all the discussions. That seemed to make the man's mind up. Apparently, it was standard procedure that any KGB operation, whether led by the military or not, must have a KGB member along. When Inga queried why it was considered so critical all she got was a stock response that it was always done that way. He then rather patronisingly, said that although she was a woman, in this case, there was no time to prepare anyone else. She would have to take Mikhael's place on the mission. It wasn't even made clear exactly what her role was other than to 'make sure the mission followed the agreed plan' whatever that meant. She got the strong impression that what he really meant was for her to make sure that the KGB couldn't be blamed if it went wrong but he wouldn't come out and say so directly. At no point in the conversation was she asked whether she had any views on being given the job. It was clearly assumed that she would just get on with it. In fact, she had reservations about the whole idea which had increasingly grown over time. It seemed to her to be enormously risky both at a personal level and also for the country. If things went wrong, the implications could literally be global. She was devoutly wishing she hadn't mentioned Ekranoplans to that Captain all those months ago. And so it was with a great deal of trepidation and no way of getting out of it that she found herself on the afternoon train to Murmansk.

When she arrived, no one knew who she was or why she was there. Eventually, she managed to get hold of the Pilot in the officer's mess and tell him of the change of plan. After that things went a lot more smoothly. She liked the rugged looking, confident man almost as much as she detested the Special Forces Major. When he was introduced and told of her role he took one long hard look at her and simply instructed her to keep clear of any of his operations. Yuri apologised for him afterwards, simply saying that all Special Forces soldiers were misogynists. It was probably something they put in their tea. When Inga pointed out that technically he was Special Forces as well he just laughed and gave her an affectionate hug that he claimed proved he was no such thing. After that he took her under his wing, arranging to get special arctic clothing sorted out and taking her over to see the massive beast that was making the whole operation feasible.

Looking up at the cockpit, she turned to Yuri. Even after so short an acquaintance, she felt she could trust this man with her reservations. 'Yuri, is this really going to work? Aren't we taking an awful risk? What happens if things go wrong?'

Yuri thought carefully. He liked this girl, she was clearly very bright as well as attractive but he wasn't convinced about the benefit of having her along. Not that he had any choice in the matter. 'Yes, it is going to work. There's no reason at all why it shouldn't be simple. My machine is more than capable of getting us there and back in the time necessary and NATO will have no chance of intercepting us.'

'Forgive me for asking this but aren't you biased by your desire to see an Ekranoplan prove itself in a real operation? As I understand it, your bureau desperately needs that sort of endorsement to keep going.'

Yuri was surprised by the question. It cut straight to the heart of his motivation. This girl was as perceptive as she was beautiful. More to the point, it made him wonder for a second whether it really had made him blind to the dangers and risks they would all be taking. He mentally shrugged. It was far too late for all that.

He laughed ruefully. 'I don't know how you came to that conclusion but you're not far off the mark for all that my dear but whatever motivations we have they are all rather redundant now aren't they? If the go ahead comes through from Moscow then we're committed, whether we like it or not.'

He was interrupted by the Major who was striding over towards them. When he reached them he said nothing, simply handing over a piece of paper to Yuri. It had one word written on it. He studied it and then looked at Inga. 'So, as I said, we must concentrate on making this mission work. We go tonight.'

Chapter 32

The Pentagon

The monster team analyst was looking at the latest Blackbird photographs. After the call from London, they had all been on high alert, hoping that their years of covert surveillance were, at last, going to bear fruit. They had managed to get a Blackbird to divert slightly on its return flight from a routine mission. The pictures were quite clear and unequivocal. There was no sign of the Eaglet in its normal berth. However, on the edge of one photograph, it had been caught travelling north towards the ice.

As soon as the picture was analysed the information had been passed to London. However, by now there was a great deal of interest in what the Brits had discovered. The same information was passed up to the top brass and a White House briefing was being prepared.

Under the Arctic Ice Cap

The Captain of Swiftsure was getting confused over what on earth his adversary was up to. A few hours ago, the Russian had gone to periscope depth and streamed his long range radio antenna for what appeared to be a routing communications window. After that, he had changed his routine and now appeared to be heading back under the icecap. And then suddenly, the Russian had started transmitting on some sort of active sonar. It had only been for a few seconds but they had managed to record it. He was now standing in the sonar control room listening to it again and again. He looked at his sonar operator. 'Any ideas Jenkins?'

'Not a clue Sir. I've never heard anything like that before. If anything, it seems to be some form of coded message but there's nothing up here to receive it.'

'We need to tell London about this. We'll get clear of the ice as soon as we can and send them a signal.'

Andrei Orlov's coded signal was received by the little sonar set that was patiently waiting in the freezing water under the ice for that one thing. As soon as it was received, a relay was made and power was instantly supplied by the batteries to start the jammer. The jammer that was connected to the antenna that had been inserted through the ice by Andrei's diving team only days ago. Limitations in size and the cold arctic water meant that it only had power for a maximum of eighteen hours but that would be more than enough. The Russian scientists had puzzled for months over how the NATO base was communicating with its headquarters. In the end, they decided it could only be some form of directional system, possibly satellite based. The issue then was how to stop it working. It wouldn't be a high power system and so a jammer didn't need to be high power either but it had to cover a large frequency range. In the end, simplicity was the key. The jammer simply made sparks. Sparks flood the electromagnetic spectrum with noise. A simple amplifier shifted the noise into the right spectrum and no one would be able to transmit or receive within twenty miles of the antenna until the batteries went flat.

London

Rupert was feeling righteously justified and terrified in equal measure. The Americans had confirmed that the Eaglet had left and now there were reports from GCHQ of some form of interference operating on the ice not far from Pickwick. Attempts at communication with the base were proving fruitless. He had activated the emergency recall system for the building and his boss was on his way. He had also warned Fleet who assured him that urgent signals were being sent to Illustrious, although whether she was in any position to do anything was debatable as all her aircraft had gone ashore that morning. The timing looked deliberate.

As soon as his boss arrived, Rupert briefed him on the situation. As they spoke, Fleet rang and told them of a message they had just received from one of their submarines. Apparently, the Victor Three they had been following had sent a strange sonar pulse out under the ice. They had no idea what it was and were returning to try and find the Russian again. Fleet's assessment was that the timing was too exact for it to be anything other than the signal that turned on whatever it was that was blacking out communications. Rupert agreed.

'What a clusterfuck,' said Rupert to his boss. 'The bloody Soviets have timed this to perfection. Even though we know it's them we'll never be able to prove it. They'll be in and out long before we can get any assets there. God, what will they do to our people?'

His boss looked resigned. 'What do you think they'll do Rupert? They need deniability don't they?'

'Shit,' and then something else struck him. 'My God Sir, Good Bowman is about to go to Defcon One isn't it? What the hell will the Soviets think?' and he immediately answered his own question. 'They'll think they've been detected and we are about to start a shooting war because of it. We've got to stop the Americans Sir.'

His boss was looking stricken. 'Rupert, you stay here. You have full authority to act as you see fit. For goodness sake see what the navy have up their sleeve. I've got to get to Whitehall. If you come up with anything leave a message for me there.'

HMS Illustrious

The Caspian Monster

Jon and Brian were pouring over some exercise signals. Defcon I had just been declared and the lengthy response signal that Illustrious had to send had just been cleared for release.

'Well, that's us all ready for all out nuclear Armageddon,' said Jon. 'Let's just hope those Orange bounders see sense and back down.'

'With any luck, the whole bloody exercise will finish soon,' responded Brian. 'The signal I'm looking forward to is the one with ENDEX on it. Then we can all go to the bar for tea and medals.'

Suddenly the loudspeaker above their heads blared into life.

'D'you hear there, Lieutenant Commander Hunt and Lieutenant Pearce are requested on the bridge at the rush.'

'Bloody hell,' said Brian. 'They never say at the rush when piping for officers. It must be something really serious.'

They both shot out of the office and made their way up several flights of ladders to reach the bridge. Breathing heavily, they entered the bridge and the Captain signalled for them to go with him into his little cubby at the back of the compartment and closed the door behind them. Without speaking, he handed Jon a lengthy signal. Jon looked at it. It had been sent with FLASH precedence, something he had only ever seen before during the Falklands War as it only related to signals about contact with the enemy. He read on with dismay appearing on his face. When he got to the end he passed it to Brian without comment. While Brian was reading he turned to the Captain.

'Sir, you asked me what the other reason for us being here was and I'm afraid it was for this contingency. But it looks like we've been made complete fools of.'

Captain Test frowned. 'Slow down Jon, what exactly is Pickwick in the first place?'

Jon caught his mental breath. The signal gave him authority to divulge all the detail on Pickwick to the ships command team and he realised he would need to do some hurried background briefing.

The Caspian Monster

'Sorry Sir, look, rather than repeat myself, would it be a good idea to get the Commander, Wings and the Air Engineer Officer in on this? They will all need to hear it as well.'

The Captain nodded and stuck his head out telling the Officer of the Watch to pipe for the officers to meet in his sea cabin below the bridge as soon as possible. They then trooped back down to his cabin where they were shortly joined by the others.

'Jon, over to you, what the hell is this all about?'

Jon started with the overall background but kept it simple. He explained about the disguised listening station and briefly described his and Brian's trip out there last year and so how they came to be on board with the information in the first place. He then went on to describe how Fleet and MI6 had concerns over the base and whether it had been discovered. It now appeared that not only had the Soviets discovered the place but were actually in the process of doing something about it.

'What the hell is this Ekranoplan that they mention. Have you heard of it Jon? You're the aviator here after all,' asked the Commander.

'Sorry Sir, not a clue but from what the signal says it seems to be some form of a cross between a hovercraft and a seaplane. I'm afraid that whatever it is, it's going to do the job before we can get near.'

The Captain was looking thoughtful. 'Jon, if the Soviets knew they had been discovered, what do you think they would do?'

'Well, I guess they would have to turn around Sir. They will need to deny they did it. But if that's the case, why doesn't the government just tell them we know what they're up to? Surely they would have to stop.'

'Not if we can't prove it Jon and they know that,' replied Wings.

'If only the aircraft were still here, they're not actually that far away. Hang on a second,' and he turned to his bridge intercom. 'Officer of the Watch it's the Captain here.' He motioned Brian to hand back the signal he was still holding.

'Officer of the Watch Sir,' came the prompt reply.

'I want you to write down this position,' and he read out the Latitude and Longitude of Pickwick from the signal in his hand. 'I know it's up beyond the ice limit but I want you to plot its position and turn us onto an intercept course at maximum revolutions. When you've worked out when we'll get close to the ice let me know.'

'Aye, aye Sir,' came the reply from a clearly intrigued voice. The Captain turned off the intercom before he could be asked any more.

'That will at least get us heading in the right direction. So, any ideas on what the hell else we can do?'

Wings was first to respond. 'I think we should recall the squadron Sir. It will take hours for them to get here and as we're now heading away from them, it may be impossible but we should at least try.'

The Captain nodded. 'Look at the speed time problem and then send a signal as soon as the meeting is over please. Now, anything else?'

The Air Engineer who had been silent up until now looked at Wings and the Captain with a strange look on his face. 'Would a Sea King be able to get there in time? If say, we could launch in an hour and half?'

The Captain looked puzzled but turned to Jon and Wings, 'Well?'

Wings answered for them while looking to Jon for confirmation. 'From what we know, yes it could but we haven't got a Sea King and for that matter, we haven't got any pilots.'

'Sorry everyone, that's not quite true. We do have one,' replied the AEO. 'We have the Hangar Queen and I thought Lieutenant Commander Hunt was a Jungly pilot.'

Chapter 33

The Arctic Sea

Yuri sat at the controls of Snezhana as she flew towards the distant ice pack. His original plan had been to get there while there was still some daylight to ensure he could pick his point of access. Although the ice surface was generally smooth and posed no problem to an Ekranoplan flying at over twenty metres there were still pressure ridges that could be of concern. Unfortunately, the weather had stepped in once again. In some ways, it was perfect. Cloud cover had set in and the wind was very light. Unfortunately, it was extremely cold. Despite their lashed up de-icing system they had already been forced to land once to clear accumulations of ice from the rear of the fuselage. However, the ice cap was visible now to the nose radar and they should be there soon even though it was now quite dark. He had already decided on one more landing just before they arrived at the boundary. He didn't want to be carrying a burden of frozen water for the next critical leg of the trip. The total loss of time would be less than an hour and that was well within his margins.

He looked over at the young girl sitting in the co-pilot's seat. He had decided to fly alone on this operation with just his flight engineer behind him for company, so he had offered the seat to Inga. It was far more comfortable than the webbing seats the troops were using in the cavernous hold behind them. And anyway he liked her company. The Major seemed to have no conversational skills whatsoever although Yuri suspected that nerves were also playing a part in his demeanour. He couldn't work Inga out. He understood the reason she was there. It had been explained that her boss had gone missing and she was the only person available to step in at the last moment. But when he quizzed her about what her role was, she seemed almost as puzzled as he was.

'So Inga, see that line on the radar scope, that's the edge of the ice. As you can see, it's not well defined but as long as we stay flying we will just glide over it. Just before we get there we'll land quickly once more and clear any ice off the tail and then we'll be on our way with a clean hull.'

Inga nodded looking thoughtful. 'Yuri, you know I didn't get involved in all your detailed technical planning. I still don't understand how we will find this place. It's incredibly well camouflaged. I know, I've seen the intelligence data.'

Yuri laughed. 'That's where our good friend Captain Orlov has come in. Some days ago he relocated it from below and has put up a radio mast nearby that is now jamming their communications.'

'I don't see how that helps us find it.'

'Ah, yes sorry, he also sent a message saying exactly how far away and on what bearing the transmitter is from the place. If you look here on the dashboard,' and he tapped a small gauge. 'This is a homing indicator. The jammer is also transmitting a signal to us which we can follow. I have already inputted the offset he gave us, so when that reads zero we have arrived.'

'But how will you stop this massive machine exactly on the spot?'

'I won't, I aim to land about two kilometres short to give us time to slow down and then taxi slowly until we're almost there. Our brave soldiers will then jump out and walk the rest of the way.'

'And if they can't find it?'

'Good question, in that case we just go home. But we'll be very close and they are very thorough people. However, my feeling is that if we don't locate it nothing will really have been lost. The base will know we were there. Snezhana is hardly quiet. Maybe it will convince them that they need to pull out now that we both know what they're up to.'

Inga smiled, 'And you will have proved the capability of this incredible machine either way of course.'

'Clever girl,' laughed Yuri. 'In some ways, I rather hope that is the outcome. I don't suppose the personnel in the base are just going to give up without some form of a fight. That's why we have troops on board after all. I'm a pilot, not a soldier and I really don't want to be involved in people getting killed, theirs or ours.'

Inga agreed. 'I may be KGB Yuri but I never envisioned being involved in an active operation like this.'

'So, why did you join my dear?'

Inga trusted Yuri. She didn't really know why. She had only met him a day ago but she had already discovered he was married with a son he was immensely proud of and that his whole life seemed to be tied up with these ridiculous machines. Before she knew it, she found herself telling him the whole story. How she had been recruited as a child and indoctrinated at the KGB school. She skipped some of the detail of her early work but explained how she had operated in Norway and started the crazy chain of events that led to her presence here in the cockpit of Snezhana. She even told him of the death of her father and how she was starting to change her view of the system she was living in.

Yuri listened in silence. He knew these sorts of things went on of course. But it was a world so far away from his, a world of flying and engineering as to seem almost on a different planet. Her description of life in Norway was astounding. Coming from anyone else he would have put it down as pure propaganda. However, he believed her, why shouldn't he? He knew she had nothing to hide. When she described her homecoming to her dying father he found he could relate to much of what she said. Yuri had always been cosseted from the harsher realities of Soviet life but he wasn't blind to what went on elsewhere. However, if even half of what she said was true about life in the West what did that say about the Soviet system? Like most Russians, he had been bought up in an

The Caspian Monster

unshakeable belief in communism. Anyway, it was rather late to be having thoughts like this. They had a job to do.

'Well my dear, you have my sympathy you really do but we have a mission to fly and now it's time for another quick landing.'

He called over the intercom to warn the passengers and then gently throttled back to allow the big machine to slowly descend towards the invisible sea in the blackness below. A sudden bump announced contact and he gradually closed the throttles even more until they were coasting slowly forward.

As Yuri taxied the aircraft on the water Inga reflected on the last two days. She knew that had he been here, Mikhael would have been revelling in the mission but she just felt confused, disorientated and not a little bit scared. It was one thing to read about this sort of thing from the security of an office desk, quite another to be along for the ride. Working in the field in Norway had been different of course. That had been fun. She had considerable autonomy and working with people was what she did. Working with machines like this was completely alien as was accompanying a load of heavily armed, mean looking soldiers, on a covert mission into effectively hostile territory. When she had sat next to Yuri for the first time as the Ekranoplan took off it had been exhilarating. The noise and power of the machine was awesome. Once they were airborne the sensation of skimming the sea's surface at such high speed was just fantastic. She had flown on commercial airliners of course but it was nothing compared to this. However, as the minutes ticked away her doubts kept returning. What would they really discover when they arrived? What would happen? Would the NATO people really give up without a fight? And if they didn't, what was the risk that the whole mission could fail?

The crewman from the tail area called to say that the ice had cleared and Yuri instructed the flight engineer to start up the two forward jet engines. They were soon airborne again. This time Yuri kept the two nose engines going and took the machine up as high as he could. Settling at just under forty metres, he knew this would give them the greatest safety margin in case they needed to clear any invisible ridges in the ice as they coasted in even though it made the flying task much harder. With such a short trip in mind, he intended to keep them operating all the way to their destination. The increased fuel consumption would be no problem. They had fuel to spare. He watched the radar and put on the aircraft's powerful landing lights. They soon spotted the white of ice floes which was soon replaced by the continual white of the ice sheet. He turned the lights off again and breathed a sigh of relief. Only just under two hours to go and they would arrive.

Chapter 34

HMS Illustrious

Jon couldn't believe what he was doing. He and Brian were dressed in full flying gear and about to man up a wreck of an aircraft and fly a mission with very little idea of the outcome except that it would be bloody dangerous. To help him he had five extra crewmen and what a team they were. One fit marine, three cripples and a Cook.

Earlier on, when the ship's AEO had mentioned the Hanger Queen everyone had looked blank.

The AEO put them out of their misery. 'The squadron embarked nine aircraft remember? They bought nine even though they only needed eight so they had spare if it was needed.'

The penny dropped. 'But hang on,' said Jon. 'Being a Hangar Queen means it's been robbed of loads of stuff to provide bits for the others. Can it even fly?'

The AEO nodded. 'I'm pretty sure it can. Hang on a second,' and he picked up a telephone. He called the Air Maintenance Control Office and asked for the duty engineer to bring the documentation for the aircraft up to the Captain's cabin as soon as possible.

Wings then spoke, 'OK, let's look at this but Jon you haven't flown for how long?'

'Er, formally the answer to that is since February last year Sir but I'd better confess that I did sneak a trip in one of the cabs when they were doing deck landing work the other day. The Squadron CO knew but I sort of hoped that no one else had noticed. It was a bit like riding a bike. It was almost like I hadn't been away at all.'

Wings chuckled, 'Well, I don't suppose that actually broke any rules if it was authorised by the CO but that still doesn't answer the

The Caspian Monster

question of whether you are up to a full night time operational sortie.'

'Don't worry Sir, I can sit next to him and make sure he doesn't get lost,' interjected Brian.

Captain Test looked thoughtful. 'You two have done some pretty good stuff together in the past. Wings, I bow to your judgement on this but if we can get the aircraft serviceable, I think we should give it a try. What's your view?'

Wings knew it was his decision. He was the senior aviator on board but he also knew that the Captain had commanded Jon and Brian during the Falklands and they had achieved some tremendous results down there. Anyway, this was a serious operational emergency. Isn't that what they trained for? 'Sir, if Jon says he wants to try then we should do everything we can to make this work.'

He was interrupted by a knock on the door. A head poked around and a young Lieutenant in white overalls handed a long black book to the AEO.

'Ah Mike,' said the AEO to the Lieutenant. 'Do everything you can to get Victor Foxtrot in a flyable state. I want her ranged and ready as soon as possible and before you ask this is an operational emergency and the rule book just went out of the window understand? I'll be down in a few minutes to give you the full story.'

The Lieutenant nodded and disappeared.

'Right, let's have a look,' said the AEO as he thumbed through the pages. 'OK, here we are, the radios have been robbed, as have the troop seats and oh dear, this could be more serious, the main ASE gyros and the radar altimeter. How do you feel about flying with no stab and no Rad Alt Jon?'

Jon saw the look on the Captain's face. 'ASE stands for Automatic Stabilisation Equipment Sir. Helicopters are inherently unstable in flight. There is a gyroscopic system in most of them that provides automatic stability making them much easier to fly. Without it, it also means some other functions like the automatic height hold won't work. The Rad Alt gives me accurate height over the sea and is normally a no go item for night flying. But to be quite honest, if the engines, rotors and flying controls work I think we should give it a try.'

'Are you sure Jon?' asked Wings. 'It's going to make things bloody difficult.'

'Frankly Sir, I often fly stab out. It keeps me on my toes and if we are going to fly over sea and flat ice the Rad Alt isn't critical. I'm up for it.'

'Right,' said the AEO getting up from his chair. 'I'm off down the hangar. I'll pass an estimate of when we'll be ready as soon as I have one.'

Jon was still thinking. 'Fine, we have an aircraft of sorts but what on earth do I do when I get up there?'

'Good question,' said the Captain. 'The key thing will be to get information. If you can get some form of tangible evidence that it's the Soviets then that will be the main aim. If you can get there before them then I suggest you simply land on, put on all your lights and let them see you. I suspect they will just fly on past.'

'What if they're already ransacking the place and shooting people? I'm going to be unarmed and rather outnumbered.'

'As I said, getting evidence will be the priority but no we shouldn't just sit and watch them committing a war crime. But I don't see what armament we could give you.'

Wings had an idea, 'Sir, Jon, we've got a few Royals left on board in sick bay. They couldn't get ashore for various reasons. Maybe some of them will be fit enough to go along. Why don't you and I go down there and see if any are suitable?'

The Captain nodded at the idea. 'Let me know as soon as you can. Meanwhile, the Commander and I will start drafting a signal for Fleet.'

The ship's sick bay was quiet when they entered. The duty Leading Medical Assistant looked surprised to see his visitors and even more surprised when they said what they wanted. He hurried

The Caspian Monster

off to find the duty doctor while Jon and Wings went into the little ward. The first face Jon saw was eerily familiar but before he could say anything the man spoke first.

'Hello again Sir. I didn't expect to see you again,' and he got up from the armchair he had been lounging in.

'Well bugger me, Sergeant McCaul. What the hell are you doing loafing about in here?'

The Sergeant smiled ruefully. 'I'm back with the lads again Sir after my little sojourn with the SBS and should have been ashore with them now but the bloody medic wouldn't let me go.'

'That's right Sergeant,' came a cheerful voice from behind as the doctor entered. 'You can't go poncing around in the snow with a broken ankle.'

The Sergeant smiled ruefully and showed Jon the plaster cast that went half way up his calf. 'Teach me to get carried away during fitness training. I don't know, we did all that stuff during the Falklands without getting a scratch and I manage to break the bloody thing running across the flight deck. I tried to tell the doc here that it's the same as wearing a ski boot but he just wouldn't have it.'

'I take it you two are acquainted?' said Wings with a smile.

'Yes Sir, the Sergeant and I had some fun together down south but it's sort of classified I'm afraid.'

'That's alright, I understand,' and then turning to the doctor he outlined his problem.

The Sergeant spoke with steel in his voice before the doctor could get a word in reply. 'I'm going. You need me and I'm the most experienced soldier on board.'

Jon agreed, 'Yes, I agree and I couldn't think of anyone I'd rather have with me, ankle in plaster or not.'

'Well,' said the doctor. 'If you'd actually let me get a word in edgewise. I was going to agree as well. We can sort the ankle out and you should be reasonably mobile, certainly to cover the short distances you seem to be talking about.'

'Sir,' said a happy looking Sergeant. 'There are three other lads here I reckon we could use. Jones had a fever but he's over it, Jenkins broke three fingers but they're on his left hand, so his trigger finger will be fine and Peterson has got a bollocksed foot like me.' He looked defiantly at the doc who nodded reluctant agreement.

'And what about me?' came a voice from the other side of the room.

'Cook Smith, what the hell are you doing here and more importantly why the hell do you think you should be included?' asked Jon who recognised the extrovert chef from his old squadron.

'Wouldn't let me go ashore Sir 'cos I've got a pier head jump draft back to Yeovilton. I've just finished a leaving medical and overheard your conversation. As to why I should be going. I'm the best shot on the squadron, probably on the ship, as you well know.'

Jon did know, he prided himself on being handy with a rifle but Smith had shown everyone up during the squadron's annual weapons test last year. So much so, that the Marine Sergeant instructor had recommended him for a snipers course if ever he could be spared. It was strange, Smith was totally wasted as a chef. He had the brains and skill to make far more of himself but every attempt to do so was met with a stubborn refusal. Smith was clearly content with life and what he did.

Jon looked at Sergeant McCaul, 'It's your decision Sergeant but I would like to have him along. He can be a right pain in the ass but my God can he shoot.'

'I'll get on it straight away Sir.'

'Here's the brief, get you guys kitted out with full arctic gear and fighting order only. We'll only be staying a few hours. Get hold of the Gunnery officer and get whatever weapons and ammunition you can get your hands on. Rifles, grenades, GPMGs, anything we have. There's plenty of room in the aircraft with only five of you. Oh and there are no seats either, so you'll just have to sit on the floor.' He didn't mention all the other missing items that would make the trip harder. There was no need to alarm his passengers any more than necessary.

And so here he was now, on the pitch black flight deck, manning up Sea King Mark Four, call sign Victor Foxtrot. Apart from a few deck landings from the left hand seat the other day he hadn't flown for a year. The aeroplane he was flying was a mess, with several normally critical systems missing and he was going to go up against an unknown enemy, who almost certainly outnumbered his team of cripples significantly and he had no real plan of action when he arrived.

Brian climbed into the left hand cockpit seat just as Jon was strapping in. 'Just like old times mate. Bet you missed it as much as me.'

Number 10 Downing Street

The Prime Minister had just put down the telephone to the President of the United States. Sitting to one side of her was the Secretary of State for Defence and on the other a senior member of the Security Services. They had been listening in on the conversation via the speakerphone

'Well gentlemen, you heard what he said, any views?'

'I'm sorry Prime Minister,' said the Secretary of State, 'but that man has an attitude problem.'

She smiled tightly at the remark. 'I'm no apologist for him but he has decided on a firm policy with the Soviets and of course this situation just plays into his hands.'

'Do you think he will really restrain himself based on our assurances? He lied to you over the Grenada affair.'

She winced at the memory. 'The difference is that he doesn't have any military forces near the place this time. Does he?'

'No Ma'am, you're right and all we have is an Aircraft Carrier with only one aircraft on board.'

'I might just have forgotten to mention that fact as no doubt you may have noticed. Now, can we really do the job? The signal from Illustrious is very upbeat and they rightly make the point that if the Soviets are really intent on a raid then any chance of being exposed will stop them in their tracks.'

The Secretary of State considered his reply carefully. 'At best, that's what will happen but only if our people can make their presence felt before they've done something silly. Otherwise, we'll just have to hope our guys can get back with some evidence of their actions.'

'I take it by something silly, you mean killing people.'

'Yes Maam, that's exactly what I mean.'

She sighed. There really wasn't anything else she could do. Illustrious had already gone ahead. She could recall them but there was no reason to do so. She may be less hawkish than the US President but she was damned if she would let the Soviets get away with such a blatant act of aggression as this.

The Secretary of State broke into her thoughts. 'Prime Minister, frankly that's not what really worries me. NATO went to Defcon One an hour ago for this exercise. How will the Russians see that? If they think it's because we know what they're up to then I'm sorry, I've no idea how they will react.'

'Nor have I and as you heard I made that point repeatedly but he sees it as a matter of strength and weakness and he just doesn't want to seem weak. At least we got him to agree not to get personally involved and attend at SHAPE. God knows how that would have been viewed by the other side.'

The Security Service head then spoke. 'Prime Minister, we are not activating any real forces for the exercise. We know that they keep an eye on all our bases. They will see we're not taking any real military action on the ground and so this must be just a headquarters exercise.'

'With the exception of a military exercise in Norway of course although we do this it at this time of year every year,' said the Secretary of State.

'And of course the other single aircraft heading in the opposite direction,' she sighed. 'So be it gentlemen, let's just pray our navy deliver the goods.'

Chapter 35

Moscow

General Secretary Yuri Andropov was meeting with the Minister of Defence, Dmitry Ustinov and his own successor at the KGB, Victor Chebrikov. The three men were the only ones who knew about the operation in the Arctic. It had been decided that the Politburo did not need to know about the raid. That was until it could be announced as a success of course.

The General Secretary wasn't feeling well. Continued kidney problems had dogged him of late but he had no intention of it either affecting his performance or of his colleagues finding out. Politics at this level were vicious enough without an obvious weakness for his enemies to latch on to.

'Dmitry, what is the status of NATO now?' he asked anxiously.

'General Secretary, one hour ago they declared Defence Condition One from their headquarters and it seems that all the NATO countries headquarters are conducting the relevant preparations. Our understanding of the NATO definition is and I quote 'Defence Condition No 1 is declared when there are obvious indications of preparation to begin military operations. It is considered that war is inevitable and may start at any moment.'

Yuri Andropov looked sick. 'But is this for real or are they just exercising?'

'Comrade Secretary, we just don't know. Since this new President of theirs came to power they have been harassing our armed forces all around the world. For the last few months they have continued to express outrage over the spying airliner we shot down. We saw an enormous increase in ciphered communications between London and Washington late last year. It could have been over the invasion of that little Caribbean island or it could have been prenuclear consultation. We have no way of knowing. And now this incredible build up of secure communication traffic and increase in their readiness state. On the other hand, I sent an urgent signal to all our sections for evidence of actual military activity. The results seem inconclusive. We have this exercise the British are conducting in Norway but they do it every year at this time. Otherwise, most bases seem quiet. But of course they can deploy their Pershing missiles within minutes and their ballistic submarines can fire at any time.'

'Right,' said the General Secretary. 'We have agreed that the only way to pre-empt a NATO strike is to strike first but I am yet to be totally convinced that we are in that situation. But I cannot and will not take any risks. All our nuclear forces are to go on full alert, aircraft, submarines and the missile silos. I will not fire first but we must be able to retaliate at a moment's notice.'

The other two men nodded agreement.

Andropov turned to the head of the KGB. 'Now Victor, what of the Arctic operation? We've allowed it to go ahead for the same reasons that we are increasing our alert status. Having our submarines bottled up is simply unacceptable. However, I am beginning to wonder whether we have made a big mistake and should call it off. If something goes wrong or if NATO finds out what we are doing it could trip this nuclear trigger we are now holding in our hands.'

'Comrade Secretary, I'm sorry but it's too late for that. They will be arriving shortly and are inside the operating area of the jamming system we set up. It can't be turned off and won't stop until the batteries powering it die. We have no way of communicating with them. I'm afraid that whatever happens now is out of our control.'

The General Secretary nodded unhappily. This was all fast becoming a nightmare.

The Arctic Circle

Snezhana was almost there. Yuri was concentrating on the homing indicator dial. Minute adjustments to the giant machines heading was keeping the needle in the middle and he watched as the range counted down. Next to him, Inga sat in tense silence looking out of the window at the white glare of ice and snow illuminated in the Ekranoplan's powerful landing lights which Yuri had just turned on.

'Alright everyone,' he called over the intercom system. 'Starting landing sequence now.'

He gently pulled the throttle levers of the two forward engines to idle and they slowed and sank down to twenty metres altitude. He then throttled back the turboprop on the tail and Snezhana slowed down even more and gently started to descend. When the speed had reduced to one hundred and twenty kilometres an hour he let her settle onto the ice. There was a sharp shock through the fuselage and then a violent drumming noise as the bottom of the hull scraped across the hard surface. She took a long time to slow down. Ice and snow has much less drag than the sea but Yuri had allowed for that and by the time they were at a fast walking pace there was still almost a kilometre to go. He throttled up the two forward jets to one third power and lowered the massive rear flaps on the short stubby wings. The exhaust gasses from the two jets were now being trapped below the wings and helping keep the weight of the machine off the surface. Yuri had also discovered it helped to blow any recirculating snow and ice away from the cockpit area and so allowed him to see better. Not that there was much to see anyway just a vague featureless plain with a few low humps of pressure ice here and there.

He taxied forward for another three quarters of a kilometre and then throttled all the engines back to idle. He called to the flight engineer to shut down the two forward engines and to keep the turbo prop running at idle. It had been agreed that there was too much risk of not being able to get a restart of the turbine engine if it was shut down and allowed to cool for several hours. Yuri and his engineer would stay in the cockpit and keep Snezhana ready for a rapid getaway if that was what was needed.

As soon as they had stopped, he called the Major to the cockpit. He pointed to the homing indicator. 'Dead ahead of us, on a bearing of three two two and three hundred and twenty metres away.'

The Major nodded and climbed back into the hold. His team had already unstrapped and were waiting for him clustered around the exit door in the side of the fuselage weapons at the ready. He was the first out and as expected the snow cover was hard and easy to walk on. He led his men to the front of the machine where he attached the device he was holding to a ringbolt on the front of the Ekranoplan. He had to smile inwardly at himself. Here they were, with all this fabulous technology and he was going to use a simple old fashioned tape measure to find his enemy. He let out three hundred and twenty metres and sighted back towards the nose of the Ekranoplan. When satisfied that he was in the correct place, he signalled to one of his team who pushed a large pointed metal pole into the ice. The search could start. He found himself having to shout to be heard by his men. Even this far away from the idling turbo prop the noise was overpowering. He understood why it had to be kept running but hadn't realised just how noisy it was. So, it was with a lot of shouting and hand gestures that he got his men searching methodically out from their datum position.

In the end, it was the Major who found what they wanted. The cloud cover had gone and the stars were out in force. There wouldn't be a moon tonight but the starlight was remarkably good especially to night adapted eyes. Even so, it was his foot that made the discovery. Without warning, he tripped over something. When he looked closely he could see a wire which was part of a series of guys holding up a small white painted pole. He called over the scientist who had come with them and asked him what he thought it was.

'High Frequency radio aerial,' he shouted over the noise of the Ekranoplan.

The Caspian Monster

A feeling of dread stole over the Major. Had they been wrong all along? Were they using simple radio after all?

'Don't worry,' said the scientist. 'The jammer will cover any frequency this thing operates on. This is temporary. They must have put it up when they lost their main communications to try and re-establish contact. The entrance to the base must be around here somewhere.'

Feeling relieved, the Major started groping around in the snow by the base of the aerial. His gloved fingers soon found what he was looking for, the wire that connected the aerial to its transmitter. He started following it through the snow. He cursed, when after a few metres it ended. Clearly, it had been cut once it was found to be useless. Nevertheless, the place should be down this line and now looking carefully in the snow he could make out faint marks in the wan starlight. The sort of thing you might do to cover footprints as you retreated. He followed the trail and with a shout of triumph, he found what he had been looking for, a small indentation in the snow and the clear outline of a hatch. He realised that without being able to follow the trail he would never have seen it. He could have walked two feet by and it would have been invisible.

This looked a difficult job. Painted white, the hatch was circular with a large unlocking ring in the centre just like you would have on a submarine. It also looked to be very substantial. If those on the other side didn't want them to get in then they could make it very difficult. He signalled his men and when they arrived they made ready with the cutting gear and explosives.

Inga and Yuri were watching from the cockpit. They saw the Major start gesticulating and it was immediately apparent that they had found what they were looking for.

'Well young lady, you've no excuse to hang around in the warm any more. It looks like we're not going home empty handed mores the pity. You'd better get down there and do whatever it is you came to do.' said Yuri in a sober tone.

Inga reluctantly agreed not really wanting to leave the warm womb of the cockpit but knowing she had no choice. She made her way down into the hold and put on her heavy arctic coat and hat before exiting out onto the ice.

Chapter 36

HMS Illustrious

Jon looked over at Brian once they had strapped into their seats in the cockpit.

'Just one minor problem old chap.'

'Whassat then, me old aviating buddy?'

'For the life of me, I can't remember how to start up this sodding machine, don't suppose you know how?'

Just for a second, Brian was worried that Jon was serious. Then he saw the look on his face.

Jon chucked him the small ring binder of Flight Reference cards. 'Nah, just a joke but I'd hate to miss something out especially when we spread the rotor blades, so just follow them through with me please. I would really hate to make a fuck up, that would really ruin the whole evening. Our passengers in the first class cabin definitely wouldn't be impressed.'

Sitting on the floor in the back, the five passengers grinned at each other in various degrees of amusement and trepidation. Still, as Jon intended, if the pilot could make light of the trip then maybe it would be alright. They were all wearing flying helmets which the ship had managed to provide at Jon's request. He was going to put the transit time to good use talking over plans as they flew north. They were all also wearing Arctic white smocks and trousers over their military gear for camouflage. In the back, under a cargo net, were an assortment of rifles, hand and smoke grenades, sub machine guns and one large General Purpose Machine Gun. Surrounding the weapons were several large boxes of ammunition.

While they were waiting for the ground power to be connected, Jon did a final check with Brian. 'So we've got the bombs and bullets. Did you manage to acquire a sat phone? I'm sure these ships carry one.'

'Yes, it's in the back with a spare battery. Let's just hope we can find out what's causing the interference so we can do something about it and then be able to use the damn thing. The ship says they'll signal Northwood and tell them we have it. That's where the UK terminal is.'

'Good, now we've definitely not got any other radios, so we will be on our own once we're airborne but we've got our personal Search and Rescue Beacons if something really goes wrong. Oh and I've got a present for you.' He reached down to his nav bag at his side and handed Brian a pair of the small binocular night vision goggles.

Brian looked confused. 'Shouldn't you be using these on your helmet?'

'I would do if they worked properly but one tube is bust, so I can't fly on them but you can look through the working tube and help find the bad guys with it. It's all the ship had as the rest went ashore with the squadron the other day.'

'Good idea,' said Brian taking the NVG. 'Oh and I found a sixteen foot load lifting stop in the cabin. No idea what use it could be but you never know, so I left it in.'

'OK, listen up everyone,' called Jon over the intercom as the ground power light came on. 'We're about to start up. Just sit tight while we get going and launch. Once we're in the cruise we will need to talk things over as much as we can. Everyone happy?'

An assortment of replies were made and Brian leaned around to look over his seat and got a cheerful thumbs up from the Sergeant.

While Jon was getting Victor Foxtrot burning and turning Captain Test put another contingency plan into force. 'Officer of the Watch, turn off our navigation lights and then order full astern please.'

The Caspian Monster

The officer grinned wickedly at the Captain. The ship had already gone to Emergency Stations in preparation and all other lights were already off with the ship in a fully darkened state.

'Aye, Aye Sir,' and he did as he was told.

A seventeen thousand ton warship doesn't respond quickly to emergency orders but even so her speed rapidly started to decrease.

The Captain went out to the bridge wing and looked aft through his binoculars.

Five hundred yards astern, the Russian AGI was taken completely by surprise. Firstly, the only visual reference she had to accurately keep station on the big ship disappeared and then it suddenly became apparent that the looming black bulk of the stern of the Carrier was approaching at an alarming rate. The deck officer in the AGI dithered and that made things even worse. He suddenly realised he had to do several things. He pushed the emergency button to summon the Captain and then ordered the wheel put hard over. He should have done it the other way round. With a mighty crash, the bow of the little ship hit a massive glancing blow on the port side of the stern of the bigger ship. The Carrier then scraped down the side with the overhang smashing several aerials and pushing the AGI over on her side. Suddenly, she came clear and righted herself in a vicious roll which almost caught a red faced, angry Captain off his guard as he came up the ladder to the bridge and sent him tumbling back down.

On Illustrious, Captain Test grinned. He called to the Officer of the Watch to resume course and speed and then went to the damage control intercom and called the Commander for a damage assessment.

'Nothing serious Sir, as expected,' came the prompt reply. 'One small dent and we're going to have some repainting to do when we get home but you should see the other guy.'

The Caspian Monster

'Oh but I did,' laughed the Captain. 'Just for once, I don't think anyone will give us a bollocking for a collision at sea.' He then went to the maritime VHF radio and put a call out on channel 16, the international hailing and emergency frequency.

'Russian intelligence gathering trawler, this is British Warship Illustrious. Oops, sorry about that. I hope you are OK. We had a little problem with our engines for a second there. Still, you shouldn't have been following so closely and of course under international collision rules you were the overtaking vessel, so you really should have kept clear you know. If you need any assistance please feel free to ask.'

There was no reply and the AGI slowly disappeared astern.

On the helicopter they had the rotors turning and were just about ready to go when they felt a slight lurch and Jon immediately realised it was Captain Test's little anti-AGI manoeuvre. Unfortunately, with no radios, he also couldn't use the deck intercom system to ask Flyco whether it had been successful. However, the Flight Deck Officer came over and plugged his head set into the side of the helicopter.

'Our Russian friend seems to taken fright and fucked off, there's a shame. You should be good for an unobserved launch. You're clear to go on the green light and good luck.'

Jon acknowledged the FDO with a 'thank you' and a thumbs up and then turned to Brian.

'Pre-take off checks please, let's get airborne.'

Fifteen minutes later and Jon was starting relax just a little. The take off had been interesting to say the least. With no stabilisation, the Sea King had lurched off the deck with the out of practice Jon having to fight the urge to over control. Luckily, they made it up and clear into the black night without clobbering the ship with the main rotors or any other sensitive part of the aircraft. Even so, it had taken him this long to start relaxing and calm his heart rate. He had climbed to a thousand feet, much higher than he would normally want to be but without accurate height information, he felt it safer to have some altitude in hand. But now with all temperatures and pressures in the green and a steady heading he felt able to start thinking ahead. Brian, with his normal sixth sense, had realised the pressure he was under and had kept everyone quiet while Jon settled down.

'Right, you chaps in the back,' he called over the intercom. 'Everything looks good and we should be able to see the whites of their eyes in about an hour. So, let's take stock and think of a few plans. Firstly, Sergeant can you catalogue all the weapons we managed to snaffle please?'

Sergeant McCaul did so and suggested that everyone should have an SLR rifle and a nine millimetre pistol. He and the three other marines would take the explosive grenades as they were properly trained to use them but he proposed that everyone took at least two smoke grenades as they were simple and reasonably safe to use. He proposed that he should take GPMG and Jon agreed as long as they shared the load of the heavy weapon if they had any distance to travel.

They had also relieved the ship of the small hand held radios they normally used for routine local communications with the ship's boats. They didn't have much range but should be fine for what they were planning. There were enough for all to have one each. Brian gave a quick brief on how to use them and told them all to use their surnames as call signs.

'Now on top of guns, Brian here has our other secret weapon. It's one of the ships Hasselblad intelligence cameras and it's loaded with special low light film. Our main aim is to deter the Soviets and if necessary get hard evidence of their actions. We really don't want a shooting war as we've no idea of their strength and there could be a shit load of them.'

'What are you suggesting then Sir?' came Cook Smith's voice which sounded slightly disappointed. 'Just go in and take photos?'

'No, that won't be enough. Look, if we get there first then it's quite simple. I'll land next to the base. A team of you can go and try to find this jammer or whatever it is. It must be on the surface nearby. We'll wait by the aircraft. The betting is that if we are seen they will just fly on by as they'll realise they've been rumbled.'

'Fucking hope so,' came an anonymous mumble.

'Yes, well that's why we get paid. Anyway, my betting is that they'll already be on the ground, so it's a moot point. If they are, they will have this weird Ekranoplan thing. Apparently, it's quite big and will be hard to miss. With Lieutenant Pearce using the one NVG we've got we should be able to spot them from a reasonable distance and land without them knowing. If we can do that, we will do so and then try to sneak up on them. The first priority will be to get some photos. But after that, it very much depends on what's going on. Somehow, we need to stop them from hurting anyone and get them to fuck off home without any damage being done.'

'And if it's too late for that?'

'We start shooting. Anyone got any better ideas?'

No one had.

Chapter 37

Pickwick

Inga gasped at the cold as she stepped into the Arctic night. She hadn't realised just what a temperature difference there was once she was outside of the warmth of the Ekranoplan. Above her, the stars were shining in the glory of a clear pollution free arctic night. It enabled her to see remarkably clearly. The snow crunched beneath her feet. The Major and his men were doing something about five hundred metres away, so she headed in their direction as she pulled the hood of her jacket over her head and quickly donned her thick arctic gloves. The whine of the turbine engine and thump of the colossal contra rotating propellers way above her head drowned out any other sounds.

As she approached the group of men, she could see they were searching the area and clearing snow from around the hatch she could now make out.

She went up to the Major. She found his impersonal hard face quite frightening but refused to be intimidated. 'So, we've found what we wanted Major?'

He smiled a humourless smile at her. 'As usual, nothing is what you expect. Look here, we have a hatch of some sort but nothing above the ice. We expected buildings of some sort. There's nothing like that. This could even be the top of a submarine except the shape is all wrong. Getting the hatch open is going to be difficult.'

'But surely there'll be an air vent of some sort? They will have to breathe won't they?'

The Major looked at her with something approaching respect for a second. 'Yes and that's what my men are searching for at the moment but frankly it is probably a waste of time. If this is submarine technology they are using they could probably stay sealed up for much longer than we dare stay here.'

'So, we have to get them to open the hatch somehow?'

'Or blow it open.'

'Won't that be dangerous to the men in there?'

He snorted in contempt. 'Don't be stupid girl. This isn't a game.'

Inga bristled at his tone, 'I thought we wanted these men as political prisoners, as bargaining chips?' she retorted angrily.

'Maybe, but that's a bit academic if we can't get them to come out. Isn't it?'

She had to acknowledge his logic even if she didn't like it much.

'Stop all that,' the Major called loudly to his men. 'We're going to try and blow it open.'

One of his men approached with a large wooden box. He opened it up and removed several tubes of plastic explosive. The Major nodded at him and indicated to get on with it while waving at everyone else to move clear. Inga, along with the other soldiers, moved several hundred metres away and waited for the preparations to finish.

Soon the Major and his explosives expert approached, trailing wire from a reel. When they reached the group, he stopped, beckoning for them all to get down while he attached one wire from the reel to one of the terminals of a small battery. When everyone was ready he held the other wire to the other terminal and there was a distant thump and a cloud of snow rose around the area of the hatch. Inga was surprised at how unimpressive it was and how little noise it had made. But hopefully it would have been enough to blow the hatch although she dreaded what it might have done to the men inside.

Weapons raised, they cautiously approached the hatch. It had blown clear and left a gaping hole. Splintered metal splayed out around the remains of the access tower. The major leaned over cautiously.

'Shit,' he exclaimed. 'This is ridiculous. They've really designed this well and if we're not careful it's going to take far too long. Which is probably what they intended in the first place.'

Twelve feet below, at the bottom of a set of rungs, was another hatch that looked identical to the one they had just blown. He called his demolitions expert over and they talked quietly for a few minutes. The other man was gesticulating and looked far from happy.

'Problems?' asked Inga refusing to be shut out of the dialogue. After all she was part of the team and technically a senior one at that.

The Major was looking frustrated. 'My man here says that if we put the same amount of explosive on that hatch it could collapse the whole structure on top of it and then we'd never get in. In fact, he thinks it's been designed deliberately that way.'

'But that would mean they couldn't get out. Surely that's just stupid?'

'Not if they have the means of staying in there for a while or even escaping via a submarine.'

'Do we know if there are any British submarines around?' she asked anxiously.

'No but it would almost certainly need specialist docking equipment. Oh God, I wonder if they have an emergency sonar beacon? If they have we may have little time.'

Inga wondered whether this had gone on long enough and said so. 'Maybe we should consider packing up. After all, we've achieved quite a lot. They'll know that we know about this now and will have to withdraw.'

'NO,' the Major snarled. 'We've come to do a job and the main part is to discover what technology they are using. Even if they get a submarine under us, there is nothing they can do. Now, unless you have something useful to contribute, just fuck off and leave me to think.'

Inga took a step back at his angry tone. The man seemed so focused as to be totally unable to listen to reason. She began to worry that in his haste he would just become more single minded and if they weren't careful they could easily run out of time. She had an idea.

'Can we talk to them? And before you start shouting again, I may have an idea.'

'How the hell would we talk to them?'

'Have we got a bullhorn or some sort of loudspeaker?'

One of the men overhearing the conversation interrupted, even though the Major glowered at him. 'There's one in the Ekranoplan. They use it to direct troops when we do operations and keep all engines running. Do you want me to get it?'

Before the Major could reply, Inga got in first. 'Yes, quickly now and before you start shouting at me Major we tell them that we understand that we can't blow the hatch but because we've come this far we'd rather destroy the whole installation than leave it intact. They will be well treated if they give up. Why shouldn't they?'

The Major thought it through. It was worth a try. In fact, the option of blowing the whole bloody thing to pieces had already crossed his mind. They had plenty of explosives after all. 'Right, we'll do just that but we'll also rig the charges anyway as a final precaution.'

Inga was taken aback. 'But why waste time doing that they will have no way of knowing we're bluffing.'

The Major smiled his cold smile back at her. 'I never bluff.'

Inga knew she would be wasting her breath. 'So, who here speaks English?' She smiled back at the bloody man when no one answered. 'Looks like that will be me then.'

The Major smirked inwardly. He spoke English as well but he saw no reason not to let the silly girl do the dirty work for him and maybe a female voice would be more effective, more reassuring.

Fifteen frustrating minutes later the charges had been laid. Two separate sets had been set. One to the hatch in case it could be successfully blown, the second to a massive charge dug deep into to the ice alongside the access tower. If that went up the whole base

The Caspian Monster

would be blown to pieces. Both sets of detonator wires were led back past the original firing point and tied to a stake in the ground. The bullhorn had been retrieved from the Ekranoplan.

Inga climbed carefully down the ladder, gingerly avoiding the splintered metal at the top. When she got to the bottom she tried an experimental twist on the hatch ring. The Major called down to her to stop wasting her time. She grinned ruefully to herself. That would have been just too easy but she would have given anything to see the look on his face if they had forgotten to lock the hatch. Placing the bullhorn to her lips, she started to talk. The noise in the confined space was deafening she just prayed they would hear it.

'NATO personnel, you know we are here and you must know what we want. You also know we have destroyed your top hatch. We are offering you the chance to surrender. But be in no doubt, we would rather destroy this whole base than leave it intact. You must understand, we can leave no evidence of our presence. This means total destruction whether you are inside or not. Surrender now or go to the bottom with your facility.'

Inga couldn't believe she had just threatened to kill an unknown number of human beings but what choice did she have? The thought made her feel sick.

She gave it a few more minutes and repeated the message. A feeling of dread went through her. Were these people such fanatics that they would rather die than just give in? It went against everything she had learnt about their way of thinking. They must be stalling for time. How long would their nerve hold? She felt hers slipping. The Major leant over again and told her she had one more chance.

Starting to panic, it translated into her voice.

'Please, we have no wish to kill you but there are enough explosives on your hull to blow you apart. Please give up.'

Nothing.

The Major ordered her up the ladder.

She made one more heartfelt plea and reluctantly started the climb. When she got to the top, the Major smiled grimly. 'I told you, I don't bluff. Time is running out. We try the demolition charges on the hatch first and if it is of no use as we expect we detonate the main charge and blow the whole thing to hell.'

Just as he finished speaking, the ring on the hatch squealed as it turned and it was slowly pushed open.

'Please don't shoot or set off any explosives, we're coming out.'

Under the ice

The Swiftsure was closing back in under the edge of the ice when its sensitive sonar picked up the distress beacon from the listening base. The operator immediately called the Captain into the sonar control room saying that he had picked up an odd warbling sound. The Captain, who was the only one on board who knew the details of Pickwick, also knew what the tone meant. Calling for an accurate bearing, he shot back to the control room and grabbed a chart. Quickly plotting his position and the bearing of the sonar tone he confirmed it was from Pickwick. The problem was that because he had had to sail clear of the ice to use his aerial to tell London what the Soviet submarine had done earlier he was now just over two hours away from the scene. He briefly contemplated turning around to tell Fleet what was going on but quickly dismissed the idea. Whatever the reason, the base would not have activated the signal unless they were either under attack or had suffered a catastrophic emergency of some sort. In either case, they needed his help as soon as possible. Quickly, he ordered an intercept course at full speed. Although the whole Pickwick operation was on a need to know basis he decided that now his crew did have that need and picked up the main broadcast microphone to brief them what was going on. With that Soviet Victor Three in the area and clearly involved in some way he wasn't going into a potential confrontation without his people understanding what the stakes were.

Andrei had done his job and knew that he should now set course for home but having invested so much time and personal effort getting this mission underway he decided to loiter in the vicinity of the base. Although unlikely, there might be some more support he could provide. Unfortunately, the ice above was far too thick to contemplate a surfacing attempt but he just felt reluctant to go until he knew his comrades above him had as well. After a time, he was glad he had stayed. A loud sonar pulse had been detected emanating from a direct bearing towards the base's position. It was like nothing he had heard before and he strongly suspected that it was some form of underwater distress signal. He was initially quite pleased as it was direct evidence that the above water operation was succeeding. However, as it continued to pulse out its message he started to get concerned. If there was a NATO submarine within detection range of the beacon it would be coming here. The last thing he wanted was an underwater confrontation. He was therefore relieved when suddenly the noise stopped. He hoped this meant that his people now had access to the inside of the base and it was them who had turned if off. It was with some alarm then when half an hour later the sonar controller called out urgently. 'Captain, we have British submarine at very high speed approaching. He clearly isn't worried about being detected, the speed he's going. My estimate is that he should be here quite soon.'

Chapter 38

Pickwick

Twelve men exited through the hatch. The Major had them herded to one side under the guard of two of his men. The prisoners were well dressed for the conditions. He decided that interrogating them was not his top priority, they could wait.

He called his scientist over and together they entered the base through the open hatch. The ladder continued for quite a great deal further until they found themselves at its base. It was pitch black and he immediately called up for torches and some of the portable lights they had brought with them. While they were waiting, he ditched his heavy arctic parka. It was much warmer down here. As soon as he could see properly he looked around. He found himself in something that looked very much like a submarine control room. Two identical monitors and control consoles lined one wall with a chair in front of each one. At one end was a large table covered in paper charts.

With dismay, he also saw what the previous incumbents had done. Although he wasn't surprised, he had hoped to prevent the worst of the sabotage he was now seeing. But it had taken so long to get them to surrender. They had clearly used the time to good effect. Both consoles were smashed to pieces. Glass and wires were strewn all over the floor. Picking his way carefully through the mess, he looked into the exposed guts of one of them. The electronics inside were as smashed as the outer casing and fizzing slightly with what he assumed must be battery acid or some other form of corrosive.

He called over his Scientist. 'What do you think? Is it worth taking any of this junk?'

To his surprise, the man was full of enthusiasm. 'Oh yes, we will only need one full set. They both look the same. I will select these least undamaged. But don't worry Major. We will still be able to

The Caspian Monster

reverse engineer the technology. It's lucky they couldn't use fire in this enclosed space. That would have made life very difficult.' He then fussed about the room until settling on one of the sets of equipment. The Major then called up for two of his men who were also trained engineers to come down and start removing the equipment.

There was only one door to choose from to exit the room, so signalling for the scientist to follow he continued his inspection. The next room was quite small, clearly for communications and strangely hadn't been subjected to the same orgy of destruction as the previous one.

'I wonder if this is a double bluff?' he mused out loud.

'Sorry, what do you mean?'

'If they wanted us to think this wasn't important when actually it is, then maybe they decided to leave it alone to make us think it wasn't worth sabotaging.'

'Hmm, let me look closer,' said the scientist as he squeezed past. 'This is almost certainly an underwater telephone. Here's an HF radio, yes and VHF. Sorry Major, I think you're wrong, there's nothing here that would be for the covert communications we know they must have used.'

'What's that?' asked the Major, pointing to a small control panel next to what they assumed was the underwater telephone. It looked intact except for a small hole on its fascia. However, a large red switch was clearly in the on position.

'My guess would be some form of distress beacon. Switches aren't painted prominently like that unless they're used rarely and for emergency purposes and that hole looks like it should have a light in it probably to confirm it has been activated.'

'Is it something we need to retrieve?'

'Not really, it's simple technology.'

The Major flicked the red switch to off and then to be sure smashed it repeatedly with the butt of his rifle. 'That's one trick they tried that didn't work. Let's move on.'

They opened the next door and he shone his light into the compartment. It was larger than the one they had first come into and once again full of smashed equipment.

'Oh my Lord, the Jackpot,' he exclaimed.

Calling urgently for more light, they were soon moving amongst a range of strange looking military equipment.

'What do you think?' he asked his expert.

'Well, the last room was for sonar, I'm almost certain of that. This looks like radio receivers and computers. Yes, look, this machine here, they weren't able to damage the front face too much, it's calibrated in radio frequencies. We're going to need to get all this out if we can.'

'We may not have too much time. Can you try and assess which is most important, particularly try to work out what they were using for secure communications?'

'Yes, of course. How about you getting a few more men down here to help me?'

The Major went back to the main hatch and called for two more soldiers to come down. He told the engineers to brief them on what to do and then come forward to help in the next compartment.

He continued exploring on his own. He entered a long corridor with doors regularly spaced to his right. Each contained two bunks and basic sanitary facilities, all clearly accommodation for the men. Although certain that they would offer up no secrets, he checked each one as he moved down the corridor. It was amusing to see the photographs of loved ones stuck over the bunks and the various forms of reading material lying around. He had to wonder what sort of men could live in these conditions for presumably months on end and shivered at the thought. Claustrophobia was already setting in even after a few minutes inside.

The rest of the place appeared to offer no further revelations. There was a communal recreation area, a galley and some showers. However, the last compartment was totally different. He had to descend a flight of stairs to get to it. Firstly, it had an airlock and it took him several minutes to work out how to get in as the inner door wouldn't open until he had secured the outer one. His ears strained and he had to clear them much as if he was descending under water as he opened the inner door. Clearly, the pressure was much higher in here. Inside, the explanation was clear. A small pool of water dominated the interior of the room about the size necessary to allow two people to enter together. He reckoned they must be at least fifteen metres under the surface here and so the pressure was necessary to keep the water at bay. As an experienced diver himself, he realised he would have to be careful leaving the room. There must be a way of slowly controlling the pressure reduction as he left, somewhere in the airlock. He was certain that the previous incumbents didn't expect to get the bends every time they left.

And they clearly knew a lot about diving. Around the perimeter of the room were several diving dry suits. Inside metal lockers were personal gear and warm inner suits. Specialised diving regulators and masks were hanging on a long rack. There was also an air compressor and other maintenance equipment.

He looked around carefully. Why did they need such a facility? Presumably, it could be used for emergency egress but that would be of no use with up to five metres of ice overhead. It must be for the maintenance or even deployment of the sensor array they were using. Quickly, he looked around at the workbench on the far side. As a diver, most of the things he saw there were familiar enough for him to recognise. Then he saw something odd. It was a triangular box about twenty centimetres in size. It had two heavily insulated wires coming from the apex next to a large ringbolt and a flat face covered in some form of plastic material. He had a pretty good idea what it was and if he was right it justified the whole mission.

He grabbed the device and with mounting excitement entered the airlock shutting the inner door behind him. He looked carefully at the outer door. There should be some form of pressure gauge and valve arrangement to allow him to vent the pressure in a controlled manner. Suddenly, with a lurch of panic, he realised that the sabotage hadn't been limited to electronics. He found the gauge. It was smashed and he found the remnants of the pressure release mechanism. The control wheel had been removed and the levers bent and twisted out of recognition. There was no other way of operating it.

Calming himself, he realised it wasn't a total catastrophe. He would need to crack open the outer door as little as possible and let the air escape as slowly as he could. It would probably be no worse than an emergency ascent and he had practiced those enough times before. It was lucky a trained diver had fallen into this little trap. Someone without the necessary knowledge could have been seriously hurt.

However, it was with no little trepidation and cursing the bastard who had put him in this position that he turned the release wheel to the outer door. It opened inwards towards him so even with it fully unlocked the air pressure held it shut. Obviously, this was for safety, so it couldn't be opened until the pressures equalised. He reached into his pocket and found his knife which he carefully put in the join between door and frame and then levered the door. The little knife immediately snapped with the strain. Cursing and with panic rising he went back into the diving compartment. Sure enough, there were no tools to be found. He suspected that they were all sitting on the sea bottom many hundreds of metres below him. If he couldn't open the door, how long would it be before someone came looking for him? More importantly, how did he tell them not to open the door too fast? And that was assuming it could be opened against a pressure of at least two atmospheres.

In desperation, he ransacked the personal lockers and with a gasp of relief found what he needed. In their haste, they had forgotten a large sheathed diving knife, the sort divers wore on their legs. This one was a monster and he doubted this would snap. Entering the lock, he shut the inner door and tried once again to carefully lever the outer door.

The Caspian Monster

A loud hiss announced the start of depressurisation. He tried to remove the knife so he could do things in stages but the pressure on the door had jammed it and it was stuck. The only way to get it out would be to lever the door more and he didn't dare do that. He could do nothing but wait. The pressure soon started to equalise and he pulled the knife free but in his heart he knew it was too late. He could already feel a sharp pain near his sinus and there was another building near his right knee. He just prayed these two bends, because he was certain that was what they were, wouldn't be too debilitating. He was a very long way from a hypobaric chamber.

Grimacing against the pain, he finally got the outer door open and went in search of his scientist.

He found him still in the communications centre. He briefly explained what he had found further on and showed him the device he had retrieved.

The scientist immediately recognised it for an advanced form of hydrophone. 'If anything will tell us how they have been detecting our submarines that is it. I congratulate you Major. Oh and we think we have the communication problem solved.'

He pointed to a small computer like device. 'We are fairly positive that this is the controller for a satellite communication system.'

'Only fairly positive?'

'As you can see it's been badly smashed. I guess you could ask one of the prisoners just to be sure. There should be some form of parabolic antenna somewhere but they may have hidden that on the surface. Otherwise, we should have all we need in a few more minutes.'

Wincing from the pain which had now travelled up the whole side of his face, he managed a neutral tone. 'Excellent, give me that satellite machine. I think it's time I spoke to the prisoners for several good reasons.'

Chapter 39

One thousand feet above the ice

'Alright everyone, we're getting close. That's assuming I've managed to fly anything like an accurate heading,' Jon announced over the intercom.

It hadn't been easy. Because of the loss of his automatic stabilisation, one of the facilities he didn't have was the ability to take his feet off the rudder pedals and let the aircraft automatically stay on the right heading. He had been concentrating really hard to keep the compass steady but it took a great deal of effort and inevitably the aircraft's heading wandered slightly. The navigation solely relied on him flying the course Brian had passed to him as well as he could. It didn't help that with no external features to monitor position along their track they were having to work on the assumption that the wind speed and direction was staying the same. All in all, after so long airborne, there were a number of things outside their control that could incrementally add to inaccuracy and lead them to the wrong place. So, it was with a great deal of trepidation that Brian was searching the horizon with the one working lens of the night vision goggles. Despite the navigation problems, the other big danger was that they would get too close and be seen. If the Russians weren't about then that was fine but otherwise they needed to keep well away until they could assess the situation.

The night was now crystal clear and starlight gave just enough light for the NVG to work. Even with the naked eye, Jon could just see the white plain of ice below him although he couldn't make out any features at this height.

The Caspian Monster

'I've got something out to port,' called Brian excitedly. 'Can't see what it is yet. Jon, come thirty degrees left.'

Jon banked the aircraft to alter their heading but could see nothing with his normal vision.

Brian continued concentrating. 'If our nav is even slightly accurate then that's in about the right place. I've got several strong white lights and I'm starting to pick up other shapes. Jon, we need to descend now and slow down once we're lower.'

Jon lowered the collective lever and started a gentle descent. At the same time, he slowed to seventy knots.

'Bugger, yes there's definitely something on the ice. I'm afraid any hope of arriving first is bollocksed. What height are we at now?'

Jon who had been giving their only altimeter a great deal of his attention immediately called back, 'two hundred feet but I'm going to go down to a hundred. I daren't go any lower until we commit to a landing.'

'We're still several miles away. How close do you think we dare approach?'

'With all those lights blinding them, which I am starting to see now as well, they'll never see us but if we get any closer they'll bloody well hear us.'

'Hang on, I can make out that hovercraft thingy now. Fuck me its big. There's a massive propeller on the back and its spinning. They must be keeping it running for a fast get away. They'll never hear us over the noise of that thing. Keep going, the closer we can get the better.'

'I hope you're right. OK, in the back, we'll be landing soon, so get ready. Once we're down I want you out of the door as fast as you can. Don't wait for instructions, just get out and take up defensive positions.'

The Sergeant acknowledged the command for them all and indicated for them to get their weapons ready.

They were starting to get worrying near the lights when Brian finally called close enough. All Jon had to do know was land, in the dark, in recirculating snow, with virtually no visual references and no accurate altimeter.

'Brian, nip down to the cabin door and call my height and watch the tail. You know what I need.'

Brian heard the tension in Jon's voice and climbed out of his seat without further comment. He went aft to the cabin door which he opened, letting in an icy blast of air as he did so. Plugging in his helmet, he started calling out what he could see which wasn't much.

Jon slowed the aircraft down even more and gave up looking at his barometric altimeter. It was far too inaccurate now. As the ground approached, he still couldn't make out any features that would allow him to assess his speed or sideways drift. *Fucking hell, this is impossible,* he thought desperately.

A shout came over the intercom. 'Pull up, pull up. You're drifting to the right.' With no other option, Jon pulled up hard on the collective and transitioned back into forward flight, turning hard to clear away from the Soviets.

'What the sodding hell do we do Jon? If you can't see to land how the fuck do we get down without crashing?'

A tight lipped, sweating Jon replied. 'We daren't use the landing lights and we must have some forward speed until the last moment, otherwise we'll just disappear in a cloud of snow and then we really won't be able to see anything. Brian, how about I try the NVG? Even with one lens working it might give me what I need.'

'Has your helmet got the fittings to clip it on?'

'Shit, no but even so, I might be able to use it.'

'It's down the side of my seat.'

'OK, got it.'

Jon tried looking through the one tube and it was suddenly like daylight. The problem now was that he didn't have enough hands to fly the aircraft. He had an idea.

'Brian get back up here. You're going to be my eyes.'

Brian came back and strapped in, taking the goggles back from Jon.

The Caspian Monster

'OK, this time I'm going to keep more forward speed on and try to run her on faster. That way, I can minimise any tendency to drift sideways.'

'And if the ground isn't flat?'

'That's your job. I want you to con me to a clear area. If it's all looking good, I'll slow her down at the last minute. OK?'

'And if this doesn't work?'

'Hey man, don't make with the negative waves,' and then more seriously. 'Look, so we crash a tiny bit. We won't be moving fast. Remember, any landing you can walk away from is a good landing. We've got to get something done. If we can get the evidence we need or get these buggers to fuck off home then we can wait it out until our mates get to us. Anyway, I'm pretty sure this will work. Now you guys in the back, make damn sure you are holding on tight. This could get interesting.'

There was no reply.

Jon turned the aircraft back into what little wind there was and started descending again. He kept his airspeed at fifty knots and when the altimeter read one hundred, feet concentrated on looking outside. He still could only just make out a horizon and a white blur below it.

Brian who could see better, started giving Jon instructions.

'OK, that heading looks good. You're drifting right again. Good, that's better. I reckon about forty feet to go. OK, slow her down more.'

Suddenly Jon could see. The whole landscape became clear and it was Brian who was blinded as the goggles whited out with an excess of light. Not daring to wonder what the hell was going on, Jon was able to flare the aircraft hard and land her with a heavy but secure thump.

'What the fuck was that? Have they seen us?' queried a very confused Brian.

Jon laughed slightly hysterically. 'Nope, look at the horizon, it's our old friends.'

The Caspian Monster

The Northern Lights were back in a magnificent display. The whole sky was alive with green purple and gold.

'Right, no time for gawping. You lot in the back get out and take up your positions. Brian, let me know when they're clear.'

Once Brian gave him the word, he reached up and slid both engine levers into the shut down position and then as soon as the rotors had slowed enough, applied the rotor brake as hard as he could. As soon as the rotor blades had stopped he unstrapped ran back to the cabin, grabbed his rifle and jumped out.

Brian was waiting for him by the step. 'Good landing and I reckon they've no idea we're here.' Indeed the noise of the Russian machine could be heard. It was quite loud even this far away. A high pitched turbine whistle and the rhythmic, growling, thump of a large propeller.

Jon indicated for all his troops to gather around.

'Sorry about the fun landing but we're down safe and sound that's all that matters. Sergeant McCaul is now going to tell us what to do.'

'Thank you Sir, no pressure then. Any idea how far away they are? I can see the lights and hear them but I suspect you know better than me.'

'No more than half a mile I reckon,' pitched in Brian. 'The terrain is mainly flat but there are a few low ridges.'

'Thank you Sir. I think our best method of approach is to come up behind that sodding great aeroplane thing. It'll mask our approach. I don't expect they'll have pickets out. They'll hardly be expecting company but we must be on our guard. With this light now, we should see them, before they see us. Everyone, make sure you camouflage gear is fully covering you. The ground is quite hard, so we shouldn't need skis or snow shoes. We'll walk carefully until we get closer and then crawl. We'll try to find some cover, so we can observe what's going on without being seen.'

They set out in a column. The Sergeant led the way. Jon was amazed at how well he was walking in view of the fact that his left foot was in plaster. He looked behind and saw that the other marine, Peterson, was also coping well. The other two marines also looked the job and Cook Smith just gave him a cheerful cocky grin. He suddenly felt a wave of optimism. With people like this how could they fail?

A few minutes later he was reconsidering that assessment.

They found the perfect way of concealing themselves when they got closer to the Ekranoplan. The snow in the last few hundred metres behind the massive beast had been piled up either side of it presumably as a consequence of the way it had arrived. Just behind it, a massive snow bank had been thrown up as it had stopped. By crawling behind it they were able to get quite close and stay well hidden. They gathered about fifty metres away and looked forward.

It was quite surreal. Silhouetted against a magnificent display of Northern Lights, the Ekranoplan looked like a giant white beached whale. The noise from its idling engine was immense. Communication could now only be achieved by shouting directly into the recipient's ear. Ahead of the machine, there were twelve men sitting on the snow with their hands over their heads and two guards standing over them with guns trained and ready. Another figure stood to one side, presumably also one of the Soviet team. Just to their left, a train of soldiers were taking things that were being handed up from a hole in the ground and putting them in the Ekranoplan through a door in its side.

Brian had the camera out and was rapidly taking photographs while the others counted the size of the opposition.

'I reckon at least eight on the surface,' Jon yelled into the Sergeant's ear. 'And there's got to be several below in the base.'

The Sergeant nodded agreement. 'We're going to have to free those prisoners if nothing else. Any ideas Sir?'

'Do you think we have a realistic chance of damaging that thing with the weapons we have?'

'Maybe Sir, if we could concentrate our fire on the engine but then we end up with a load of stranded and severely pissed off Russians and there's twice as many of them as us.'

Jon nodded but before he could reply something was happening. A figure climbed out of the hole. He had something in his hand. He strode towards the prisoners.

'We'd better see what this guy is up to first.'

Chapter 40

Pickwick

When the men came out of the hatch, Inga stood to one side not sure whether to be triumphant or dismayed. The looks on their faces varied from hostile anger to naked fear. She could empathise with both. The Major had them herded to one side. She decided she couldn't face going down the ladder, so to make herself useful she took out a notebook and went to get the prisoner's details.

The look of disdain on the guard's face when she told them what she intended didn't put her off. She marched up to the first man and demanded his name and details. The look he gave her when he was confronted by a woman was quite startled but didn't last long. After all, it had been a woman who had talked them out in the first place. It was the same with all the others. They freely told her their names, serial numbers, date of birth and two admitted to being military officers but after that, they refused to say anything more. Still, it was a start. She tried to reassure them that they would be well treated but was met with nothing but hostile silence.

After that, she stood with the guards and waited. The sudden onset of the Northern Lights should have intrigued her but she had too much on her mind and anyway she had seen them many times before. It wasn't long before equipment was being transferred out of the hatch and taken to the Ekranoplan and then some time after that the Major reappeared. He was carrying something in his hand and his faced looked like thunder but she also noted he was limping. Something must have happened but there was no chance to find out what as he brushed past her as though she was invisible. He shouted for the guards to line the prisoners up. He said something to one of the guards but she couldn't hear what he had said. It was quite a surprise when he started shouting at the prisoners over the noise of the Ekranoplan in fluent English.

'You are prisoners of the Union of Soviet Socialist Republics. You have been spying on us for too long and will be dealt with as spies.'

One of the men interrupted, shouting back angrily that they were in international waters.

The Major pulled his pistol and put it to the man's face.

'No one argues, understand?'

The man turned white and nodded.

'I need some answers. Is this part of your communications system?' and he held up a strange piece of twisted metal. He was met with stony silence.

'You managed to sabotage most of the place but I need to know what this is.'

Silence.

'OK, who was the bastard who sabotaged the diving lock?' As he said this he looked at all their faces carefully. The last but one man on the left covered a quick smirk with a straight face. The Major strode over to him and stood toe to toe.

'You may think it's funny but that could be considered an overtly hostile act.'

The man laughed in the Major's face. 'You are joking, what the fuck do you think you lot are doing? I consider it an act of war you Russian bastard.'

The Major took a step backwards and looked at all the prisoners. The pain in his face was starting to blur the vision in his left eye. He didn't have time for involved interrogations and he needed some answers. He reached down, pulled out his pistol again and before anyone could react, shot the man through the forehead. A fountain of blood and brains erupted from the back of his skull and he fell backwards onto the bloody snow. Both guards then presented their rifles at the remaining prisoners who were reacting in various degrees of shock and rage at the sheer callousness of the act.

'How many more have to die before I get the answers I need?'

Inga was as shocked as the rest and very quickly as angry as well. She walked up to the Major.

'What the hell are you doing? We need to take these prisoners back with us. Are you mad?'

He turned towards her his face strangely lopsided. 'Shut up you stupid bitch. Did you really think they would be coming back with us? Once I have what I need, the remainder will be going back into their base to enjoy the little explosion we have arranged. We can't leave any evidence now can we?'

Feeling sick, Inga didn't know what to say as the Major turned his back on her to continue the interrogation.

Before she knew what she was doing she pulled out her own pistol and pointed it at his back. It was a stupid thing to do but she couldn't think of anything else.

'Stop this now Major. I know what the mission brief is and so do you.'

He turned to her, contempt in his eyes. Before she could react, he simply snatched the gun from her hands and then swung it back and hit her across the face with it. She fell to the ground with blood pouring out of a cut in her temple.

He looked down at her with contempt. 'Go back to the Ekranoplan little girl. This is man's work.' And he emphasised it with the toe of his boot.

The pain was immense and for a few moments she was dazed and could barely think. Slowly, she came to her senses and she realised she simply didn't know what to do. Part of her was screaming in helpless rage and shame but another colder more analytical part of her was telling her to get up and leave. Bleakly, she realised that there was nothing she could do here. Maybe if she talked to Yuri she could head off the tragedy that was about to occur. She felt sick in her soul as it dawned on her that this had been the plan all along. Mikhael would have known, she felt sure. Oh God, did Yuri know? She suddenly realised there was probably no one she could turn to. As she walked, it was as if a switch had been made in her head. All the doubts that had been building up since her father's useless, stupid, dismal death, all the misgivings over the indoctrination she had been receiving since childhood came to a head. She now finally understood that the idealised world that her father believed in never existed or if it did, it was dead now. The vocation she had taken on because of it was a fabrication and a lie. She walked like a zombie lost in thought not looking where she was going. So it came as yet another shock when strong arms went around her neck and mouth stifling her instinctive scream. Something else jerked her off the ground and a fist slammed into her stomach.

Jon and company had been as shocked and angry as everyone else when the prisoner fell to the ground and then the report of the gun was heard.

'Fucking, fucking bastards,' he muttered with the sentiment being echoed along the line of men lying on the snow bank. He started to turn towards the Sergeant who waved him back to the scene being played out in the snow before them. There was clearly an altercation going on. At least one of the Russians was disagreeing with what had happened. They saw the bigger one turn and knock the dissenter to the ground. A few seconds later, he got drunkenly up and started walking slowly back roughly towards where they were hiding. Brian looked really angry but looking at Jon he pointed to his camera and then to the scene on the ice and gave a grim thumbs up.

Jon made a snap decision. 'Right Sergeant, I want that man. Do whatever it takes but get him back to us in enough of a state to answer some fucking questions.'

The Sergeant nodded and beckoned to Jones and Jenkins.

'You two, you're the most mobile. Move along the bank and get behind that bloke. When he's past you, grab the bastard and get him here in one piece. Frankly, be as rough as you like but the boss wants a word, so make sure he stays conscious. Got it?'

The two marines nodded grimly and slithered further along the snow bank as instructed.

The Russian wasn't paying much attention and passed only a few metres by the two camouflaged marines. Quickly checking that everyone's attention was on the prisoners, they sprinted out of cover. One marine put his arm around the Russian's head. The other rugby tackled him around the knees and then punched him hard in the gut for good measure. Within seconds, they held the struggling body tight and dragged him back over into the cover of the snow bank. It had only taken a few seconds and none of the rest of the Russians had paid the slightest attention.

The two marines were surprised, both at how light their captive was and how passive he seemed. Not prepared to take any chances, after what they had just witnessed, they kept him firmly clamped and dragged him to the waiting officer. They also managed few more surreptitious punches to the midriff on the way. Partly to keep him subdued, partly for the satisfaction.

He was dropped by Jon's feet spread-eagled on his face.

'Right turn him over lads. Let's have a little chat.'

When they turned him over they still couldn't see a face. It was part covered by a fur lined hood and a mask or scarf over the mouth. There was also a lot of blood. The man was gasping and heaving from the winding given him by the two marines. Jon didn't feel the slightest sympathy. He pulled the hood back and was shocked by the release of a nest of blonde hair. He pulled down the mask starting to get extremely confused. Despite the blood, he could hardly fail to recognise the face. The last time he had seen it, it was lying under him panting in exertion but for far, far different reasons. For a moment he was completely disorientated. How could this be happening?'

'Inga?'

She looked back through pain filled eyes with disbelief and then hope. 'Jon?'

Chapter 41

Under the ice

'Revolutions for five knots, assume silent running state.' The Captain of Swiftsure was not going to charge into an unknown situation like a bull in a china shop. At full speed not only was he announcing his arrival to anyone in the local vicinity but he was also deaf to their presence. A submariner always had to balance risk against the likelihood of success. In this case, he needed to know what the risks were before he could even contemplate achieving anything.

The giant undersea machine glided to a gentle five knots and the passive sonar arrays started to listen. The Captain made his way to the sonar operator and looked over his shoulder at the waterfall array that showed all the noises being received. Initially, the screen simply looked like static on a television and represented all the things that were making noise underwater, from snapping shrimps to the echo of waves out in the open ocean. It was immediately clear that the emergency beacon had stopped. Then slowly, some dark lines started to appear at the top of the display. Every underwater machine made noise of some sort and each had their own distinctive signature. The speed of the propeller, the pumps that provided coolant to the reactors, all the whirring machinery inside the hull contributed to a unique signature for each craft. The Captain had seen this one before. The sonar operator who had been listening to the raw sound through his headphones looked up at the Captain.

'Same Victor Three Sir, the one that was with the fleet and made that strange sonar signal. He's on a bearing of three four eight and going very slowly. He's still quite a long way away.'

The Captain thought carefully. The Russian almost certainly knew he was there, at least up until he had slowed down. Even the

Russians couldn't have missed that. The bearing he was on was directly towards Pickwick and the distress beacon had stopped. He could only conclude that the Russian was involved and may have done some harm to the base although for the life of him he couldn't see how. Whatever was happening, he was going to bloody well find out.

Andrei saw the trace of the British submarine disappear as it slowed down. Not surprisingly, it vanished from his screens as it started running silently. However, Andrei was not sanguine that he wasn't still visible to the enemy submarine and with a start, he realised that the term enemy was how he now saw them. To keep in touch, he needed to get closer and he knew pretty accurately where they had been until very recently. He ordered a closing course and increase in speed. Slowly, as the distance between the two massive nuclear leviathans reduced, he started to pick up the British submarine's sonar signature. They didn't seem to be trying to evade. He realised that they couldn't be here only because of a direct response to the sonar beacon that the base had been transmitting. There wouldn't have been time unless they were already in the vicinity. That meant they had probably been tracking him already. His only course of action was to try to get them to follow him away from the area of the base.

Turning on a westerly heading away from the position of the base, he watched the sonar trace carefully. Sure enough, they turned as well.

Unfortunately, the trace then disappeared. All submarines irrespective of the quality of their sensors have a blind spot dead astern due to the water disruption caused by their propellers. As soon as the British boat got behind them they were blind again. Andrei gave it half an hour and then turned to check the trace. He was still there. Half an hour later he turned again and got a shock. The British had closed right up.

The sonar operator called urgently with something close to panic in his voice. 'Sir, I just heard them open a torpedo tube. Water discharge. I've got high speed propeller noises. Oh my God, they've fired a torpedo.'

Pickwick

Jon looked down at Inga, trying to work out what the hell was going on. The Sergeant and others were looking at him strangely and Brian who had met Inga once was frowning with recognition dawning on his face.

'Inga, what the hell are you doing here?'

'Oh Jon, I really don't know anymore.' She was still gasping and whooping for breath but managed to sit up with Jon's help.

'OK, everyone, believe it or not, I know this woman. We met in Norway last year,' and then it dawned on him. 'You bitch, you're KGB. You fucking set me up and now that's why you're here. You found out something from Bardufoss and now you've come to murder our people.'

Inga visibly flinched at the word bitch. 'Jon, believe me, I'm sorry, so much has happened since we last met. Look, my God, how did you get here? No, never mind. That horrible man is going to kill all the prisoners. I didn't come here to murder defenceless people. Please let me help you.'

The Sergeant was looking sceptical. 'Come on Sir, we need to find out everything they're planning and before they start shooting our people again.'

'Thank you Sergeant McCaul, I know that but I think this lady will tell us without any further coercion.' And turning to the frightened looking girl. 'So, Inga what are you bastards planning?'

'Jon, it's not me, it's that Major. I think something happened to him when he went down into the base. He looks ill and he's in a really vengeful mood,' she realised she was babbling with fright.

'For fuck's sake girl, stop dithering what is he planning?'

Inga was getting terrified now. She could see that Jon was getting even angrier and the soldiers around her looked murderous. Without conscious thought, she reverted to speaking Russian. 'He said they would be put back in the base. They were never going to take them but I wasn't told. My boss knew but he never told me.'

Brian looked alarmed. 'What the fuck was that all about Jon? Get the stupid cow to talk English.'

Jon grabbed Inga's shoulders and shook her. 'Inga, get to the bloody point and stop speaking Russian. I'm the only one who understands you.'

She looked vacant for a moment then pulled herself together. 'It's been wired with an enormous amount of explosives. They're planning to set it off just before they leave. Jon, please believe me. I knew nothing about this. They told me the prisoners would be taken back to Russia.' The last words were accompanied by a wrenching sob.

'It's alright guys, I think we can trust her,' as he said it he looked meaningfully at the girl praying that he was right. 'You may not have heard it over the noise of that bloody machine but she said that they are going to put them back in Pickwick before they leave and blow it to bits with them inside.'

'Sir, look,' called Cook Smith. 'Seems she was right.'

They all peered over the snow bank. The last of the Russian soldiers had climbed back into the machine with the exception of those guarding the prisoners. A loud whining sound came from the Ekranoplan and a blast of jet exhaust hit the snow near the nose as the forward engines were started. The prisoners were being herded by their guards towards the entrance of Pickwick.

'Gentlemen,' called Jon. 'Cook Smith claims to be the best shot here. Frankly, I think he's talking bollocks like he usually does. I reckon I'm better but let's find out. The range is about two hundred metres. The priority is the two guards, once you can get a clear shot, then that bloody officer. Any questions?'

Seven 7.62 millimetre Self Loading Rifles poked over the snow bank. Seven really pissed off people sighted on the Russian soldiers and waited their moment.

Under the Ice

The Captain of Swiftsure was totally fed up with the bloody Russian. He had turned away and it soon became clear that he was trying to force him away from Pickwick by making him follow him. It was confirmed when soon after the chase began, the Russian slowed and turned to clear his rear arcs. It was now a balance of priorities. Something had happened at Pickwick and he needed to get back there. Not that there was much he could do. He knew there was a diver's access in the base but his boat didn't carry any specialist cold water diving gear. He could get his men to use the normal equipment they carried but there was a significant risk of their regulators freezing solid in the extremely cold water. He might have to risk it and he was sure his men would volunteer anyway but first he had to get rid of the Russian. If he turned back he didn't want to be followed and possibly harassed by the sodding man.

He ordered the submarine to speed up and get as close as was safe. It was time to get heavy handed.

'Attack team, make ready,' he called to the control room and immediately got some startled expressions.

'I want a Mark Eight made ready to fire on my command.'

That really got some strange looks.

The Executive Officer came up to him. 'Sir, a Mark Eight, surely we should use a guided torpedo?'

'I don't want to sink the bugger. I'm just going to scare the living daylights out of him.'

The XO grinned as the idea sank in.

The Captain pulled down the submarine's main broadcast microphone from its clip by his head. 'This is the Captain speaking. As you know the Russian we have been following has something to do with the distress signal we heard from our guys on the surface. I'm going to blind fire a Mark Eight torpedo past him. Hopefully, he will get the message and sod off. Either way, we will then head back to Pickwick. Once we have turned. I want the diving officer to report to the control room. That is all.'

'Sir, the Russian is slowing again.'

'Alright, revolutions for five knots please.'

He's down to five knots as well Sir and he's turning.'

'Open tube one doors. On my mark, fire on a bearing of two seven zero.'

The attack team acknowledged the order and made all the switches.

'Fire.'

There was the rarely heard thump through the hull as the massive World War Two vintage torpedo was forced out of its tube by a slug of pressurised water. It was followed quickly by the whine of its propeller as it got under way. The sound quickly faded as the torpedo shot down the bearing it was programmed to follow, straight past the slow moving Russian and off into the distance.

The control room waited in tense silence.

'Sir, target is increasing speed and now turning north. She's accelerating very fast. Indeed the whir of the Russian submarine's propeller could actually be heard in the control room. There was a cheer from the assembled men. She wouldn't be doing that if she wanted to continue playing silly buggers.

'How long to get back to Pickwick at full speed please?'

The Officer of the Watch did a quick calculation. 'Twenty five minutes Sir.'

'Make it so and tell the diving officer to meet me in my cabin.'

For a moment Andrei stood frozen with panic starting to rise. Surely the British couldn't really be firing on them? If they had, then they only had seconds to live.

'Sir the torpedo bearing is changing fast,' the sonar operator shouted with surprise in his voice. 'It's going past us.'

Relief flooded through Andrei and he could see the same look on his men around him in the control room. But Andrei took the message. The British Captain was not prepared to play the game of cat and mouse that normally took place between them. He could understand why and he now had a decision to make. A submariner always had to balance risk against the likelihood of success and he had already succeeded in all his mission objectives. Time to go. And then something else struck him.

'How long will it take him to get back?' he asked his navigator.

'Twenty minutes to half an hour Sir.'

Well, that could make things interesting for them if they decided to get involved. 'Navigating officer, take us home please as fast as you like.'

Pickwick

'Get out of the way, get out of the fucking way,' Jon was muttering under his breath. The Russian guards were ushering the prisoners back towards the hole in the snow. The problem was that the prisoners were in the way of a clear shot. They didn't dare fire without serious risk of shooting one of their own as well. A 7.62 bullet was more than capable of going through one human being and taking out the next one in line as well.

'Hold your fire,' called the Sergeant, echoing Jon's frustration. 'If we have to, we wait until they're all back inside then the field will be clear.'

'Inga, come here,' called Jon.

She crawled next to him.

'How are they going to set off the explosive charges?'

She pointed to the left of the officer. 'If you look you can see a stake in the ground there. The wires are tied around it. He uses a battery to fire the detonators.'

The Caspian Monster

'Thank you, now get down.' There was no warmth in his voice.

'Sergeant, no matter how long we wait we mustn't let that officer near that stake in the snow. See it there,' and he pointed.

Sergeant McCaul nodded. 'I understand Sir. I heard what the girl said.'

By now there was some form of altercation happening at the entrance to the base. One of the guards raised a rifle butt and clubbed one of the prisoners over the head. He fell to his knees but slowly the others started to climb down.

'Steady guys,' called the Sergeant. 'There's plenty of time. That guy will only have a headache. Let's not make it any worse. Jones and Jenkins, you take the one on the left. Peterson you and I will take the one on the right. Smithy and you Sir take the officer. Lieutenant Pearce, can you hold fire and follow up on any misses please.'

Smith grinned at Jon. 'Now we'll really find out Sir.'

Jon smiled but said nothing. He was too busy sighting his rifle on the distant figure.

Very soon, the last man's head was disappearing out of sight. The field of fire was clear. The two guards were still looking down the hole in the ground when the Sergeant called time.

The noise of the rifles was shockingly loud but it was too late for anything else now. The two guards dropped to the snow. One started to crawl away but Brian was able to finish him off.

To Jon and Cook Smith's total disbelief, their man crouched into the snow just as they fired and they both missed.

The Major was wondering how they could keep their prisoners confined long enough to fire the charges when he noticed the hatch cover they had blown off earlier lying in the snow near his feet. It would be perfect. He would jam it down the shaft, it was distorted enough to fit. It should be enough to impede any thoughts of a quick exit. He was just bending down when he heard the all too familiar wicking noise of bullets flying past followed almost immediately by the crash of rifle fire. Automatically, he hit the snow and almost without thought pulled the hatch cover up to shelter from the direction he thought the fire was coming from. Sure enough, he felt the impact of several rounds striking the metal. Looking quickly behind him, he saw the two guards lying prone with blood stains in the snow behind them. Putting all thoughts of how the hell an enemy had got here, he looked over at the Ekranoplan. It was about a hundred metres away. The stake with the detonator wires was off to one side. What should he do?

He decided on the machine. There was no way he could set off the explosives when under heavy fire like this. He would be lucky to get away as it was. Carefully, using the hatch as a shield, he crawled and slithered towards the machine. He almost made it when the cramp in his leg forced him to stop. The agony caused by the small bubble of nitrogen in his knee was way beyond belief. He cried out in pain and just for a second the hatch cover he was holding slipped. Two bullets hit him simultaneously. One took off the side of his face and the other hit him so hard in the upper arm it was almost severed. For a dazed second, he realised that he had stopped feeling any pain whatsoever and then he slumped to the ground with his vision fading. The last thing he saw was the Ekranoplan disappearing from view in a white explosion of snow.

'Don't shoot at the Ekranoplan,' yelled Jon anxiously. 'We probably won't be able to stop it and I've got an idea that might sort it out for good. Inga, how long does it take for that thing to turn around?'

She confirmed his suspicions when she told him of the weakness in the design.

'Sergeant, get the guys out of the hole and then all of you get clear, well clear, as far away to one side as you can manage, got that?'

The Sergeant was about to argue but thought better of it when he saw the look in Jon's eyes. 'Right Sir.'

'Brian, come with me, I'm going to need your help.' And he started running back towards the helicopter.

Brian jumped up and quickly caught the running Jon. 'What the fuck are you up to Jon?'

Jon told him between gasps as they ran.

'Fuck me,' said Brian. 'I'd have never thought of that, Ekranoplan fishing.'

Chapter 42

Pickwick

Yuri had seen the two guards go down. He had also seen the Major's ploy with the hatch cover, so stayed his hands on the throttles. He watched with admiration as the man inched his way towards Snezhana with the white puffs of bullets striking all around him. He, like everyone else, was wondering how the hell anyone had found them and had managed to sneak up so successfully.

Turning to his flight engineer he told him to climb into the weapon turret above his head and look around for anything. It was a shame there was no gun in the turret but it was one of the things that they hadn't deemed necessary for a covert mission. That was proving to be a costly mistake.

The engineer called down excitedly. 'Yes, half a dozen soldiers in the snow bank to our rear and wait, yes I can just see a large helicopter parked behind us about five hundred metres away.'

Yuri started thinking furiously. He immediately realised that by keeping the turbo jet running he had provided the cover that the enemy needed to sneak up on them but who would have thought they could have had a helicopter in range? Pushing potential recriminations to one side, he concentrated on what they could do now. If they disembarked their remaining troops there would be a fire fight which they might not win, especially if the people in the listening base worked out what was going on and joined in.

He looked out again and saw the Major go down. Yuri really thought he was going to make it but then for some unfathomable reason, he literally dropped his guard for just a second and the enemy soldiers had him.

'*Whoever they were, they bloody well knew how to shoot,*' he thought grimly. With no reason to stay further, Yuri slammed all

The Caspian Monster

three throttles forward to get clear of any weapons fire. The germ of an idea formed in his mind as he did so.

The Sergeant, the Major's second in command, came up into the cockpit demanding to know what the hell was going on. Yuri told him to sit in the co-pilot's seat and gave him a headset. He told the man what had happened to his superior. The Sergeant took the news surprisingly stoically. He seemed far more concerned over what they were going to do now.

'We have to go back we can't leave any evidence,' he said anxiously.

'I know that,' said Yuri angrily. 'But what you don't know is that they came in by helicopter. We saw it parked up behind us. I have an idea on how to sort it out and take out a lot of their people as well. Then we can land back there and tidy up.' He went on to explain his idea. The Sergeant was no pilot and knew even less about Ekranoplans but immediately understood Yuri's plan. He readily agreed and Yuri started to turn Snezhana around as fast as he could using the technique he had developed so long ago and so far away in the Caspian Sea.

Jon had a stitch and was sweating profusely despite the intense cold by the time they got back to the Sea King. He hardly noticed. For a desperate moment, he thought they would never find it. The cloud of snow and ice blown up by the departing Ekranoplan had caused a white out of enormous proportions. But it had cleared just enough for him to follow its old track back to the helicopter. Brian already knew what to do, so Jon threw himself in the pilot's seat and started making switches as fast as he could. Even though he knew it would take a while for the Ekranoplan to come back, he also knew that gave him very little time to get airborne. Of course, he was gambling that it would come back but he couldn't see the Soviets just running away. There was too much of a mess. Too much evidence for them to clear up to just meekly go home with their tail between their legs. If he was in their place he would regroup and come back ready to fight it out.

The number one engine started and then the number two. He breathed a sigh of relief. Leaving them to cool for so long and with only battery power to start them up was always a risk. He knew he should wait for Brian to get clear but as he didn't even know where he was he couldn't wait and let off the rotor brake to spin up the rotors to normal speed.

Everything was working and he was just starting to wonder where Brian was when he reappeared and started to climb into the left hand seat.

Jon waved at him and made him plug in his helmet.

'Brian, don't take this the wrong way but please fuck off. I don't need your help to do this and there's no point in risking you as well. It's going to be bloody dangerous.'

'If you think I'm letting you.....'

He didn't get to finish. Jon shouted him down. 'I need you on the ground to take charge if it all goes pear shaped. I know the Sergeant is capable but he doesn't have the bigger picture. Now for God's sake go. I haven't any more time.'

Brian hated the idea of letting his friend do this alone. He could just strap in anyway. There was nothing Jon would be able to do about it. But in the end, he knew that Jon was right and there was no time.

He tapped Jon on the helmet. 'Don't go fucking up now Jon.'

Jon just grinned and gave him a friendly finger. Brian ran down to the cargo door jumped out and slid it shut behind him. He ran out from the whistling rotors and gave Jon a thumbs up from outside.

Jon didn't hesitate. He pulled the collective lever up firmly, corrected the yaw with the rudder pedals and when high enough, lowered the nose and transitioned in the direction where the Ekranoplan had disappeared.

'*Right, you bastards*' he thought grimly. '*Time for a little surprise.*'

'Why are you now turning the other way?' asked the Sergeant when Yuri reversed their turn after only a short while.

'Oh sorry, I should have explained. We turn sixty degrees one way and then reverse the turn. That way we end up going back along the same track we came up on. I want to ensure we fly directly over the base and helicopter.'

He was climbing the machine and turning as fast and hard as he could before they wallowed back to low altitude. It was by far the quickest way to turn around but even so it was taking quite a time. He just prayed the helicopter would still be there when he flew over it with all his engines flat out and as low as he could. It should be, you couldn't get such a large machine off the ground in a hurry and anyway they would be far too busy getting the prisoners out of the base and sorting themselves out. They wouldn't be expecting him back so soon and capable of doing what he intended. An Ekranoplan flew on a cushion of air and the downdraft from its stub wings could be ferocious. He intended to make it even more so by keeping all three engines running but forcing the machine as low as he could. Anything underneath would be subjected to enormous pressure damage, helicopters and men included.

After four turning cycles and keeping the wings banked far longer than he ever dared before, with the wingtips brushing the snow on several occasions, he had Snezhana heading back to her destination. He pushed the throttles to their maximum and then forced the machine down to less than ten metres. Glancing out of the side of the cockpit, he could see an enormous plume of snow and ice being thrown up by the ferocious blast under the machine.

He glanced over at the Sergeant. The man was staring out of the cockpit window looking white in the face. Presumably, being up here in the cockpit and seeing what really went on was a new dimension for him. The Northern Lights were still helping him see and he found he didn't even need to look at his homing indicator which was still working as he had now found the trail in the snow they made on the way out. It was a physical beacon leading him directly back. He had never felt so alive in his life. This was real flying. Every nerve taught and in total concentration, he kept Snezhana as low as he dared while also looking out for any sign of the base. He risked a glance at the homing beacon and saw they had less than two kilometres to go.

When he looked up, he couldn't believe his eyes. Amazingly, the helicopter had appeared from nowhere and was right in front of him. They were closing incredibly fast. The helicopter was much higher. What the hell was the pilot doing? Yuri saw the machine pass overhead. He caught a glimpse of something but before he could feel relieved that they had passed clear, all hell broke loose.

Jon knew he had only minutes at best. He needed to get clear of the men on the ground as fast as he could. Looking ahead, up its track in the snow, he eventually spotted the returning Ekranoplan in the distance. Actually, it wasn't the machine he was seeing it was a massive plume of snow with the lights in the sky being reflected off it, a beautiful, strange and menacing sight. Then he picked out the machine itself, the machine and that massive spinning propeller. How big was it and how high off the ground? He had no way of knowing and no accurate height information even if he did know. This was going to have to be pure seat of the pants stuff and there was only one chance to get it right. As Brian would have said, it was time to do some real pilot shit. He slowed down and let the Ekranoplan come to him, keeping it dead centre. Even if its pilot had worked out what he was up to it was far too late. The massive machine could never get out of the way now.

Jon adjusted his height and prayed it was correct as everything speeded up. The Ekranoplan was suddenly massive in the cockpit windows and then shot below him. He hit the cargo release button but had no idea whether he done it in time.

He hadn't.

The Caspian Monster

Slung underneath the Sea King on a sixteen foot long lifting strop, was a cargo net that Brian had filled with anything he could find from the aircraft's cabin. This included several heavy ammunition boxes full of 7.62 rounds, a case of hand grenades and the flotation canisters he had removed from the aircraft's stub wings. It was as heavy as he could make it. Even so, it was swinging like a pendulum underneath the Sea King when it passed over the Ekranoplan. The swing didn't matter. The propeller was so large and the helicopter so close, it was certain that something was going to go through it. In fact, one of the blades hit the boxed ammunition squarely and promptly disintegrated.

The instantaneous and massive imbalance immediately caused the turbo prop to tear itself loose with debris flying in all directions. A complete intact blade penetrated the cabin and literally cut one of the soldiers in half in a spray of blood and gore before anyone even realised what was going on. The others looked on in horror for a few milliseconds before the violence of what came next took all their attention. The damage wasn't confined to the inside of the Ekranoplan either as some more of the debris flew up and cut the tail completely off the Sea King as it passed overhead.

Yuri felt the impact but had no idea what it was. The Ekranoplan sheared violently to one side and he automatically corrected with his rudder pedals. They had no effect. He slammed all three throttles shut and tried to keep some semblance of control. He had none. He lost control of his bladder just as the nose of the machine hit the ground and everything went black.

Jon felt the aircraft start to spin and immediately realised he had lost all yaw control. His cockpit warning panel lit up like a Christmas tree and he saw he had no hydraulics. He was a passenger. He did the only thing left to him and slammed both engine levers to shut off and then braced himself for impact.

The Caspian Monster

Brian had just caught up with the Sergeant. It had taken far too long to convince the crew of Pickwick that the cavalry had arrived but eventually they had been extricated. They were now all running to get clear when they heard the Ekranoplan returning. The Sea King had already passed them and was well clear when the Russian machine passed underneath it. Although Brian knew what might happen and had told the others, no one expected such extreme violence.

Brian saw the helicopter spin out of control but realised there was nothing he could do while the Ekranoplan was crashing before his eyes. It hit the ice in a vast cloud of snow with a thump they all felt through their feet. It was already yawing sideways and on impact, the whole nose section broke free at the weak point where the hinges were that it used to open up for loading. The rest of the fuselage turned at right angles to its direction of travel and started to roll, spinning faster and faster, shedding debris until it was wracked by an enormous explosion as the fuel tanks went up. A blazing, cartwheeling, pyre of death that no one could possibly survive. All the time there was the sickening, tearing, wrenching sound as the massive machine tore it itself apart in front of them.

The nose section was luckier. Thrown clear of the main wreckage, it carried on into the snow bank it had made earlier and came to a wrenching halt, twisted and almost unrecognisable.

As soon as he dared, Brian got to his feet and started running to where he thought the Sea King had come down. Despite his plastered leg, Sergeant McCaul managed to catch him up. 'I've sent a couple of my guys to check out that front bit and the rest of us are coming with you.' Brian just nodded in acceptance although he was surprised to see the Russian girl running with them.

The Sea King was in a snow drift. Or rather what was left of a Sea King. It was on its right side, the tail section completely missing and the main rotors just broken stubs. There was no sign of movement but mercifully no sign of fire either. Brian ran around the front. All the cockpit windows had smashed and he could see that

The Caspian Monster

Jon was still strapped into his seat but ominously still. Brian ripped at the remaining window supports and managed to get to his friend. With enormous relief, he could see that he was still breathing although his left arm was at a horrible angle.

'Jon, can you hear me?' there was no response. Brian reached down and undid the harness quick release, supporting the body as Jon's weight was freed. There was a crash to his left as Sergeant McCaul kicked in what had been the cockpit roof and suddenly there were enough hands to carefully extricate Jon's unconscious body. They laid him out in the snow and Brian checked him over. Inga tried to get in to help. Brian took one look at her. 'Why don't you just sod off little lady. You and your lot have done enough already.' With pain in her eyes, she stood back out of the way.

Jon's eyes flickered open. 'Hello matey, did I get the bastard?'

'You could say that. He's smeared all over the snow behind you. Now don't you go nodding off again, we need to find the damage and do some first aid.'

'Oh fucking hell, not like we did on that last first aid course. I don't stand a chance.'

Chapter 43

The remains of Pickwick Base

They made a jury rigged stretcher for Jon out of the helicopter cabin door and took him back to the area around the base. One of the men went back inside and retrieved a large first aid kit. Because the Russian explosives were still in place they made a camp on the ice well clear until they could ensure that they had been made safe.

Jon appeared to have a very badly broken arm and had taken a heavy blow to the head. Judging by the damage to his helmet it was pretty severe. He was conscious now but in pain. What was more worrying was that he was spitting blood. Brian was really worried there were some internal injuries that he could do nothing about. He had given Jon a shot of morphine which seemed to help the pain but he needed hospitalisation and soon.

Surprisingly, there was also a survivor from the Ekranoplan. The pilot had been found in the half crushed cockpit. At first, they thought he had been severely injured. When they pulled him out, half of one of his legs was missing and then they realised it was because the artificial half was still stuck in there. In fact, this was probably what had saved him. If it had been a real leg, it would almost certainly have been severed and then no first aid would have saved him.

They sat the two pilots together while they debated what to do next. The satellite phone had been retrieved from the wrecked Sea King and seemed to be working but that damned jammer was still operating. Sergeant McCaul was about to detail his three fit men to start searching for it but in this vast wilderness, no one was sanguine that it would be found quickly. Strangely it was the Russian pilot who solved the problem. He had started chatting to Jon in Russian and when Jon explained what they needed he told them the range

The Caspian Monster

and bearing to look for it. The three men set off with their compasses.

All this time Inga had been sitting to one side in misery. She suddenly realised she had no home, no friends, no country, nothing. They wouldn't even let her help Jon despite the fact that she told them she was skilled in first aid. She so wanted to talk to Jon and apologise. To tell him why she had done what she had done and how sorry she was. To tell him that she shouldn't have been here, anything to see even a hint of forgiveness in his eyes. All she got was looks of contempt or open hatred. What was worse was that she completely understood their feelings. In their place she would have felt the same, so she could hardly complain. What future did she have now? The answer was none at all. Deep in despair, she nevertheless listened to the conversation about possible rescue. They seemed to be saying that more helicopters were a long time away. Their best chance in the short term was a submarine. There should be one in the vicinity. But the ice was too thick apparently. She had an idea and quickly made up her mind. She would force their hand. No one was taking the slightest notice of her. There were several torches lying around on the ice. She took one and opened it up, removing the battery.

She knew roughly where the stake had been in the ground. Unfortunately, it was directly under where the Ekranoplan had crashed. Nevertheless, she went to where she thought it had been and then slowly wandered towards the hole in the ice scuffing her feet as she did. No one took the slightest notice of her.

She was only a few feet from the hatch itself when she found the wires with her foot. Reaching down, she picked them up and started walking backwards. All too soon she came to their end, still too close to the hatch. So be it, she had no life anyway. She reached into her pocket for the battery.

Jon was in a drug induced euphoric state. He had been talking to Yuri and found the man strangely likeable. He seemed to bear no ill will to Jon for his successful attempt to crash his beloved Snezhana, as Jon discovered she was called. Jon asked why Inga was on the mission not letting on that he already knew her. Yuri didn't really know except that she was filling in for her boss who had gone missing at the last moment. Jon then looked around wondering where she had gone. He saw her several hundred metres away fiddling with something in her hands.

He called over to Brian. 'Hey Brian, what's my beautiful ex bloody girlfriend up to over there?'

Brian looked over to where Jon was pointing but before he could speak, Pickwick blew up.

There was an enormous crash and pieces of metal and ice flew hundreds of feet into the air. Inga was picked up by the blast and flew backwards over the snow. When the explosion had subsided there was a large hole in the ice and no sign that Pickwick had ever existed. Before anyone could stop him, Jon managed to get to his feet and half stumble, half run to Inga's broken body. He fell onto the ice next to her and pulled her to him. Maybe it was the morphine, he wasn't sure but suddenly he felt really shitty about the way they had been treating her. He cradled her head on his lap, tears pouring from his eyes.

'You stupid, stupid bitch, you didn't have to do that. Why'd you have to blow yourself up? You could have come home with me' he said looking at her still face. It was covered in dried blood in places but reflected in the glow of the lights in the sky. He thought it looked quite beautiful.

Hands grabbed him gently from behind. 'Don't be such an ass Jon,' said Brian. 'You're all drugged up on morphine. Look, she's not dead, that is unless corpses can breathe.'

Half an hour later, Jon was back talking to Yuri. The Northern Lights had stopped at last and the night was now dark and clear. Inga was still unconscious and being attended to by Brian but he reckoned she would survive. Jon had been given strict instructions to sit down and behave and also given some more morphine. He was actually feeling quite good now.

Yuri, whose injuries were far less serious, seemed more upset over the loss of his machine than anything else.

'Bloody hell, Yuri it was only a lump of metal my friend.'

'To you maybe but my life is tied up with these machines. I fear this will be the end of them. You people in the West have nothing like them, do you?'

'Well no, we have some hovercraft but nothing like that thing. You Russians really have some brilliant engineers I'll give you that.'

Yuri smiled at the compliment. 'Well of course and I still have a chance.'

'Sorry, what do you mean?'

'Who's to say one of my countries submarines won't appear through that hole first?'

Jon hadn't thought of that. The satellite radio was now working and they had been told to expect help soon but the big Russian had a point. Could it all go wrong even now? That would be a right bitch.

Before Jon could respond, there was a ripple and then a stirring in the water in front of them and the fin of a submarine slowly rose up dripping water. For the life of him, Jon had no idea whose it was.

Then a man at the top appeared and looked down on them. In clear English he called, 'hello you lot, seems you need rescuing. Lucky we were around. Mind you, that explosion was a bit close for comfort but at least it got our attention.'

Epilogue

SHAPE Headquarters

'ENDEX', the signal all the staff officers had been waiting for had finally arrived. Good Bowman was over. They could all get back to normal life away from the frantic exercise that had kept them at their desks and operation rooms for so many weeks. No doubt there would be endless wash up meetings and lessons learnt briefings and the rest but all in good time. Within half an hour the Officers Club bar was packed.

No 10 Downing Street

The British Prime Minister picked up the telephone.

'Ronald, yes a good exercise and it all went well. I just hope we didn't give the Soviets too much to worry about.'

'The incident in the Arctic? Yes, that's all sorted.'

'No, I don't think I need to say any more than that.'

'Now listen, you decided I didn't need to know about your little foray into our Caribbean island. So frankly, I've decided you don't need to know about our little operation in the Arctic.'

When she put the phone down, there was a look of quiet satisfaction on her face.

Moscow

A stunned silence descended over the Politburo. An hour ago, all NATO signal traffic had reverted to normal peacetime levels. Just like that.

The General Secretary closed the emergency session by summing up. 'Gentlemen, it appears our concerns were unfounded, at least for the moment. It was just an exercise after all. I propose we stand down our forces from full alert. I will be forming a committee to look into this and ensure that somehow we never get into this position again. Would the head of the KGB and Defence Minister stay behind please.'

When everyone else had filed out he turned to his two colleagues. 'What news of our rather precipitous raid gentlemen?'

'Not good, not good at all. The jammer stopped suddenly but we have had no word. However, we know a British submarine is now in the area. Preliminary reconnaissance indicates the Ekranoplan crashed and is burnt out.'

'Right, get me the British Prime Minister on the telephone.'

The two other men looked extremely surprised but quickly arranged for the telephone to be connected.

The General Secretary took the receiver once contact had been made.

'Prime Minister, good morning, I think there is something we need to clear up.'

'Yes, exactly.'

'Indeed.'

'Thank you.'

He put the phone down, with a sigh of relief and looked at the other two men.

'What did she say?'

She said 'What raid?'

Haslar Naval Hospital Gosport

Jon stared out of the window, bored to tears. His left arm was supported in a cast. The operation on his ribs and damaged lung had gone well and everyone said he was going to make a full recovery. He grimaced at the thought of being stuck here for another three weeks but at least he had the prospect of a flying job when he was fit again.

The Caspian Monster

His bed was surrounded by flowers and get well cards, some of which he had tried to hide when he saw the coarseness of the contents even if they were actually quite funny. However, the Nurses had found them all and had great fun at his expense reading them and asking for interpretations of the remarks. There were chocolates in the cupboard and courtesy of Brian, a bottle of malt whiskey, carefully hidden behind them. He suspected the girls knew about it but he was prepared to put up a fight if any of them tried to remove it.

Cook Smith and the rest of the team had all called in. Despite arbitration by Sergeant McCaul, there was fierce debate over whose shot had first got the soldier using the shield. In the end, it was decided to call the competition a draw but Jon and Smithy both agreed there was some unfinished business to sort out in the future.

Yesterday, he had been visited by Rupert and the Fleet Captain. As far as the world was concerned, the activities of the last few weeks had never happened. The Soviets were playing along and that was it. The Captain apologised that this meant that Jon, Brian and their team, would never have their efforts acknowledged or rewarded but he made it plain that it was known by those who mattered. Jon realised that he couldn't care less.

Rupert told him that Yuri, the pilot of the Ekranoplan, had asked for asylum having made a good recovery from his injuries which had all been minor. Not only had it been granted but the Russians were being unusually helpful in allowing his family to emigrate as well.

Visiting time was about to start and he wondered who would appear around the door this time. His parents had been this morning and were now having to head home, so he would probably be only seeing them at weekends from now on. Brian might pop in later but Yeovilton was quite far away and he had a job to go back to so maybe not. He sighed and lay back, the ache in his arm was starting again. He wondered if that cute blonde nurse was on duty again if so it would definitely be worth asking for some more painkillers.

He heard some footsteps approaching and looked around to see who his visitor was now.

She looked radiant and fully recovered. He knew she had also been granted asylum and couldn't have been more pleased.

'Hello Inga.'

Author's notes

Hands up all those who didn't know that the world almost ended in 1983? Thought so, me too.

Being in the British military then was a bit of 'happy time'. We had seen off John Nott and his defence cuts post the Falklands. No one was talking about military reductions any more. When I started researching this book I knew something had happened through vague recollections of stories I had heard. At the start of writing, I was considering a story to remind people about the Cold War in general and how we in the Royal Navy felt about it. After all, it is now a generation ago. When I drilled into the reality I was appalled. The Cuban missile crisis in the sixties was bad enough but at least that was played out in the open. The incidents of 1983 were played out by both sides in almost total ignorance of what the other thought was going on. Add on top of that some terrible coincidences which became widely misinterpreted and the possibility of Armageddon became a definite reality. With the exception of the Ekranoplan raid, everything in this book really happened. Exercise 'Good Bowman' was actually called 'Able Archer' and took place in the autumn rather than after Christmas but that is the only liberty I have taken. So consider the following factors:

1. Ronald Reagan really disliked the Soviet system and allowed his military machine to go into overdrive with their Psychological Operations. This probably marked the nadir of general relations between the two powers.

2. A culmination of this approach was Fleetex 83 which took place in April in the Pacific. The largest fleet exercise since WW2.

3. The Soviets were led by old men with no understanding of the western world beyond a paranoid feeling that the West was overtly hostile.

4. The man who started Operation Ryan to try and find out what the Americans were up to and so by definition was one of the most paranoid, ended up leading the USSR during the period of highest tension.

5. The US deployed Pershing missiles into Europe. Capable of being operationally deployed within minutes and flying self correcting profiles, they were a true first strike weapon and the Soviets knew it. They were there to counter the threat of the Russian SS20s, but these had been in the field since 1975, so it was seen as another attempt by the US to alter the balance of power in their favour. The first physical deployment actually occurred while exercise Able Archer was going on (see item 9. below).

6. In March, Reagan announced the Strategic Defence Initiative – 'Star Wars'. He may have seen it as purely defensive. The Soviets certainly didn't. They saw it as an escalation of the arms race into space. In the same month, in a famous speech he labelled the Soviet Union an 'Evil Empire'.

7. In September, the Russians shot down the Korean airliner. From their side, it came at the time of a sensitive missile test and there were other spy planes in the area. From the American side, they had a member of congress on board and couldn't see how the Soviets failed to identify it as a civilian. The Soviets attempts to hamper the search and rescue operation were extremely provocative.

8. In October, for whatever reasons, the US invaded Grenada. The build up in signal traffic between the US and UK seemed extremely odd to the Soviets. They weren't to know that the US decided to invade a country whose Head of State was the Queen of England without telling them.

9. To cap it all, in November Able Archer started. It was a full blown NATO exercise to practice the procedures for a full nuclear release which even included the personal participation of the German Chancellor and British Prime Minister. Staggeringly, it happened concurrently with the first deployment of live Pershing missiles in Germany. Thank God someone persuaded the Americans

The Caspian Monster

not to become actively involved. Had Reagan actually participated, who knows what might have happened.

The Soviets had always suspected that if the West was to attempt a first strike then it would be in the guise of an exercise and that their only possible counter would be to strike first.

How close do you think Andropov's finger was to the big red button?

One final note about the situation. The Russians had just commissioned a space based ballistic missile detection system. On several occasions in the summer it malfunctioned and produced false alerts of weapon firings from the west. It was only because of the actions of local commanders who realised it was the system that was malfunctioning rather than a real attack that the Russians didn't initiate a response. Had it happened during Able Archer..........

Ekranoplans are just wonderful and I had so much fun learning all about them. I've known about them in general for years but for most people they are a surprise. The 'Caspian Monster' was the name they were originally given for obvious reasons. I have put a few photographs in the next section so their true nature can be appreciated.

For many years, the US talked about being able to launch an amphibious strike from 'over the horizon'. They spent billions developing things like the V22 Osprey tilt rotor aircraft and the like. Imagine how capable a fleet of Ekranoplans; some with troops and equipment, some with missiles and guns would have been. However, my personal assessment is that they were very much the fruit of early post war thinking. The thing is, you can use a V22 for other things. An Ekranoplan is very limited in its deployment roles. Couple this to the problems they had with lateral stability and enormous turning circles and you can see why they withered on the vine. I've kept as close to the truth about them as possible. The original prototype crashed as described and was never salvaged as it was far too heavy for any lifting equipment. The cause was because the pilot inexplicably failed to use full power during take off although I have not been able to find out the real reason for that. The massive Lun with the missiles on its back was built and flown but only as a one off. A second was never finished and that was going to be used for search and rescue. The prototype still exists and is sitting derelict in the naval station in the town of Kaspyisk. If you thought Eaglet was a slightly unrepresentative name, 'Lun' means Duck.

Out of one hundred and thirty ordered, only three Orlyonoks made it into active duty and saw limited service. In 1985, Ustinov the Defence Minister died and his successor effectively ended the Ekranoplan programme. However, today if you go to the web site of the Volga shipyard and look at their portfolio they list the Orlyonok Ekranoplan as one of the current products. Who knows, maybe we'll see them on the transatlantic run sometime in the future. They would look good in Virgin livery!

As far as I know, they were never used in the Arctic..........

The Jungly world is as I remember it although I am now waiting for the first person to tell me that the 'Milliways' base at Bardufoss hadn't been built in 83. I know but as I served there a few years later it was easier for me to describe it as I experienced it. The Royal Marines are a wonderful service for which I have nothing but admiration. However, on occasions, I did feel that they looked on the RN as their smaller cousin not the other way around. And sometimes they did get their sense of humour tweaked by 'Jack'. The 'Radio Controlled marine' story is actually true. I can honestly say it's the closest I've actually come to wetting myself with laughter.

Naval parties can (and hopefully still do) get out of hand. When you work as hard as we did then playing hard was expected too. I should apologise to 829 Lynx Squadron from Portland for pinching their story about the Father Christmas pudding competition but it was too good not to use.

Underslung loads are a subject in their own right. I've lifted most things in my time from 105mm Howitzers to bags of bread. The worst were target drones. You had to be very careful that they were lifted in such a way that they didn't start to want to fly themselves alongside you or even up into the rotors. Getting a swing going, especially when the load was very heavy, could be a nightmare. You often wondered who was flying who as the load started to make the helicopter sway in sympathy. I needed a way for Jon to take out an Ekranoplan. In those days the Sea King 4 was completely unarmed and carried little in the way of the systems they have fitted today. Not hitting the side of your ship with a swinging load was always good. So I had the idea of using the bloody thing as a weapon just for once. I reckon it would have worked too.

Submarine listening stations did exist, they probably still do. My invention of Pickwick is just that, an invention but I don't see why it couldn't have worked. Early Russian submarines were terribly noisy. I flew ASW Sea Kings when we first used passive sonar buoys. Clanking Ruskies were easy to pick up, so much so that when we operated against our own machines, they had to have noise makers fitted to simulate the Russians. Unfortunately, they eventually got wise to the problem and things got a lot harder. The Russian harassment of our exercises was frequent and often quite intrusive. In a Carrier it would be extremely odd not to have a 'tattle tail' AGI in close company at all times.

The story of donating smelly socks and porn to an AGI is true although it was from HMS Hermes not HMS Illustrious. I wonder who actually got the porn in the end? I bet it wasn't the sailors who retrieved it……….

The Caspian Monster

Ekranoplans

The original 'Caspian Monster', in one of its several configurations during its life.

The 'Lun' or Duck in NATO parlance with the SSN 22 Sunburn missile containers on the back

The smaller (relatively speaking), Orlyonok or Eaglet, star of the book which had the largest diameter propeller of any flying vessel in the world.

Cocaine

Jon and Brian fly again in the next book in the series about operating in the Caribbean and conduction anti-submarine and anti-drug smuggling operations:

America is being flooded with drugs and the US Coast Guard can't find out why. HMS Chester is in the Caribbean conducting trials and is tasked to aid a new anti-drugs Task Force. Helicopter pilot, Lieutenant Commander Jonathon Hunt and his Observer Brian Pearce become involved when it is decided that the war needs to be taken to the enemy. The strength of the British and American military is pitted against the ingenuity of the Columbian drug smuggler cartels and results in a dramatic confrontation off the coast of Columbia.

Once again the story is based on the Author's own experiences of flying in the Caribbean theatre and conducting anti submarine operations around the world.

Printed in Great Britain
by Amazon